A——————

CANDLELIGHT REGENCY SPECIAL

Candlelight Regencies

581   THE DAZZLED HEART, *Nina Pykare*

586   THE EDUCATION OF JOANNE, *Joan Vincent*

587   MOLLY, *Jennie Tremaine*

588   JESSICA WINDOM, *Marnie Ellingson*

589   THE ARDENT SUITOR, *Marian Lorraine*

593   THE RAKE'S COMPANION, *Regina Towers*

594   LADY INCOGNITA, *Nina Pykare*

595   A BOND OF HONOUR, *Joan Vincent*

596   GINNY, *Jennie Tremaine*

597   THE MARRIAGE AGREEMENT, *Margaret MacWilliams*

602   A COMPANION IN JOY, *Dorothy Mack*

603   MIDNIGHT SURRENDER, *Margaret Major Cleaves*

604   A SCHEME FOR LOVE, *Joan Vincent*

605   THE DANGER IN LOVING, *Helen Nuelle*

610   LOVE'S FOLLY, *Nina Pykare*

611   A WORTHY CHARADE, *Vivian Harris*

612   THE DUKE'S WARD, *Samantha Lester*

613   MANSION FOR A LADY, *Cilla Whitmore*

618   THE TWICE BOUGHT BRIDE, *Elinor Larkin*

619   THE MAGNIFICENT DUCHESS, *Sarah Stamford*

620   SARATOGA SEASON, *Margaret MacWilliams*

621   AN INTRIGUING INNOCENT, *Rebecca Ashley*

625   THE AVENGING HEART, *Janis Susan May*

626   THE HEART OF THE MATTER, *Diana Burke*

627   THE PAISLEY BUTTERFLY, *Phyllis Taylor Pianka*

631   MAKESHIFT MISTRESS, *Amanda Mack*

632   RESCUED BY LOVE, *Joan Vincent*

633   A MARRIAGEABLE ASSET, *Ruth Gerber*

637   THE BRASH AMERICAN, *Samantha Lester*

638   A SEASON OF SURPRISES, *Rebecca Ashley*

639   THE ENTERPRISING MINX, *Marian Lorraine*

643   A HARMLESS RUSE, *Alexandra Lord*

644   THE GYPSY HEIRESS, *Laura London*

645   THE INNOCENT HEART, *Nina Pykare*

649   LORD SATAN'S BRIDE, *Anne Stuart*

650   THE CURIOUS ROGUE, *Joan Vincent*

651   THE RELUCTANT DUKE, *Marilyn Lowery*

655   LOVE'S TEMPEST, *Elinor Larkin*

656   MISS HUNGERFORD'S HANDSOME HERO, *Noël Vreeland Carter*

657   REBEL IN LOVE, *Veronica Howard*

Bride of Vengeance

Rose Marie Abbott

A CANDLELIGHT REGENCY SPECIAL

Published by
Dell Publishing Co., Inc.
1 Dag Hammarskjold Plaza
New York, New York 10017

Dell ® TM 681510, Dell Publishing Co., Inc.

ISBN: 0–440–10819–5

Printed in the United States of America

First printing—June 1981

Bride of Vengeance

One

Miss Cherry Hilliard raced up the back staircase, the train of her green merino habit draped awkwardly over her left arm. Her right hand, besides grasping the crop of her riding whip, was trying to prevent the tall, precariously balanced riding hat from falling underfoot and tripping her.

She burst through the door of her bedchamber, threw down whip and high-crowned hat, and began fumbling hurriedly with the fastenings of the tailored riding coat that encased her slender form.

"Hetty! Where are you? These buttons won't open. I must reach Uncle before he leaves."

"Here I am, Miss Cherry." The elderly maid laid down the gown she was mending and stood up resignedly. "Let me do it, miss," she said soothingly, and soon Hetty's patient fingers succeeded where her mistress's impatient ones had failed.

"There you are, miss. It goes much faster if you don't rush things."

"That's silly, Hetty. How can things go faster if you do them slower?" Stepping out of the skirt about her feet, Cherry Hilliard plumped herself down in the wooden chair near the foot of her bed. "Bring me the plainest gown I have, please, Hetty. Uncle Geoffrey is so conventional he would frown on anything but the plainest black."

She began tugging at her riding boots. "They won't come off, Hetty," she exclaimed pettishly.

The maid, accustomed to her charge's impatience, remained unruffled, merely stating, "Miss Cherry, stand up and let me dress you. Then I'll pull off the boots."

As Cherry obediently rose, Hetty thrust a black crepe gown over her head, did up the series of hooks, and tied the sash. Then she gave her mistress a gentle shove. When Cherry sank backward into the chair, Hetty easily drew off her riding boots. "There you are, miss."

Only when she was fastening the satin ribbons about Cherry's slim ankles did the maid ask, "You gen'lly try not to see your uncle, Miss Cherry. Why do you want to see him now?"

"I haven't missed him, have I, Hetty? I saw Uncle Geoffrey's coach from the east pasture, but you know how slow Molly is. She positively refuses to do more than a slow walk. He is still here, isn't he, Hetty? Has he come to tell us we can return to London?"

"Return, miss? What good would that do? The Season is over, and besides, you can't go to any parties, not now."

"I know, I know, but just being in London would be ever so much better than rusticating here. All my life I've lived in Leighton Buzzard, Hetty, where nothing ever happens. It was so much more enjoyable in London, didn't you think so, too?" As Cherry spoke, she stood up and started to move across the floor toward the door.

"Wait, miss. You can't go with your hair mussed. You

10

will just have to wait, Miss Cherry," she added at sight of a faint pout.

"Oh, very well, Hetty, but hurry, please."

The maid drew a comb through the tangled curls, reflecting that the new short hairstyle was most becoming to her young mistress, but wisely refraining from airing this view: Miss Cherry might have her head turned by too much praise.

"Thank you, Hetty," Cherry called over her shoulder as she rushed headlong out the door and down the front staircase, only pausing to catch her breath outside the drawing room doors. She knew her uncle did not approve of what he called her "hoydenish" ways, and since his approval as head of the family was necessary for a remove to London, she did not wish to ruin her chances by making a bad impression.

Her breathing steadied, Cherry tapped on the door, then opened it slowly. "Mama, are you busy?"

A soft, breathless voice greeted her. "Cherry, dear, please come in. Your Uncle Hilliard is here with some wonderful news for us."

Wonderful news? Cherry held her breath. Could it be true? "Of Papa? Has he been . . .?" Her voice faltered; she could not continue. Cherry stood rooted just inside the doors. Could her father possibly be alive?

"No, no, dear, I fear there's been no change in that." The black-gowned figure on the worn velvet sofa raised a trembling hand and wiped her eyes with a black-bordered handkerchief. Never a strong woman, Amanda Hilliard had taken to her bed at the news of her husband's death. Now only an event of extreme importance, such as her brother-in-law's visit, could draw her from the sanctuary of her bedchamber. "Come and greet your uncle, Cherry," she murmured faintly.

11

As Cherry approached and curtsied to the well-fleshed peer sitting in her mother's sturdiest chair, she perceived a look of triumph on his face. Uncle Geoffrey was feeling smug about something. Was Agnes finally betrothed? But surely he would not come all this far to inform them of such news. What could it be?

She didn't have long to wait. "Cherry." Lord Hilliard spoke her name with distaste. He had never approved of giving a female such a highly improper name. Thankfully her hair had darkened with age and was no longer the vivid red that had occasioned her outrageous name. Why should one wish to call attention to such garish locks? In his opinion all proper young ladies had much more modest adornment.

"Cherry," he repeated, "I have personally journeyed to Leighton Buzzard to inform your mother of the great honour bestowed on our family."

He paused, smiling complacently, and Cherry's words tumbled from her lips. "Honour? Is Papa to receive a medal?"

Lord Hilliard frowned. "Of course not. John was mentioned in the dispatches. That should be sufficient. No," he smiled again, "this concerns you."

"Me?" Cherry's green eyes widened. "I don't understand, Uncle." How could a country miss bring honour to the family?

"I have received an offer for you from Lord Varian," he announced.

"Offer? For me? From Varian?" Cherry shook her head. "Oh, you must be mistaken, Uncle Geoffrey. Lord Varian has never once spoken to me. He can't possibly want to marry *me*. He must want Agnes, or . . . or Lizzie."

Lord Hilliard shook his head emphatically. "No, he

distinctly said, 'Miss Cherry Hilliard, daughter of John Hilliard.' "

Cherry stared at her uncle, trying to see in his pale blue, close-set eyes some clue to this strange announcement. Then she shrugged. "Well, it doesn't signify, does it? I can't possibly marry him."

"*Can't,* you say, miss. What do you mean by *can't?*" roared his lordship. His normally florid face had darkened to a bright red at her unexpected response.

Cherry was quite taken aback by her uncle's violent reaction and hastened to explain. "But I'm in mourning, Uncle. No gentleman ever approaches a lady in black gloves."

The same point had not only occurred to his lordship but had given him some anxious moments. However, he was not in the habit of having his decisions questioned, especially by a female barely out of the schoolroom. "I don't need you to teach me manners, miss," he retorted. "Lord Varian offered for you and I accepted."

"You accepted?" Cherry's head swung around so swiftly that the red curls whipped around her face. Her eyes narrowed, showing a thin green line. "You did what, Uncle? A man who has never spoken to me, a complete stranger in fact, offers for me and *you* accept for me?" Her hands were clenched so tightly her nails were biting into her palms in an effort to keep from bursting into tears. "How dare you, sir?"

In her agitation Cherry neither heard nor heeded a strangled gasp from her mother. Her eyes were fixed on her uncle, who had been brought to his feet by her defiance. "How dare—how dare—" he sputtered, breathing heavily. "You mannerless chit, you—you—" Words failed him momentarily, but he recovered. "I'll have you know, miss, that were you one of my daughters, such words would earn the beating they deserve. *I* am the head of the family and *your* guardian, miss. Your marriage is *my* responsibility."

"Mama." Cherry rushed to the side of her silent mother and, throwing herself on her knees, grasped her mother's hands. "Mama, is this true?"

Amanda Hilliard smiled tremulously. "Of course, Cherry. Your uncle is just taking the place of your father. Had he lived . . . But you know this, child. After all, didn't we introduce you this Season for the express purpose of finding a husband?" She was trying desperately to be reassuring. Amanda had warned her brother-in-law that Cherry was not likely to take this unexpected arrangement with meek obedience and had pleaded with him to delay telling Cherry. However, he had overruled her and now *she* must try to soothe her upset daughter.

"Yes, Mama, but I imagined, in my naïveté, perhaps, that any man wanting to marry me would at least *speak* to me and tell me he cared for me. Lord Varian and I haven't even been introduced," she wailed.

Amanda Hilliard patted her daughter's hand sympathetically. "Lord Varian has behaved with the utmost propriety, Cherry. It is highly improper to speak to a young lady about marriage before obtaining her guardian's permission, you know." Then, as Cherry's rebellious expression did not change, she added, "It is an excellent match, Cherry, much better than I had ever hoped for. Your portion is small, my dear," she reminded her daughter. "And you will be a countess," she coaxed.

Only a few of her mother's words penetrated Cherry's perturbed mind. "Excellent match, Mama?" She pulled her hands from her mother's and rose to her feet, her breath coming quickly. "Have you taken leave of your senses, Mama? The Earl of Varian is a rake. Even *I* heard the gossip about him."

"Cherry! You will not use such words to your mother. Apologize at once."

Cherry's head whipped around at her uncle's commanding voice. The sight of his glaring eyes and horrified expression made her realize the extent of her bad manners. Impulsively she bent down and kissed her mother's cheek. "I'm sorry I used the words I did to *you*, Mama, but I won't apologize for speaking the truth. Can you deny, Uncle, that he openly parades his . . . his bit of muslin at Vauxhall and the Park? That he prefers *her* company to *ton* parties? Or that he spends the rest of his time drinking and gaming, laying wagers on anything?" Only her mother's shriek stopped Cherry's rash speech.

"Cherry! My vinaigrette! Where did you learn such vulgar speech?" Amanda lay back against the sofa, gasping in horror. "Not from my lips, I can assure you, Geoffrey."

His lordship, not wanting a vapourish female on his hands, moved to intervene. "His amusements are no concern of yours, miss. He offers you an honourable position as his wife."

Cherry steadied herself and tried to speak calmly. "A position I do not want, Uncle." Then, as the colour rose in his face, she burst out, "I can't imagine why he wants me as his wife, he hasn't even made the effort to meet me."

His lordship, imagining the trouble to be a female's more delicate nature and sensibility, spoke patronizingly. "Now, now, my dear. Perhaps his lordship has been a bit wild since his return from Spain, but all gentlemen have their amusements. It is of no consequence."

Then, as Cherry returned no answer but continued to look rebellious, he asked sharply, "You're not such a ninnyhammer as to let his lack of an arm dissuade you, are you, miss?"

By now Cherry was pacing the floor in her agitation. "I don't care whether he has *three* arms, Uncle. You may inform Lord Varian that I have no wish to be his wife."

Hilliard's short temper, held in check by his own awareness of the impropriety of Varian's offer, now exploded. "You have no wish! You, miss, are the outside of enough! Well-bred children obey their elders and you, miss, will obey me. You will marry his lordship." He strode forward to stand threateningly over her, his face so red Cherry feared an apoplexy. She realized suddenly that only a thin thread prevented her uncle from physically chastising her. She stared at him, her eyes enormous green globes, her lips quivering with anger and words she dare not speak.

Then, with a sob, she turned and rushed toward the doors. Her impatient hands slipped from the handle before she could grip it tightly enough to turn it. Open, please open, she silently begged, again grasping the handle. The door open at last, she ran upstairs and threw herself on her bed, fists beating the pillow in frustration. Only when she was sufficiently exhausted did tears come, tears and sobs that shook her entire body.

Two

As the door slammed shut behind Cherry's retreating form, Mrs. Hilliard raised fearful eyes to her brother-in-law's quivering frame. "The poor child is upset, Geoffrey. You must admit our news was a great shock to her. But her words don't signify, you know. She has always been exceedingly impetuous, but," she assured him, "she's always been a good girl. I don't know what I would have done without her help all these years." Amanda Hilliard's blue, pleading eyes, framed by guinea-gold curls that had lost none of their youthful sheen though now covered with the black lace cap of a widow, silently begged for generosity of spirit from her irate relation.

Lord Hilliard was pacing the floor in helpless fury. The girl should be soundly beaten to teach her proper manners. Such defiance of her elder's authority was not to be condoned. Why had not Providence seen fit to make the child like her mother? *She,* at least, was a proper, well-bred, obedient female who knew her place.

"I regret exceedingly that my brother never saw fit to

live with his family, Amanda. He should have sold out years ago. That girl needs a firm hand. I said so before and I say so now." He stopped his pacing in order to emphasize his next words. "One reason, indeed the main reason, I accepted Varian's offer was that he would be firm with her. An officer in command of troops does not stand for disobedience."

"Oh, dear, Cherry will be his wife, not a soldier under his command, Geoffrey. You don't think he will be too hard on her?" Amanda Hilliard's voice faltered. "Perhaps break her spirits?"

"Of course not, Amanda," he assured her, but privately his lordship thought that broken spirits would be a much needed improvement in that chit. "She will soon learn to behave with propriety. All will be well then, I'm sure."

Though his words were encouraging, his hearty tone of voice seemed to stifle Amanda. "Please sit down, Geoffrey. Such energy is disturbing to someone of my poor constitution. I have never been well, as you know." And Amanda placed a hand on her breast to still her fluttering heart. When Lord Hilliard had seated himself, she continued, speaking hesitantly, for she did not wish to appear critical. "Perhaps we should have waited to inform Cherry of Varian's offer."

"Nonsense. The chit should be pleased. I never expected an offer from an earl, not with her portion! I must confess, Amanda, I was almost thrown for a loss when I realized what Varian was after. Thought at first he wanted to ask me to—" Then, remembering that he was speaking to a sheltered female, Lord Hilliard interrupted himself. "Well, never mind, that's not important. Point is, it's a magnificent match for that chit. Varian could have any female he wanted, and I can't pretend the Hilliard family is of the first rank. Solid, of course," he added expansively, "never a hint of scandal, but not first rank."

Intent on mollifying her brother-in-law, for he still appeared agitated, Amanda explained, "It's just that it's so unexpected, Geoffrey. After having her spirits raised at the prospect of a marriage, and then having them dashed to the ground at the news of John's death, Cherry has had to reconcile herself to the lack of a betrothal this year, which she has done very nicely. And now to have the totally unexpected news of a betrothal! You must admit it has been hard on her. With the Season just begun, all the excitement of her first *ton* parties and her first visit to Almack's, not to mention all those gowns your mother provided, just when she was meeting eligible young men, hoping for an offer, *all* had to be abandoned." Mrs. Hilliard sighed in exhaustion from this unusually long speech and again wiped her misting eyes with her handkerchief.

"I realize that, Amanda, but the entire family has had to do the same. I hope you haven't forgotten that Agnes was brought out this year also. She, too, had begun her first Season in hopes of an offer. And Elizabeth will have to wait another year." Lord Hilliard privately wondered why the Earl of Varian should prefer a headstrong miss with such unnatural looks to his obedient daughters with their typically English complexions, but deemed it wiser not to voice these thoughts to his vapourish sister-in-law.

"I think it was most inconvenient of John to die during Cherry's first Season." Amanda wiped tears again. "It's been so hard to raise the child alone."

Alarmed at the prospect of more tears, his lordship hastened to reassure the distraught woman. "No one blames you, Amanda. The child has too much of her father's spirit. She needs a man's hand, always has. I blame m'brother. He could have sold out. There was nothing keeping him in the military, not after his marriage. I don't hold with these military campaigns. A man's family should come first." It was all due to John's being a second son—he did not have to grow up with the knowledge that the responsibility of an estate would be his. *He* could afford to indulge the wilder side of his nature!

Mrs. Hilliard, placed in the dilemma of either agreeing with her brother-in-law and thereby criticizing her dead husband or disagreeing with him and speaking an untruth, tried a new topic of conversation. "Why did Varian have to offer now, Geoffrey? It's most improper, I'm sure you'll agree. It's just not done. A well-bred gentleman respects a female's mourning. And why did he offer in the first place? Cherry was right, you know. He never once asked to be presented, not once. And we were in London for over a month. He could have made some effort to meet her!"

"You surely can't expect him to dance at balls, Amanda!"

Exasperated with typical masculine denseness, Amanda explained, "Of course not, Geoffrey, but he could put in an appearance. Many men don't dance, as you very well know. And he could have called, or just left his card."

"I admit it was not at all proper, Amanda, and I didn't like it, but what could I do? Not only was it the first offer for the chit, but an excellent one. On what grounds could I have refused him?"

Mrs. Hilliard's murmured "I'm sure I don't know" was lost as Lord Hilliard continued, "She will be a countess and the wife of a wealthy man. I don't know what Varian's fortune is," he mused, "but he has several estates, and he was most generous," he assured the future mother-in-law. "Her jointure is much more than customary, and he mentioned a sum for pin money that was more than generous. I can't fault him there."

"Perhaps he wanted to ensure a betrothal before you received any other offers. Cherry did make a most favourable impression, Geoffrey. There were several young men who were clearly smitten. If John hadn't died, I'm sure she would have had several immediate offers."

"Thought of that m'self," Lord Hilliard admitted. "It's the only reasonable explanation, but I couldn't ask his lordship, of course. Couldn't very well tell him he shouldn't be offering, either, though, mind you, I did insist that no announcement be made until the year is up. And the wedding itself must wait until the family is out of black gloves." Lord Hilliard, sufficiently shocked at the impropriety of an offer during the year of mourning, could not conceive of further stretching of the bonds of propriety.

"That was very thoughtful of you, I'm sure, Geoffrey. By then Cherry will be reconciled to it. After a year in mourning she will be thrilled at new bride clothes." Amanda Hilliard's voice was wistful: her financial affairs did not allow for such nonessentials as new gowns.

Hilliard thought it time to bring the conversation back to necessities. "You heard her just now, Amanda. For a chit barely out of the schoolroom her language and behaviour are shocking. She shows no respect for her elders and no gratitude for my efforts in her behalf. I am persuaded that I did the right thing by accepting Varian's offer. He will provide the firm hand she needs. Now, now," he hastened to reassure his sister-in-law as Amanda showed signs of further tears, "I am not blaming you. Can't expect a woman to be firm."

"I'm sure you've done the best thing for Cherry, Geoffrey, and I'm grateful to you, truly I am. Will you be staying the night?"

"No, no, don't put yourself out for me, Amanda. I must

return to London today. We'll be removing to the country shortly." His lordship pulled out his watch to verify the hour. "There'll just be time to return by dinner if I leave now."

"Dinner? Oh, yes, town hours are later, I keep forgetting. We spent so little time in London." Again Amanda's voice was wistful. Except for a short wedding trip and her daughter's aborted Season in London, her entire life had been quietly spent in the village of Leighton Buzzard, and occasionally she found herself longing for Society. Her health had improved immensely during their stay in London, and Amanda wished with all her heart for the opportunity of returning to that healthful clime.

Lord Hilliard rose. "Varian indicated he would present himself shortly. I hope by the time he arrives Cherry will have learned some manners and greet him properly."

"I'm sure she will, Geoffrey. It is an honour for her, as I'm sure she will soon realize," Amanda said hopefully as she held out her hand to her brother-in-law.

Three

Hetty, coming into her mistress's bedchamber and finding her charge sobbing hysterically, sat down on the bed and engulfed her in loving arms. "There, there, Miss Cherry, don't cry."

Poor child! So full of life she was, but life lived only on her own terms! For a female such a course promised only heartache. "It can't be that bad, miss," Hetty rocked and soothed. She had come into the Hilliard household as nurse to the infant Cherry and remained as personal maid. Consequently she had had a great deal of experience attempting to soothe her mistress's disappointments, for Cherry's volatile temperament, combined with an unthinking impetuosity, was not conducive to accepting life's adversities.

"There, there, it can't be that bad," she repeated, then warned, "You'll ruin your face if you don't stop crying."

"That's nonsense, Hetty. Who's to see what I look like?" Cherry muttered, but sat up, wiping her eyes with the handkerchief provided by Hetty. "I don't have to marry him, do I, Hetty?"

"Who, miss?"

"Lord Varian. Uncle Geoffrey says I have to marry him. Do I?"

"I'm sure I don't know, Miss Cherry. His lordship, Lord Hilliard that is, is your guardian now that your papa is dead."

Cherry jumped off the bed. "Don't remind me of that, please, Hetty. Is my uncle still here? I can't bear to face him again. He's always so full of his own disapproval of me. I just know someday I'll tell him exactly what I think of him, and that would be disastrous."

The elderly maid wisely ignored Cherry's confidences and answered her question. "No, miss. His carriage left long ago."

"Where's Mama?"

"In her sitting room, Miss Cherry. I had to help her upstairs as soon as his lordship left."

Cherry sighed. "Poor Mama. Papa's death was hard on her. Who will care for her if I marry?" Impulsively, Cherry ran across the room and hugged her maid. "Thank you, dear Hetty. I'm better now, but I must speak to Mama."

Cherry was almost at the door when she was stopped by her maid's voice. "Not before you wash your face, miss."

Cherry whirled around and stared at her image in the mirror atop the walnut dressing table. Her face was even paler than usual. Across the bridge of her nose a band of freckles stood out darkly, a mute reminder that her outdoor trips were usually undertaken too hastily to remember parasols. Her eyes were red and listless and tears glistened on her lashes.

Tempted to forgo a washing—for what did it matter

how she looked?—Cherry glanced at her maid, who was standing patiently waiting, her hands on her hips. "Oh, very well, Hetty. But it won't help."

Feeling somewhat refreshed, if not looking better, Cherry sped down the corridor to her mother's sitting room. There she opened the door cautiously so as not to waken her mother if she was sleeping.

Mrs. Hilliard was reclining, as usual, on the worn brocaded couch, her face turned toward the wall. At Cherry's entrance she languidly turned her head, then shrieked, "Cherry! You poor dear! Your face! You've been weeping!"

"What did you expect me to do, Mama?" Cherry asked as she crossed the room.

"I know you were surprised, child, as I was, at your Uncle Hilliard's news, but it's nothing to weep about." Her eyes surveyed her daughter anxiously. "It is really an excellent match, Cherry. Much better than I had ever hoped for you. You'll be a countess and the envy of all the girls in London. I'm sure neither Agnes nor Lizzie would be in tears if Varian offered for either of them."

"No, Mama," Cherry agreed dutifully, then burst out, "unless it were tears of joy, for no man would ever look twice at either of them."

"Hush, child, that is unkind in you. A person's looks are a gift of the Almighty and are not to be criticized."

Cherry bowed her head in swift apology. However, she couldn't understand why she should rejoice at an offer just because her cousins would.

"Must I marry him, Mama?" She threw herself on the floor beside the couch, her eyes raised pleadingly.

Mrs. Hilliard hesitated. She had never really understood her daughter, for not only were Cherry's high spirits alien to her timid parent, but in addition, Cherry's extremely volatile nature—down in the dumps one moment, then immediately up in the bows—made it difficult to keep up with her. Mrs. Hilliard never knew exactly how Cherry would react. In the past all she could do was soothe her hurts. Now, however, Cherry's persistence in refusing such a brilliant match was totally beyond her comprehension. "I don't understand your reluctance, Cherry. Most girls would be ecstatic over marriage to a young, handsome earl, and a wealthy one at that."

Cherry regarded her hands, which were tightly clasped in her lap. "I don't care for him, Mama," she muttered. Surely her mother, of all people, would understand! How could she marry a man she didn't love, a man, moreover, whom she had never spoken to?

"Not now, Cherry, but you will."

Cherry's eyes flew up in astonishment. "How can you know that, Mama?"

"Varian is a very handsome man, child. You've seen him, haven't you?"

Cherry nodded. "That's what hurts, Mama. I've only seen him twice, both times in the Park, driving with that woman. He never was at any parties we attended. If he wants me as his wife, why hasn't he had the courtesy to meet me, to speak to me? As it is, I'm a stranger to him. How can he know what I'm like?"

Mrs. Hilliard patted her daughter's hand. "Most girls of our class are in the same position, child. Most marriages are arranged, you know."

"Yours wasn't," Cherry protested.

"No, Cherry, mine was a love match." Her mother smiled fleetingly. "I truly loved your father and he loved me, but that is exceedingly uncommon." Amanda Hilliard, who had spoken often to her daughter of her love for the dashing dragoon officer, could not now bring herself to admit that a love that had flared so ecstatically could be so suddenly extinguished.

John Hilliard had spent his inheritance in buying a commission in the army. Hotheaded and wild, he made a perfect cavalry officer—but a poor husband, as Amanda Wilton discovered soon after their marriage. His interest in his family might have been kindled had his child been a son whom he could instruct in the arts of riding, shooting, and swordplay. But a girl, even one with hair of flame, was of no interest to him. His visits to his family became farther and farther apart, ending when he accompanied Sir Arthur Wellesley to the Peninsular War.

Cherry jumped up, took a few steps, then faced her mother, her hands clenched tightly. "I want a marriage like yours, Mama. I don't want to marry a complete stranger, but the man I love, just as you did. You must help me," she pleaded. "You must tell Uncle Geoffrey to refuse the offer."

Mrs. Hilliard's face crumpled into the helpless look Cherry had so often seen. "Oh, Cherry," she wailed, "you can't refuse now, not after the offer has once been accepted. A woman can't jilt a man, it's highly improper. No one else would marry you, child. It shows a flighty nature and a lack of proper respect. It's just not done."

I should have known better than to ask Mama for help, Cherry told herself. Mama has never made a single decision in her entire life, let alone stood up to anyone. I'll wager it was Papa's decision to marry, not hers. How could *she* possibly help me now?

An apprehensive mother watched her silent daughter for some moments, expecting an outburst. Cherry was so volatile! When none came, she said hesitantly, "Please, Cherry, please, don't cry anymore. Think of all the pretty gowns you will be able to have, for I'm sure Varian will be generous, and think of your position. As the Countess of Varian—it's an old title—you'll outrank most women in London, except for the few duchesses and marchionesses."

Cherry stared at her mother. She didn't know exactly what marriage between a man and a woman meant, but she was sure that it entailed more than rank and gowns, and she knew she didn't want to spend the rest of her life living with a man too occupied with another woman to even look at her.

Four

Nicole Claude tossed down the novel she had been trying to read. It was a stupid romance, really, about an insipid heroine who kept defending her virtue. Didn't authors ever write true-to-life romances? If she ever wrote a novel, it would not be about some silly innocent who knew nothing of life.

She glanced at the ormolu clock gracing the mantelpiece and sighed. Varian had been gone over four hours. She disliked being left to her own resources while he amused himself at White's or Boodles'. To be sure, there were compensations: he generally gave her his winnings, and whenever he left her after dinner to try his luck at hazard or faro, he returned to spend the entire night with her.

Deep in her practical French soul, she had to admit it was the only thing he could do. Varian couldn't make casual love to her, as so many other gentlemen did, expecting their mistresses to welcome them at any hour and then going off to the races, a cockfight, or their constant gaming.

Varian's handicap prevented him from tying his own cravat or shaving himself. He also needed help in donning his fashionably tight-fitting frock coat and in removing his boots. And Nicole, though adept at undressing him, could not tie a cravat.

She had tried, but the results were deplorable. Thus, whenever he came to the house he had purchased for her, he was invariably accompanied by his valet and planned on staying the night.

Restlessly Nicole began to pace the opulently furnished bedchamber. She herself had selected the furnishings, for Varian had given her carte blanche. Generally just to be in *her* room filled her with great satisfaction: only the deed to the house itself could please her more. The huge four-poster bed was swathed in shell pink gauze curtains hanging from a heavily embroidered canopy; the floor was covered with a rug so thick it reached her ankles when she walked barefoot, as she did now; the fireplace had a marble mantel sculptured in the Adam style; the chairs and the daybed were painted gold and covered in rich brocade; she had ivory-handled brushes for her hair and silver-mounted perfume flasks. In this room she felt like a lady, not a man's plaything.

But now, annoyed that Varian would put games of chance above her, she paced back and forth, her novel and her beautiful surroundings forgotten. Why didn't he come? She wanted him, *now*.

Varian was a most satisfactory lover. He could arouse her passions as no other man had done. And he wasn't a lout either. Some men, as she well knew, had no consideration for a woman's feelings and were concerned only with satisfying their own brutish passions. But not Varian. He never forced himself on her, preferring to delay his pleasure until her response could match his.

Nicole beat her hands together in frustration, then continued her pacing. Where was he? With her other lovers she had never been so impatient, but then, they could not compare with Varian. However, if she was honest with herself, she knew that even if she had not found Varian satisfying as a lover, she would still have remained his mistress. He was extremely generous, never begrudging her a gown or jewels.

Yes, Nicole, she told herself, the wisest thing you've ever done in your life was to become Varian's mistress. Certainly he was an improvement over Lord Blessington, who had become tightfisted as he became impotent, then blamed her for his inadequacies. A man who thought nothing of wagering three hundred pounds on the turn of a card, he begrudged her a like sum for a gown and beat her when she asked for one.

Yes, all in all, it was a most satisfactory arrangement for her, she thought complacently. Then a slight sound caught her ears and she swung around with a glad cry. "*Chéri*, finally you have come. I have been so *distraite*. It grows late."

The Earl of Varian stood just inside the door that gave onto the dressing room, still clad in the evening attire of a gentleman of fashion. Only the pinned-up left sleeve of the well-fitting blue superfine coat made him different from his peers. To be sure, not many of them had his tall athletic figure, which filled the coat and skin-tight pantaloons to perfection. Nor did their faces bear such a sardonic expression, as if his lordship viewed the world with bitter mockery. Now, however, the sight of Nicole brought a smile to his lips. He tossed a rouleau of guineas to her. "Will this ease your suffering?"

She caught it easily. "Ooooooh!" she exclaimed, then curtsied playfully. *"Merci,* milord." The low neck of her dressing gown parted as her knees bent, revealing her amply rounded breasts. "It is just that I miss you, Damon," she pouted. "And I do not like to compete with games of chance. Do I not offer more than White's?"

Her words brought a quick frown to his brow and a cold look to his dark eyes.

"Qu'est-ce que c'est?" she whispered. Varian had been moody ever since his return from Spain. She blamed it on the loss of his forearm. After all, one couldn't expect a man with his proud nature to accept such a loss with equanimity. But her words couldn't have provoked him, could they? They had been said in play.

His lordship's lips turned up slightly. His smile was bitter. "Your choice of words brings to mind some unpleasantness, Nicole."

Nicole tossed aside the guineas and slowly, deliberately slowly, so as to gain his attention, she moved toward him. She was wearing a pale pink silk dressing gown, so pale as to be almost flesh coloured, so diaphanous as to reveal the curves of her body. Her lips curved in a warm smile. "Let's not think of unpleasant thoughts now, *chéri,"* she murmured, her words low in her throat. She entwined her arms about his neck, pressing her body against his. "With us, there should always be pleasant thoughts, *n'est-ce pas? I* have been waiting so long, *mon amour."*

Varian stared down at the face raised so invitingly to his. A cascade of black ringlets covered Nicole's head and tumbled down to fall on her white shoulders. Her face was of singular beauty: she had huge blue eyes that darkened to a sapphire shade when she was angry or disturbed; a patrician nose with a most amusingly disdainful cast; and lips that were warm and inviting. Now, as his gaze fastened on them, her mouth opened slightly. The tip of her tongue emerged to moisten her upper lip, which glistened in the candlelight. Gad, the wench was desirable!

Nicole began to untie his cravat with fingers that trembled slightly from impatience, but Varian put up his hand to stop her. "I must talk to you, Nicole. As I said, your words reminded me of something that must be said."

She stared at him, trying to read the unfathomable expression on his face. What was more important than their love? Or was he planning to end it? No, it couldn't be that. He was still enamored of her, of that she was positive. As experienced as she was in the ways of love, surely she would know if a man had lost interest in her. "What is it, Damon? What is this unpleasantness?"

"I have just returned from calling on Lord Hilliard. I offered for his niece."

The bald words hung in the air. Slowly Nicole pulled away from him, dropping her arms to her sides. Then she repeated his words, as if repetition would make them more believable. "You offered for his niece."

She shook her head slightly to clear it. He was going to marry another woman. She couldn't believe it. If he wanted marriage, why did he not marry her? She was well born enough for marriage. But he was waiting for a response. Careful, Nicole, she warned herself, don't ruin everything by saying the wrong thing.

"I thought you were happy with me, *mon amour.*" She spoke tremulously, her hands gesturing helplessly, her eyes widening.

"I am," he agreed.

"Then why, Damon? Why do you wish to marry another woman?"

"One generally marries to provide an heir," he said dryly.

Nicole's eyes narrowed. This was no answer. Any woman could provide an heir. Even she, if necessary.

"Who is she, this girl?" she demanded. "Do I know her?"

"I doubt it. She was presented this Season."

"So? A schoolroom miss! And what does she have that I don't, eh, my lord Varian?" Nicole thrust herself forward, hands on hips, daring him to find fault with the perfection of her body.

"I wouldn't know, *ma chérie.*"

Her hands dropped, she stared at him. "You wouldn't know." Nicole found herself repeating his words again. She felt utterly confused and at a loss, a singular situation for her. "Why don't you know?" she demanded.

"I will see the chit for the first time tomorrow."

Nicole laughed then, a great peal of laughter, slightly hysterical from relief. There was nothing to worry about after all. A marriage of convenience, it meant nothing.

But her laughter was a mistake, for Varian's face darkened, his jaw set. "This amuses you, Nicole?" he asked coldly.

She hastened to reassure him. "*Non, non, mon amour.* I am relieved, that is all. I feared I was to lose you."

"Oh, no, you won't lose me, Nicole." Varian stepped forward, picked up her hand, and pressed the palm to his lips.

"When is this marriage to be, my lord?"

He shrugged. "The chit is in black gloves for most of a year. Hilliard insisted on the conventions being followed, so next spring some time."

She smiled a satisfied smile and almost purred, "So there is no hurry?"

"I've waited this long, I can wait longer."

"And afterward?" she asked, so softly he had to bend his head to hear her.

"Afterward?" He too smiled, but his smile was tinged with malice. "Why, afterward, Nicole, since Lady Varian will be available to act as hostess, there is no reason you cannot move in with us."

She felt stupefied, as if she had suffered a blow to the head. Something was definitely not right. In a typical marriage of convenience both partners lived in amicable civility, for no emotions were involved. Each went his own way, discreetly of course. But such an unemotional situation did not square with Varian's devilish smile. But then she shrugged. So long as Varian did not love the chit, it meant nothing to her.

"There are times, Damon, when I think you are aptly named. Only a *daemon* could think of such a trick to play on a new wife.

"Come, *chéri.*" Nicole began to unbutton his shirt. "I accept your invitation gladly, but that is for the future. For now," she said as she drew off his coat, "do not keep me waiting longer, *mon amour.*"

Five

After leaving her mother, Cherry paced the bare floor of her bedchamber, too restless to sit still. Never before had she felt so vulnerable, so helpless, so alone. Years before, she had become accustomed to being without a father, for Major Hilliard was much too occupied with his military duties to have time to spend with his family. Thus, it was Cherry who made the everyday decisions in the Hilliard household, but all of them had been supported by her mother. When she had made mistakes, Cherry had never felt bad, for Mama was there to sympathize with her and comfort her. And when things happened over which neither had any control, Cherry could always count on her mother's support.

All monies from their small property went to Major Hilliard, whose expenses as a cavalry officer were prodigious. As a consequence, Cherry had, from early childhood, been forced to wear hand-me-down gowns from her cousins. Lady Hilliard sent over boxes of outgrown gowns regularly. To be sure, the gowns were the wrong colour for

Cherry's vivid hair and had too many ruffles and flounces for Cherry's active life, but they covered her and she was grateful for them. But not for her cousins' manners. Both Agnes and Lizzie, whenever they saw her, took pains to gloat over Cherry's wardrobe.

And Cherry, mortified that her plain, mousy cousins had cause to gloat, would come in tears to her mother. Then she would be comforted by her mother's arms and her reminder, "You must remember, dear, that your papa must keep up appearances. His expenses are truly heavy. I'm sure he appreciates your sacrifice and his appreciation is much more important than your cousins' bad manners. You want to help your papa, don't you?" And Cherry, knowing she was helping her father, would wipe her tears, firmly resolved to ignore her horrid cousins.

But now, there was no one! Her mother had deserted her. Instead of trying to talk Uncle Geoffrey out of the betrothal, she was trying to convince Cherry to accept it! She wouldn't! She would never accept such a marriage, but who would help her? She had no brothers to turn to. She was alone, with no one to help her fight against this hateful marriage. A female, alone, could do nothing. She must have help.

If only Papa hadn't been killed. He would not have accepted an offer from such a dreadful man! He would have asked her opinion of it. Oh, why did Papa have to be killed in the middle of her first Season? It would have been so much easier if she hadn't known what the *beau monde* was like.

It had been so exciting, the first time she'd been to London to her very first parties. There had been balls every night, at the most popular hostesses', too: Lady Jersey, Lady Cowper, Lady Sefton, and even Countess Lieven. It had been just wonderful, she'd had partners for every dance. Cherry had worried about that at first, fearful that a country miss would not know how to get on in the *ton,* but she'd had the satisfaction of dancing while her cousins were sitting out.

Cherry's face became wistful as she remembered those glorious days. Though she had missed being presented to the queen at a drawing room, she had been to Almack's. Even in Bedfordshire she'd heard of Almack's, and Grandmama had impressed upon her the importance of correct behaviour, lest the hostesses deny her entrance. She'd been thrilled when Lady Jersey had called to proffer a voucher, but disappointed when she got there. The three rooms were elegant, of course, but somehow she had expected Almack's to be more grand from the way everyone spoke of it in hushed tones.

She had met Edward Bennet there. He hadn't been to the coming-out ball given for herself and Agnes. "I had another engagement that evening, Miss Hilliard," he told her as they waltzed. "I regret exceedingly that I wasn't able to make your acquaintance at that time."

"Why, Mr. Bennet?" she'd asked, smiling up at him.

"I could have had four dances with you by now. As it is, I'll only be able to stand up with you once again this evening."

And when she'd looked surprised that he should want to dance with her, he said, "My mother warned me not to single out any young lady for particular attention. It's not considered good *ton,* you know."

Cherry could not bring herself to inform her partner that he had misinterpreted her expression, so she murmured something noncommittal and accepted his invitation for a ride in the Park.

Mama had objected, thinking it improper for an unchaperoned young lady to drive in public with a gentleman, but Grandmama had overruled her. "Now, Amanda, it's perfectly proper if a groom is in attendance. After all, they will be in full view at all times. There is no chance of any impropriety occurring."

Edward was such a nice young man, rather serious-minded, but pleasant. He seemed especially attracted to her hair, for he found so many occasions to refer to it. "It's like fire, Miss Hilliard, like living fire."

It seemed to Cherry that people reacted quite strongly to the unusual colour of her hair. They were either attracted to it, like Mr. Bennet, or they hated it, like her Uncle Geoffrey.

She had even caught Mr. Brummell staring at her, his quizzing glass raised. He had turned away after making a comment to a friend, a disparaging remark, Cherry surmised, for his friend had laughed nastily.

Somehow Cherry had always taken her hair for granted. It had never seemed unusual to her, just something she had, like her greenish-blue eyes and her ivory skin. But she soon discovered that she was the only female in the *ton* with hair of such brightness. Most girls had hair of a light brown colour. Of course, there were a goodly number with darker hair, and quite a few with guinea-gold locks, but only a small number had red hair, and those were mostly of dark auburn. She had even overheard someone ask, "Is that colour natural, or is she wearing a wig?" and had been hard put not to giggle.

Now, as Cherry stood lost in thought, a pensive smile on her face, for she had truly liked Mr. Bennet and had thoroughly enjoyed the few weeks of her London Season, her thoughts suddenly veered to Lord Varian and she began pacing again in agitation.

She had seen his lordship several times. He had been pointed out to her in Hyde Park by Lizzie as they rode in

Lady Hilliard's barouche. Her cousin, eager to display her greater sophistication labouriously earned during her previous Season, had been regaling Cherry with choice bits of gossip, when they had come upon a smart curricle driven by a dashing female.

"Don't look at her, Cherry, she's not respectable," Lizzie hissed. "It's highly improper for a delicately bred female to display any knowledge of a gentleman's mistress," she further explained, "though everyone knows of their fancy women, and the chaperones at all the parties spend all their time talking about the muslin company. That particular lightskirt," she confided, "is entertaining Lord Varian, who lost an arm in the Peninsula."

Cherry, obedient to Lizzie's command, had refused to look at the female, though she couldn't resist a glance at his lordship. Impulsively she had felt sympathy for the tall, well-built man with the empty sleeve. It must have been a terrible shock to him to lose an arm at the elbow. But later, overhearing the gossip from the chaperones at various balls and parties of Varian's hard drinking, gaming, and wenching, her sympathy had vanished.

Once, just once, she had met him face-to-face. Riding in the Park in Mr. Bennet's high-perch phaeton, they had come abreast of Varian and that woman. Cherry, curious to see the most talked of mistress in London besides Harriette Wilson, decided to ignore Lizzie's advice and risk a look. She had glanced up to meet dark, smoldering eyes, eyes that seemed to dare her to pity him. She had been so disconcerted that she had quite forgotten to look at the Frenchwoman.

Now this rake had offered for her and, more importantly, been accepted by her uncle. He was an earl, and rich, too, according to her mother and uncle. Cherry knew that wealth did not weigh with her mother, for she herself had not married for money; but Lord Hilliard, Cherry knew, would enjoy the added prestige coming to him from being allied to a wealthy family.

Her mother was pleased, for Cherry's sake, she had to admit; her uncle had been obviously smug about the business. Agnes and Lizzie would be jealous at first, then hopeful that the new relationship would help them find husbands. Everyone was happy over this marriage, everyone but Cherry.

Why had Varian offered for her? He couldn't want her dowry; she had only a small portion and he was wealthy. He couldn't want to ally himself with an influential family, for Uncle Geoffrey had no political connections. It was not possible he was in love with her, a girl he'd never met. Could it be that Varian wanted to marry her for her hair? Had he asked who she was after seeing her with Mr. Bennet?

Don't be silly, Cherry told herself. It's only in novels that such things happen, not in real life. She had probably made no impression on him at all.

To be sure, all her other suitors had appeared smitten by her hair. They had complimented her profusely until her cheeks burned, begged her for waltzes and rides in the Park. Most of them were rather silly, of course, gazing at her with heartsick expressions, stammering and stuttering; but at least they had approached her and wanted to be with her.

Cherry stopped pacing. No, Varian was not like them. He was different. He hadn't once asked to be presented to her. He'd never even seen her except that time in the Park, and then he hadn't known who she was. Of course he couldn't dance, except awkwardly, and a man with such eyes would have too much pride to appear awkward in public. However, he could at least have attended parties

41

and spoken to her there, or he could have called on her grandmother.

Grandmama! Why hadn't she thought of her? Here she'd been allowing her thoughts to drift to her Season and had forgotten her grandmother's importance. It was she who had supplied Cherry's new clothes. "The chit needs gowns, Amanda. She cannot be introduced in last year's castoffs. I refuse to be seen with her if you persist in dressing her in rags. You will forget your pride and allow me to supply them."

Her grandmother had helped then. And more importantly, the Dowager Lady Hilliard was not known for holding her tongue. Uncle Geoffrey would listen to her. If only she could be brought to support Cherry. She would write immediately, Cherry decided. No! It would be much more effective to plead her own cause. She would go to London to see her grandmother!

Six

"Hetty, when does the stagecoach stop in the village?" Cherry asked the next morning.

"The coach, miss?" Hetty stopped brushing Cherry's hair to ask suspiciously, "Now, why should you wish to know that?"

"Because I am going to take it to London."

"Lunnon! Now, Miss Cherry." The face of the elderly maid plainly showed the consternation she felt. Though never before able to dissuade her charge from any course of action, she nevertheless felt it her duty to make the attempt. "You can't go to Lunnon, miss, not on a public coach. It ain't fittin'."

"Other people ride on them, don't they, Hetty?"

"Not unescorted well-bred young ladies," stated Hetty emphatically as she placed the hairbrush on the dressing table. She would need all her wits and no distractions to win this argument.

"But I won't be unescorted, Hetty. You will be coming with me and I shall be a governess."

Hetty chose to ignore Cherry's first words. She preferred to attack where she had some chance of success. "A governess, miss? You can't be a governess. No married woman in her right mind would hire you, you're much too pretty."

Cherry giggled. "I don't want to be a real governess, silly. It would be much too boring. Just a pretend one on the stage. I'll wear my plainest gown, a black shawl, and a black bonnet with a veil, Hetty," she added triumphantly. "No one will recognize me."

Hetty shook her head. "And where will *we* be goin' in Lunnon?"

"To my grandmother's. I thought it out last night, Hetty. Mama can't help me. She has never stood up to anyone in her life, especially Uncle Geoffrey. And he wants to marry me off as quickly as possible. That's why he accepted the first offer made for me. I think he's jealous that I had more suitors than Agnes or Lizzie. Uncle has never liked me because I don't act like those mice he has for daughters. All they ever say is 'Yes, Papa.' The only one left to save me from Varian is my grandmother."

Hetty had resumed the hair brushing as Cherry spoke. The situation was not as bad as she had feared. It was possible the Dowager could succeed where others had failed and persuade the child to accept the inevitable. Certainly the old lady had more spirit than either of her daughters-in-law, or her son, if truth be told. If anyone could manage Cherry, it was the Dowager.

Cherry interrupted her maid's musings. "Go to the Swan Inn, please, Hetty," she coaxed. "And book two seats to London for Miss Aubrey and companion. I shall be Miss Aubrey. If anyone asks, you can explain that Lord Hilliard brought my old governess for a short visit and she's returning, with you as an escort, to make it all proper. When she was here, Miss Aubrey didn't often go to the village, so I'm sure no one will recognize me."

"I don't know, miss. It's not at all proper for you to travel on a public coach." Hetty's face expressed her misgivings. "And your mother will be worried. Who's to take care of her with you and me gone?"

Cherry sighed. Hetty's disapproval was an unexpected obstacle. She had been so involved in her plans, she had quite overlooked Hetty. Nothing for it now but to take her objections in order. "You know I can't afford to hire a post chaise, Hetty. The cost is enormous, even if it is only forty miles. And I'll leave a note for Mama, telling her where we're going. She can get Annie Wryson to help. We'll only be gone a few days. Please, Hetty, please go."

As a reluctant maid set off to walk the mile into Leighton Buzzard, Cherry hurriedly selected the few items of clothing she would need. She could take only one small portmanteau for herself, for any larger bag would be too heavy for her to carry and she couldn't expect Hetty to carry two bags on a mile journey.

This small chore accomplished and the note written for her mother, Cherry Hilliard waited, impatiently pacing the floor. She was still waiting, hours later, when, dressed in a black bombazine gown and her mother's black bonnet, she sat in the private parlour of the Swan Inn next to a grumbling Hetty. The landlord had informed "Miss Aubrey" that the stagecoach was late. "I told Hetty this morning that the coach usually got here by two o'clock, miss, but it's way behind the time bill. You can wait in here, not fittin' for you to stay in the common." And Cherry, in the guise of a governess, had perforce to act like one and wait with the outward semblance of patience.

Though the landlord had looked at her strangely, she knew no one could possibly recognize her. Her face was shadowed by the veil, which hung down past her chin, and the bonnet covered her hair. Not one flaming strand showed. Cherry, overcoming her habitual impatience, had taken particular pains to hide her curls. She had ruthlessly shoved them under a cotton mob cap and then forced the cap under the concealing bonnet.

But doing something, anything, was far easier than waiting. She couldn't even tap her foot, but must be sedate, as a governess is. Why didn't the stage come? Why did it have to be late today, when she had to get to London? Soon her mother would be waking from her afternoon nap. Would she discover Cherry's note too early and send the groom after her? How humiliating it would be to be discovered.

When she was sure she couldn't sit still another minute longer—only the fear that she'd be recognized had prevented her from running out to look up the street—a loud noise and much bustle announced the coach. The landlord called, "The stage, miss," and hurried out, carrying a tray covered with foaming pints of ale.

Now that the stage was here, Cherry entered the courtyard hesitantly. She had never traveled in anything but Uncle Geoffrey's carriage and watched nervously as the lumbering black and red coach was pulled to a stop.

The coachman remained on his box, as did the roof passengers. They all reached down gladly to accept the glasses offered by the landlord, tossing down coins onto his tray. One group of ostlers was leading away the exhausted horses, while another group was bringing up a new, more spirited team. The change of horses was rapid. The descending travelers had barely caught their bags—tossed to them from the boot by the guard—when it was time to go again.

As Cherry stood hesitating, trying to find courage to

46

enter, the guard jumped down, took charge of their baggage, then opened the door of the coach and all but shoved her inside. "There's plenty of room inside, ma'am," he announced.

Four pairs of eyes stared at her. Thankful that the veil shielded her features, she stood wavering. Perhaps she shouldn't . . . "Make room," shouted the guard, and Cherry felt herself pushed from behind as Hetty was precipitated into the coach.

With much reluctance the passengers moved a few inches. Just as Cherry and Hetty were seated, the coach started up with a lurch. The fat woman sitting next to Cherry fell away from her, and Cherry quickly shoved herself back against the squabs. In her ignorance of public travel she had not imagined that the coaches would be so crowded.

Behind the protection of the veil, she looked at her fellow passengers surreptitiously. Not one of them would she have met in the course of her daily life. Cherry had led a sheltered life. During the eighteen years she had lived in Leighton Buzzard she had met very few villagers. Except for Parson and Mrs. Dudley and Squire Hatton, she knew no one. Mama had refused to socialize with her social inferiors and had no funds to entertain her peers.

Seated directly across from her was a man who seemed to be staring at her, as if trying to see through the veil. As she encountered his stare, she hastily lowered her eyes. It was not proper to stare, even through a veil, and besides, he gave her the most uncomfortable sensation. His blue eyes appeared to be devouring her.

Cherry laughed to herself. Perhaps in her relief to be finally on her way, she was getting imaginative. It was probably just ordinary curiosity on his part.

"Are you traveling far?"

Startled to be addressed by a stranger, she looked up.

That man was still eyeing her. While she debated the wisdom of speaking, she had time to examine him more closely. He was wearing breeches and top boots, as did most men, but his coat was not new, or too clean. Neither did it fit well, although that could be due to the cramped quarters of the coach. His face was browned, as if he had spent much time outdoors; his hair was graying over the temples. All in all a quite ordinary man. Only the piercing quality of his gaze and his intent look were disquieting.

As she hesitated, unsure whether she should speak to a stranger, he smiled, a warm, winning smile, and, reassured, Cherry answered, "Just to London, sir."

Then, belatedly remembering the story she planned to relate, she started to explain, "I'm taking a new post," when Hetty spoke up belligerently, "And I'm escortin' Miss Aubrey to her new employers."

The fat woman, fanning herself with a handkerchief, sighed. "I for one will be pleased to arrive. This journey has been plagued by late starts and poor driving. I declare, never before have I been on a more poorly driven coach, and I travel regularly to Dunstable to visit my daughter."

One passenger was sleeping, leaning back against the squabs, a handkerchief over his face. Across from him was a young man, his face pockmarked. When Cherry turned her gaze on him, he hurriedly turned his eyes away and nervously plucked at the buttons of his coat.

By now her earlier hesitation had vanished. The passengers looked harmless, and she did have Hetty for protection. However, she had no desire to converse with them, and she was tired. Sleep had been long in coming last night. Her mind had been much too occupied with her plans: first the details of her masquerade as her former governess, and later, all the things she had to tell her grandmother, all the reasons why Varian's offer should be

48

refused. Cherry had decided that a calm, reasoned approach would be much more effective than her usual spontaneous speech and had marshaled her arguments, but it had taken time, time ordinarily spent in sleep.

She leaned back against the none too clean squabs and closed her eyes. It seemed as if she had just dozed off when she was aroused again as the coach drove over the cobbles of a courtyard and the guard called, "Dunstable."

The fat woman descended, pushing past Cherry, and Hetty quickly moved across to sit next to her charge. No other passengers entered. Again the coach started off with much swaying and heaving and Cherry slept, leaning against Hetty. By tonight she would be in Berkeley Square under her grandmother's protection, safe from Varian.

She awoke with a start as the coach gave a violent turn and she was thrown against Hetty. "What is it?" she gasped. "Hetty, what's happened?"

The coach stopped so suddenly Cherry was thrust back into her seat. She could see the man across from her holding onto the leather strap to keep himself upright. Only then was she aware that the coach was leaning precariously to one side, and she was almost atop Hetty.

The guard jerked open the door, grumbling, "He must'a bin blind, not to see us. But that's the way wi' t'Quality, no carin' for the likes o' us common fo'k."

"What happened?" demanded the man sitting across from Cherry.

"We's lost a wheel," answered the guard. "It's lucky we be, that t'coach didn't overturn. Had to swerve, we did, to miss a gent's curricle. Best get down, fo'ks."

"Oh, dear. How long before it can be repaired?" inquired Cherry.

"Don't know, ma'am. T'Wig an' Bottle is just down t'street," he informed the passengers. "Ye'll have to stay the night here in St. Albans. T'morrow we can get a new coach t'take ye on to Lunnon."

In the gathering dusk Cherry and Hetty, carrying their bags, trudged down Market Street, following their fellow passengers. Cherry was moving almost automatically, for she was still not fully awake and the accident had happened too fast for her to comprehend. Jostled by a rough-looking man to an awareness of her surroundings, as she passed through the door of the inn she looked about her curiously. The entrance gave directly onto a room filled with many oak tables at which more rough-looking men were occupied with their dinners. The din was prodigious, as all seemed to be talking at once.

The innkeeper coming toward the group of passengers had to raise his voice to be heard. "Wot kin I do fer ye's?" he asked, wiping his hands on a none too clean apron.

One of the passengers stepped forward. "The London stage has lost a wheel, and we"—he gestured to include the group behind him—"require beds and dinner."

The innkeeper nodded. "Can be done, sirs, can be done. Course, ye'll ha' t'share a bedchamber," he cautioned. Then his eye fell on Cherry and Hetty. "Don't always get ladies here, but I do ha' a private parlour for your dinner. How many be there?" He started counting, then yelled, "Ten extra for dinner, Annie."

The floor was dirty and there was a strange odor in the air. Cherry did not like the looks of this inn and moved closer to Hetty.

"If ye'll come wi' me, I'll show ye yer rooms," announced the innkeeper, turning to lead the way up the staircase. "The parlour's in there." He pointed to a door to his right. "Win ye're ready come on down."

The first bedchamber was assigned to Cherry and Hetty. Within its privacy, Cherry sank onto its only chair, opened her reticule, and counted the few coins in it. She groaned. "There's just enough to pay for our lodging and dinner, Hetty. What will we do? I won't be able to hire a hackney, and we can't walk to Berkeley Square."

"Don't you worry, Miss Cherry. I've a few pennies saved. Now wash your hands and face. The water's cold, but 'tis better than nothin'. We had best get our dinner."

Cherry brightened and obediently followed her maid's orders. Then, feeling more the thing, she descended to the mutton pie and cold sirloin provided for their meal.

The other passengers were already seated at the long table in the parlour, busily eating their dinners. Most of them hardly noticed her entrance with Hetty, but as Cherry seated herself and pushed up her veil, she again felt the piercing gaze of her fellow passenger fixed on her face. Why did he have to be sitting across from her again? she asked herself. However, her attention was switched to her dinner, as the innkeeper shoved a plate of food in front of her.

"A most inconvenient accident, wouldn't you say, miss?"

Directly addressed, there was little she could do but answer. Cherry glanced up, then swiftly lowered her eyes. "Oh, indeed, yes."

"I trust you won't be inconvenienced by arriving late to your destination," he continued.

"Oh, no," she assured him, keeping her eyes on her plate. She wished he would stop looking at her. She began to feel extremely uncomfortable.

"The name's Jack Keene, miss," he introduced himself, then leaned forward and lowered his voice. "I'm going to London myself. Be glad to look out for you. It's not safe for a young girl, especially one as pretty as you, to travel alone."

Hetty, sitting two chairs down, had kept her eye on Cherry. She hadn't held with this escapade, but the sooner the child got to her grandmother's the better. Now she spoke up. "Miss Ch—Aubrey is not alone, sir. I'm looking out for her and she's goin' to her new fambly, which is expectin' her."

It must be her imagination, Cherry decided, but she had the distinct impression that Mr. Keene was not pleased at Hetty's words. At any rate, after giving her a long look he applied himself to his meal, no longer trying to engage her attention.

Cherry could not eat. The food looked none too appetizing. The mutton fat was beginning to congeal on her plate, and the sirloin, when she tasted it, was full of gristle. She pushed at the food, then impulsively rose from the table and with a murmured "Excuse me" hurried up the stairs to the bedchamber.

She felt keyed up and restless inside. All she'd done today was wait: first for Hetty to return with the tickets, then in the inn for the coach to arrive, and now, now she must wait for tomorrow before she could see her grandmother. She wanted to scream from frustration. Everything was going wrong! Instead, she had to be content with activity. She began to pace back and forth across the small room, from the leaded window from which she could see down into the empty courtyard, past the narrow bed, to the door, and back again. There was only the one chair and a small table in the barely furnished room, nothing to hinder her steps.

How she hated waiting! At home she could always ride or go walking or help Hetty with the cooking. Had she been wise to come on this journey? There was nothing to do here but wait, nothing to see but this room, smaller and barer than her own room at home.

It didn't help her impatience to have Hetty undress her as soon as her maid arrived. "I'm not sleepy, Hetty," she protested. "I slept on the coach. Why do I have to go to bed now? It's not even dark yet."

Her protest was overlooked. "We'll be waked early, miss."

"Oh, Hetty, this isn't turning out the way I'd hoped. Do you suppose the accident was an omen, a bad omen?"

"I'm sure I don't know, miss," Hetty said stolidly as she dropped a muslin bedgown over Cherry's head. "I don't gen'lly hold with omens and such like."

"Well, first the coach was late, and now the wheel's off. . . . Oh, Hetty, maybe we shouldn't have come," Cherry wailed.

"Rather late for that, miss, I'd say." Hetty was vigorously brushing the mass of orange-red ringlets. "Your hair needs croppin' again, Miss Cherry," she announced, hoping to turn Cherry's thoughts in a new direction.

"Oh, Hetty, what difference does it make how long my hair is? I'm not in London where it's important to be fashionable. I'm in mourning, remember?"

"Well, there you are, miss," said Hetty, handing a dressing gown to Cherry. "I'll just go down and get a hot brick. The sheets is probably damp," she sniffed disparagingly.

Cherry sat on the edge of the bed, not wanting to sleep. She hadn't really wished that she hadn't come on this journey. It was just that the day had been so frustrating. If she hadn't come, it would have meant acceptance of Varian's offer of marriage. And she couldn't do that.

Not that she was in love with anyone else. There hadn't been time to fall in love. She had only been in London a little more than a month. And though there had been scores of eligible young men surrounding her at balls and assemblies, to be honest with herself, she had to admit being bored by many of them, even Mr. Bennet.

Her father had been a soldier, a cavalry officer who died heroically fighting for his country. Most of the young men she met seemed callow youths compared to Major John Hilliard, late of His Majesty's Dragoons.

A soft knock sounded and the door opened slowly and silently. Cherry glanced up, expecting to see Hetty with a hot brick. She was amazed to see the man with the piercing eyes standing in the open doorway. Thinking he had mistaken her bedchamber for his, she called, "Go away. You are mistaken. This is not your bedchamber."

He smiled, revealing yellowish teeth, then reached out and closed the door behind him.

Seven

Cherry shivered and drew the folds of her dressing gown tighter. His gaze had become more and more like that of a beast about to devour its prey. She felt extremely uncomfortable and jumped from the bed. "Go away," she repeated. "You have no business here."

"It is very much my business to be here," he said softly, leaning against the door. "I was sure that bonnet and veil hid a beauty, and I wasn't mistaken," he added smugly.

What could he possibly want with her? She had to get rid of him. Cherry drew herself up to her full height. "Leave at once, sir, or I'll scream," she warned.

"Now why should you want to do that, my pretty? I have no intention of hurting you."

Cherry relaxed slightly. "You haven't? Then what do you want?"

"Just a bit of fun. Surely that's not new to you. I can't believe a governess with your looks would still be . . ." he paused, "unspoiled?"

She stared at him, not understanding his words, but instinctively mistrusting him. She shook her head decisively. "Go away, Mr. Keene."

Her words appeared to anger him, for he straightened up from his negligent pose and took a step toward her. "Now don't get high and mighty with me, miss. You can share your favours with me as well as your employers."

Still not understanding him, but beginning to fear this intruder, Cherry stammered, "No, no, no. G-go away," as she backed away from him.

Keene's face darkened. He took a quick stride forward and reached out for her.

Cherry screamed, "Hetty! Help me!"

She tried to get away from him, running toward the window, but there was no room to run. He was upon her with a growl, grabbed her by the arm, and put a hand over her mouth to stop her cries.

Cherry jerked her head, trying to get free of his cruelly tight fingers. He was holding her so close to him, she was almost touching his body! She pulled her arm with all her strength and tried to shake her head free, but her resistance only resulted in his grasp tightening. Cherry began to know real terror. Was he about to kill her?

For an instant she felt helpless. Her senses reeled, she felt faint and stopped struggling. He was so strong and she was so weak. How could she fight against him?

"That's better. You must like a man to be rough with you, eh?"

Like *him*? His words roused her. She would not tamely submit to such a man! Her right hand was free! She reached up and slapped him across the face—then reeled as he slapped her.

In the sudden silence voices could be heard. "No woman of that name here, my lord." It was the innkeeper! "The only young woman on the London stage is a governess, a Miss Aubrey."

"Nevertheless, I insist you open the door." It was a commanding voice, one Cherry had never heard before, but it made her assailant pause. A strange look appeared on his face and he released her arm. A moment later he brushed past her, threw open the window, and disappeared out of it, just as the door opened and Hetty entered. "Miss, what happened?"

"Oh, Hetty." Cherry threw herself at her maid. "He came in—I thought—I thought it was you—he tried to—he wanted to—" She couldn't continue, but put her head on Hetty's ample bosom and, held tight in her maid's warm embrace, sobbed at the full realization of her narrow escape.

"Hetty, it was dreadful," she choked. "He was beastly. I feared he would kill me." Cherry's whole body shuddered in reaction; she gulped, then took a deep breath. She had to talk to Hetty. Maybe she could explain what that awful man wanted in her bedchamber.

Cherry pulled back from Hetty's embrace, raising her streaming eyes, but the pursed look on her maid's face drove all thoughts of questions from her. Something was amiss!

She looked past Hetty's form and saw a pair of black Hessians with a mirror finish and cream-coloured pantaloons encasing muscular legs. Her eyes widened and her gaze traveled upward. She could see, leaning against the door of her bedchamber, a blue-coated figure. Her eyes slid over the wide shoulders, the buff waistcoat, and white cravat, and came to rest on the left sleeve, pinned up at the elbow. Varian! What was he doing here?

He was watching her, his lips curled in a cynical smile. His dark eyes, as he met her gaze, were full of mockery. "I came to present my respects and found my betrothed had flown."

His voice was harsh, not at all pleasant. Neither was his expression welcoming. "I should have expected that, perhaps," he muttered.

This enigmatic expression went unexplained as he straightened up and came toward her. "Now, you will please dress, Miss Hilliard. We leave shortly."

His voice was soft, not raised, as Uncle Geoffrey's ofttimes was, but his request sounded amazingly like an order, and who was he to give her orders? How could they leave now, when she had just escaped being assaulted? She needed comforting, not harsh words.

"Leave? Don't be silly," she exclaimed, moving away from Hetty to stand confronting him, her face tearstained, her hair disheveled. "I can't leave with you."

"No?" Again his lips curled slightly. "Yet you allow a man to visit you, or"—he paused at her gasp, his eyebrows raised—"am I mistaken?"

Cherry's head rose. She stamped her foot in vexation. "Oh," she exclaimed, her hands clenched tightly at her sides. How she wanted to hit him! "You do mistake, my lord. That a stranger entered here I can't deny, but I did *not* invite him in, and . . . and I can't go with you, I'm going to my grandmother's."

"So you said in your note." Then Varian's voice dropped. He spoke under his breath, his words barely audible. "London is closer than Leighton Buzzard. Very well, Miss Hilliard. I will escort you to Berkeley Square."

Cherry was surprised that he knew her grandmother's direction, since he had never called there. "You will? But why?"

"Surely that is obvious. I do not wish your presence here to become known. Fortunately you traveled under an assumed name, but your—ah—hair is not easily overlooked. Now"—he gestured with the hand holding his high-crowned beaver, and though he continued to speak in a soft voice, it was a very determined, almost implacable voice—"you will get dressed."

She stared at him. Cherry was not acquainted with many men, and this man was different from those she knew. Instinctively she sensed that he would not respond to coaxing or pleading: he would be immune to a feminine smile. She shook her head slightly. Just when she had discovered the power of her smile and the attraction of her emerald green eyes, especially after being lowered behind her dark lashes, she had to confront a man immune to them!

Varian misinterpreted her head shake. "Miss Hilliard, you may as well learn now, I do not like to repeat myself and I do not like to be kept waiting."

His voice was still soft and barely audible, but there was more menace in it than in the blustery tones of her uncle or in Jack Keene's growl. Instinctively she knew that here was a man to be feared.

But contrarily, knowledge of this only made her more defiant. She raised her chin. "How can I dress with you in my bedchamber? There's no screen in here."

His eyebrows rose. Then he smiled. Cherry had the curious feeling that she was facing Lucifer himself when she saw that smile. It was an evil, threatening smile, just a slight lift of his lips that did not reach his eyes. They remained cold. Seeing those eyes, Cherry shivered.

"I assure you, Miss Hilliard, the sight of your—ah—charms, will not embarrass me."

She stared at him, for a moment not comprehending. Then, as the full implication of his words hit her, she blushed, covering her brilliant cheeks with her hands. "Oh, you are horrible," she gasped.

He merely shrugged and stood waiting. Cherry would not move. He had no right to expect her to remove her bedgown in his presence. He was a stranger, not her husband.

Hetty, up to now a silent witness, was fully acquainted with her mistress's determination. She also sensed the implacability of his lordship and feared further confrontation. Miss Cherry might be hurt. And 'twere better that his lordship escort them to Lunnon—Miss Cherry was not safe here. She moved to intervene.

"If you please, m'lord"—she spoke hesitantly, coming forward and bobbing a respectful curtsey—"if you would turn your back?"

He laughed then, but walked over to the open window, where he stood gazing out.

Cherry was caught. She couldn't refuse to go, not if he would really escort her to Grandmama. Besides, it would be more pleasant traveling in a private carriage. But once under her grandmother's protection, Cherry would tell Varian exactly what she thought of his manners in coming into her bedchamber and ordering her about.

She allowed Hetty to dress her, but dawdled, taking as much time as possible, though Hetty shook her head in silent disapproval.

Cherry knew that she should thank Lord Varian for rescuing her, for his appearance had caused her attacker to flee, but she refused to do so. He had no right to give her orders. He was certainly not her guardian, and with her grandmother's help, he would not be her husband.

At last the bonnet was on her head, its black veil covering her face, and the shawl wrapped around her shoulders. Her nightclothes were packed again in the portmanteau. She was ready to leave and walked over to the door.

Eight

Varian held open the door, and Cherry slowly descended the stairs, followed by Hetty with the bags. She wanted desperately to run away from the cold, hateful man to whom she was betrothed, but knew that would be useless. Where could she go in a strange village?

The innkeeper stood waiting at the foot of the stairs, a suspicious expression on his face. Should she appeal to him for help? But somehow his hands, tangled in his dirty apron, repelled her. He could be worse than Varian. He could be like Jack Keene. Cherry shuddered.

A carelessly thrown guinea from Varian produced a wide smile and an obsequious bow. That's what he was waiting for, Cherry decided. He wasn't worried about me at all. I would have made a fool of myself if I had appealed to him for help.

A large traveling carriage was waiting before the door of the Wig and Bottle. At their appearance, a groom sprang down from the box, took the bags, then opened the door.

"Dalton, we shall proceed to the White Hart to change horses. By now my team should be sufficiently rested to enable us to reach London without too much delay. Desire Chawley to proceed to number fifteen Berkeley Square."

"Very good, m'lord," murmured the groom, then threw a quick glance at Cherry as he assisted her into the carriage.

More than ever glad that she had her face covered, Cherry sank onto the blue velvet seat of the coach. She felt extremely mortified that his lordship's servants should witness her forced removal. Across from her, another servant, his lordship's valet perhaps, was keeping his face carefully blank. Whether he approved his lordship's actions or not, Cherry knew she could get no help from him.

Varian entered, then Hetty. The carriage started smoothly, not at all like the lurching of the stage. It was only a short drive before it stopped again to change horses. Cherry, reminded that Varian's plans must have been considerably disarranged by her flight, refused to feel apologetic. How was she to know he would immediately come to call? He had never before thought it important enough to call on her.

The journey from the White Hart Inn in St. Albans to Berkeley Square, London, was made in silence. Cherry, though admitting to herself that it was indeed more comfortable riding in the earl's well-sprung carriage than in a public coach, leaned back against the well-padded squabs, closed her eyes, and refused to look at her escort. She had no intention of being a well-mannered young lady and conversing politely. Besides, what did one say to an arrogant lord who was all but abducting you?

His lordship, too, was silent. He was hungry, having missed his dinner chasing after Miss Hilliard, and angry. Who would have thought the chit would run away from such an advantageous marriage? He turned his head slightly. In the waning daylight he could just see her resolutely closed eyes behind the veil. Miss Hilliard was not at all what he had expected! She had already disrupted his plans. Well, it was early times yet, and perhaps now, while his anger was still hot, would be a better time for their marriage.

The lights of London woke Cherry from a very pleasant daydream in which she had the Earl of Varian at her mercy, ready to plunge a sword through his breast! She looked eagerly out of the window.

There was exhilaration just in being in London. The streets were crowded with pleasure seekers. The oil lamps glowed, making the streets almost as bright as day, so Cherry had no trouble in seeing.

Pedestrians lurched drunkenly along, some carrying bottles from which they drank. Many of the men had their arms about women. Other men were the targets of approaching females. As Cherry watched, one woman, a child really, so tiny she was, ran up and kissed a portly man in breeches, to be flung down into the street. Before Cherry had time to react to this cruel act, her attention was caught by another man, who was yelling, "Stop, thief!"

Cherry watched, fascinated. This was one aspect of London hitherto concealed from her. She had gone only to Almack's or to private parties, escorted by her mother and grandmother to the fashionable section of the city. She had never seen men in their cups before or known that thieves operated so openly.

But remembrance of Almack's and her own brief Season brought renewed awareness of her own predicament. But surely, she told herself, Grandmama will help me. She had helped before. It had been the Dowager Lady Hilliard who had borne the cost of Cherry's new wardrobe. Moreover, her grandmother would be the one person to understand Cherry's reluctance to enter into a marriage without love.

According to her mother, Lady Hilliard had been the only support when her son John had fallen in love with Amanda Wilton and wished to marry. She had not forbidden the match, nor had she held out for a richer bride. Yes, Cherry was sure her grandmother would not want her to wed a stranger, a hateful, odious stranger, at that.

Before she met Lord Varian, Cherry had been most reluctant to wed him. Now, having met him, she wanted it even less. She detested him; a man so arrogant he cared naught for her wishes would be a dreadful husband. In the light of the streetlamps she glanced at him, his face shadowed by the brim of his hat. She shivered as she met the gaze of his cold, dark eyes.

They had turned off Oxford Street and were traversing quiet residential streets. It could not be too much farther. Cherry leaned forward as if urging the horses on. She wanted to be free of Varian's presence.

The carriage stopped. A flambeau was still burning outside number 15, Berkeley Square. Cherry watched as the groom mounted the steps. At sight of the door knocker, a feeling of relief swept over her. It had not earlier occurred to her that her grandmother might not be in London. What would she have done had she arrived here to find her grandmother gone?

The groom returned to inform his lordship that the Dowager had just retired but would be told that her granddaughter had arrived. He held open the door of the carriage. Varian descended, then held out his hand to assist Cherry.

She drew her shawl about her—she didn't want him

touching her—and stepped down carefully. She wouldn't give him the satisfaction of catching her if she fell. She swept into the house.

There a sleepy butler, hiding a yawn behind a gloved hand, said, "Her ladyship sent word, miss, that she would receive you tomorrow. I've already sent up the maids to make up the bed."

"Thank you, Whaley," Cherry replied. She wanted to tell him that her late arrival had not been her fault but held her tongue. The less servants knew, the less gossip there would be. "I'll go straight up, Whaley. Good night."

She sensed that Varian had entered the house behind her, but refused to turn to look at him. Quickly she walked across the hall and almost ran up the stairs. She was free at last!

Cherry entered the bedchamber she had left just a short month ago. It was twice the size of her bedchamber at home, containing not only a four-poster bed draped in blue brocade, a dressing table, and a large wardrobe, but several comfortable chairs, a writing table, and a chaise longue as well.

She waltzed around the room. "Oh, Hetty, I'm here. Isn't it wonderful?" Her spirits soared. She felt like singing. She was safe! Her grandmother would know how to break the betrothal.

Here in this room she had dreamed of a husband: kind, loving, and gentle. From here, dressed in the new gowns from the most elegant modiste on Bond Street, she had gone to gay parties, smart assemblies, and the most fashionable balls.

But all the gowns were gone now, packed away in boxes. Cherry quickly sobered and sat down. Her brief moment of happiness was over. Life was so unfair to give her happiness for such a short time, then take it away. She felt tears well up, but then she rallied.

Cherry Hilliard, she told herself, you should be ashamed of yourself, thinking only of gowns and parties. You should be proud to wear black for your father. He was a hero. Didn't Mama receive a personal letter from Lord Wellington, telling her that Major the Honourable John Hilliard had died a hero's death?

She glanced up to find Hetty patiently waiting. Cherry smiled ruefully. "I'm sorry, Hetty, you're tired. I'll go to bed now."

Hetty shook her head, her cap jiggling. "Oh, no, miss. His lordship's carriage was so comfortable, I slept most of the way," she admitted, then frowned at Cherry's sudden grin. "Now that's enough, Miss Cherry. A body like me don't have many rides in fancy coaches. And it's you who need sleep, not me. Into bed, now."

After Hetty closed the curtains, Cherry lay quietly, dreamily listening to the noises of London. A carriage rumbled by, its wheels grating on the cobbled streets. Inside the house, a door closed, hurriedly and noisily. From afar off, the watch called.

Today had been an ordeal for her, and she was content to rest, confident that tomorrow would bring rescue.

Street noises woke her. Though Berkeley Square was an enclosed residential area and escaped most of the customary traffic of the London streets, there were still sounds of milkmaids bringing milk, water boys hawking fresh water, and bakery boys calling at the tops of their voices. Cherry liked the excitement of the city. There was always something to see. It was not at all like the country, where riding and walking were her sole recreations.

Soon Hetty arrived, bringing a cup of tea and a plate of toast.

Cherry sat up and smiled gaily. "What o'clock is it, Hetty? Did you sleep well?"

"It's ten, miss, and your grandmother's beds is most comfortable."

Hungrily Cherry ate her breakfast. "Oh, Hetty, it's so good to be here. Perhaps I can stay with grandmother." Cherry's spirits were high: even Hetty's frowning brow and tight-set lips could not lower her spirits. She felt all bubbly inside. Her problems were solved. She was here!

Her toilette was leisurely. There was no need to hurry, for her grandmother was a late riser, never appearing before eleven o'clock. Chatting to Hetty, she dawdled over her bath. "There's so many things I didn't see when I was in London before. With all the parties I had to attend there was no time for the wild animals, or the Elgin marbles, or the theatre. Do you know, Hetty, I have never been to Covent Garden?"

Only her choice of gown was rapid. Having brought but two gowns with her, she need not spend hours deciding what to wear.

At half after eleven Cherry descended to the Dowager's sitting room. As she opened the door she could see an elderly lady, wearing a silk gown in the style of the preceding century, a powdered wig on her head, sitting erect on a damask settee, her wide-spreading skirts covering its expanse. She looked up at Cherry's entrance and laid aside the latest *Lady's Magazine*.

"Well, miss, what's this I hear? You arrived last night in a gentleman's carriage?"

Somewhat taken aback by these sharp words, Cherry curtsied, then came up to plant a dutiful kiss on her grandmother's rouged cheek.

"Yes, Grandmama, it was dreadful. He insisted that I

come with him, even though I explained that I was coming to see you."

Cherry's far from clear explanation brought a play of expression to the elderly woman's face, ranging from outrage to puzzlement. She held up a hand. "Of whom do you speak, miss? But first, sit down, child. I don't like you towering over me."

Cherry obediently complied, sinking into a nearby chair. "Why, Lord Varian, Grandmama."

"Varian, that—" She swallowed the words.

"Yes, Grandmama, that *rake*," Cherry supplied, "and Uncle Geoffrey has accepted his offer." Then she jumped up, ran over to the settee, and threw herself at her grandmother's knees, clutching at her hands. "I don't have to marry him, do I?"

"Varian?" murmured the Dowager, then threw a sharp glance at Cherry. "Not one of your suitors, was he?"

"No," Cherry declared emphatically. "I have never been introduced to him. We have never exchanged two words, not until last night," she amended bitterly.

"And what happened then? No, no, sit down, miss, such emotional outbursts tire me."

Cherry reluctantly returned to the chair, where she sat clutching her hands together. "Well, Uncle Geoffrey said I had to marry Lord Varian. He had offered for me and Uncle accepted without consulting me. And *you* said, Grandmama, when Papa died, that there was no need to stay in London, for a gentleman couldn't make an offer during a time of mourning."

The Dowager frowned. "Yes, I did say that. Go on."

Cherry's resolve to provide a calm and reasoned explanation failed her at this curt command. "I can't marry him, truly I can't!" she wailed.

"Why not, miss? He's an earl, and well off from all

69

reports. He's still young, of good breeding, and a handsome lad to boot. You're not," she inquired sharply, "so missish as to let his injury turn you off, are you, gel?"

Cherry shook her head emphatically. "No, Grandmama, I don't care how many arms he has, but he's never cared enough for me to even seek an introduction, and besides," she hesitated, then said in a rush, "I've heard all sorts of horrible things about him."

"Gossip never has anything good to say about anyone," the Dowager replied dryly, then asked, "What things?"

"He has a French mistress and he's always seen with her. He even allows her to drive his team. He never goes to *ton* affairs and when he isn't occupied with *her,* he's gaming, playing high and accepting all sorts of wagers and dares. There was even mention of dueling. I know, I know," she responded to the Dowager's questioning look, "no one has been specific, but everyone who talks about him sounds horrified."

"There's nothing unusual about that, gel." The Dowager's voice held relief. Trust those gossips to make a situation seem worse to young ears, but if no details were mentioned, the chit could be reassured. "All men and most women gamble, and any man worth his salt has a mistress. It doesn't signify."

Was everyone to tell her his mistress meant nothing? "But, Grandmama . . ."

"Well?"

"Mama and Papa loved each other before their marriage."

"Yes, so they did," the Dowager agreed flatly, "but theirs was a most unusual match, child. Most gentlemen marry to provide an heir for their estates, or to provide the estate. Love doesn't enter into it at all, not in our class, gel.

Providing there's no aversion, people of breeding can deal amicably together, as your grandfather and I did."

Cherry's eyes grew into round orbs as she stared at her relation. This was the first information she'd learned concerning her grandparents' marriage. What was it like to live with a strange man? Her unruly tongue almost blurted out these words, but she held back for fear of a tongue-lashing. Instead, Cherry burst out, "But he's arrogant and hateful!"

"How do you know this, miss?"

"I started to tell you. I couldn't get Uncle to change his mind and refuse Varian's offer, so I decided to come to you for help. Mama wouldn't stand up to Uncle Geoffrey."

The Dowager chose to overlook this last statement as a truism and concentrate on the important portion of her granddaughter's words. "And how were you going to do that, pray?"

"By coach," Cherry said innocently.

The Dowager was so shocked she could not speak, but stared at her granddaughter in horror.

"Well, how else was I to come?" Cherry asked. "I couldn't afford to hire a post chaise. And I would have arrived, too, but the wheel broke off and we had to stay at St. Albans, and . . . and . . ." Cherry hesitated, then decided to forget the unpleasant attack at the inn. "Varian came, and told me to get dressed, that I had to leave with him. But when I said I was coming to you, he agreed to bring me here. He said it was closer than going home. He was horrible, Grandmama, coming into my bedchamber when I had on my bedgown, ordering me around like a servant, and he didn't even leave the room when I dressed!"

"What was Varian doing at St. Albans?"

Of what importance was that? Cherry wondered, but

obediently answered, "Well, he said something about coming to pay his respects and finding me gone, so I suppose he arrived at home and Mama showed him my note, but I really don't know. I had no desire to speak to him."

"I see. He must have wanted you enough to go after you, gel."

"He can't want *me,* he has a mistress. He can't want my fortune, for I have none. Besides, there are other girls in London who are prettier and have more money. Why does he want me, a female he'd never met?"

The Dowager looked at her granddaughter. Cherry's head was covered by a mass of fiery ringlets framing bright green eyes, her lips were pouting, her chin determined, and her head was erect and defiant. She appeared to be just exactly what she was, a firebrand, high-spirited, impetuous, and too independent for most men to manage. She would need a firm hand on her bridle, or she'd lead a man a merry chase. Life with her would not be easy. Why indeed did Varian want her?

The Dowager's musings were interrupted as the footman threw open the double doors and announced, "Lord Varian, m'lady," then withdrew discreetly.

"Oh, no!" Cherry jumped up from her chair and ran over to stand behind her grandmother. From the protection of the settee she could see the man approaching them. As her grandmother had said, he was tall and handsome, if one overlooked those eyes, which were dark and full of some emotion Cherry couldn't define—hate? bitterness? scorn?—she didn't know what it was, only that it was unpleasant. He was wearing top boots and breeches.

"Forgive my attire, ma'am," he said, bowing. "I rode over for the sake of privacy. There was enough fare for servants' gossip last night."

"You're Varian," the Dowager announced as she held out her hand. For the moment she ignored his last words, but resolved to discover their meaning later.

He took the wrinkled, beringed hand in his, bent his head, and carried it to his lips.

"How'd'do? Sit down," she commanded, gesturing toward a chair, then waited until he was seated in the chair Cherry had vacated, leaning back slightly, his legs crossed, a picture of ease. How can he look so comfortable? Cherry fumed. He was hateful, ruining her life, and showing not one sign of guilt.

"My granddaughter tells me you've offered for her?"

"That is correct, m'lady."

"Hmmmmmm. You haven't been too eager to meet her, I hear."

His black eyebrows rose almost to meet the black locks that were cut in the fashionable Windswept style. "I believe it is correct procedure, ma'am, to first approach a young lady's guardian."

"So as not to raise false hopes, my lord?" the Dowager asked, her voice silky.

Cherry held her breath. Grandmama was baiting him! She very well knew that few guardians would turn down a connection with the Mallory family. Cherry watched him. Beyond a brief glance at her, Varian kept his eyes on the Dowager. If he doesn't want to look at me, why does he want to marry me? she asked herself, her hands tight on the wooden frame of the settee. She wanted to scream questions at him, but held her peace. Her grandmother was more able than she to deal with the Earl of Varian.

"It has been known to happen," he answered coldly.

"Your concern for proper behaviour is commendable, my lord, but your concern falls short. My understanding is that mourning is not the time for betrothals."

73

That hit home, Cherry could see. His lordship frowned, but then he looked the Dowager in the eye and said softly, "And it is my understanding, my lady, that there is precious little mourning for your son."

Ohhhhhh! Cherry had to bite her lips to keep from crying out. She wanted to slap that dark, satanic face. How dare he imply that no one mourned her father? Why didn't Grandmama say something to put him in his place?

Instead, the Dowager answered lamely, "The conventions, I'm sure you'll agree, my lord, should be upheld."

"In most cases, my lady, I agree, but not in this. I've come to ask your permission for an early marriage."

Cherry gasped, so shocked she barely heard her grandmother's question.

"How early?"

"Within the month."

No, screamed Cherry silently. No, no, no!

"And your reasons, my lord?"

"To prevent another possible scandal."

"Scandal? Whatever do you mean, sir?"

"Has your granddaughter forgotten so soon? Or neglected to inform you? When I arrived at the Wig and Bottle—yes, you may well raise your eyebrows, my lady, it was a decidedly second-class inn—there were sounds of screams coming from Miss Hilliard's room, and signs of a struggle. I believe, and Miss Hilliard confirmed my suspicions, that a man was in her bedchamber, though not by her invitation, I must admit."

"Which you do most reluctantly, my lord." Cherry could not keep still a moment longer. "Since you disapprove so much of my behaviour, I give you leave to withdraw your offer."

"Is this true, Cherry?" The Dowager turned a scowling face toward her granddaughter.

"Yes, Grandmama," she admitted. "He was a passenger on the coach and came in after Hetty went to get a hot brick. I didn't lock the door, thinking Hetty would return shortly. He wouldn't go and I screamed."

"I believe my arrival prevented a—situation from developing," his lordship said delicately. "Miss Hilliard should not have been there. Her impulsive behaviour in running off to London, without first ascertaining whether you were still in residence, speaks of an unstable nature that might lead her to other unconventional behaviour."

"Faddle," Cherry spoke up again. "If you don't like my behaviour, why marry me?" She could not keep still, but moved around the settee to sit next to her grandmother, grasping the Dowager's hands and raising her eyes pleadingly. "Grandmama, he disapproves of me. He can't want to marry me. Tell him he can't."

The Dowager gazed down at the stricken face of her granddaughter, eyes bright with unshed tears, then across at the implacable lord, who was staring at Cherry, a brooding quality to his gaze. "My granddaughter raises a valid question, my lord."

"Childish qualities often disappear when a girl becomes a woman, my lady."

Ohhhh! How she hated this cold man with his pompous words. It was all because women were supposed to be submissive, passive, and obedient. If they showed any signs of the spirited behaviour that would not only be accepted but praised in a man, they were considered childish. It was unfair! Didn't her grandmother understand? Moreover, couldn't she see how dreadful he was?

The Dowager sighed. She was unsure of the correct course of action. On the one hand, Cherry needed firm handling, kind but firm. She was much too headstrong. It was the fault of a too lenient upbringing, and that, of course, was John's fault, falling out of love as easily as falling into it and soon losing interest in his wife and daughter. However, one couldn't undo the past. The important question now was whether Varian was the right man for her. He had acted properly in going after the child and bringing Cherry to her relations, but he seemed such a cold, unemotional man. Then, as her gaze centered on his tightly held lips, she amended her judgment: a man with emotions held rigidly in check.

"How soon would you wish the marriage, my lord?"

For a moment Cherry could not believe her ears. Her grandmother, whom she had counted on for support, had capitulated! To this treachery, Cherry screamed, "No, no, no!"

She jumped up from the settee and stood, her eyes wildly moving from her grandmother to Varian and back again. Her breathing was ragged, her eyes so brilliant they could have lit up a darkened room. "I won't marry you, I won't, I won't," she stormed. "You're hateful, you don't care for me at all." Then she ran past Varian and out of the room, ignoring the Dowager's words, "Cherry, come back here this instant!"

Cherry raced up the stairs, tears blinding her eyes. In her bedchamber she closed and locked the door, then threw herself on the bed, sobbing hysterically. Her grandmother had betrayed her! She had been in Cherry's favour until Varian told her about that man, that awful Jack Keene. Was she afraid that Varian would gossip about that and blacken Cherry's reputation? It was not her fault he had come in. She had not invited him. And besides, who was Varian to complain of her behaviour? He had had the effrontery to offer during mourning. If he had at least approached her, courted her, it would not have been quite so bad. Most girls were not in love when they married, she knew that, but at least most men showed some interest in the girl they wanted.

On this occasion Cherry's sobs did not last long, for she had no time to waste in crying. Not with Varian asking for a marriage within the month. She sat up. Well, if Grandmama won't help me, I must find someone who will, she decided. The only problem was *who*. She didn't know that many people in London, not well enough to ask for help anyway. She had few relations: her mother's sister, who was as helpless as Amanda Hilliard; her cousins—wait a bit! Dobbin would help her. Her cousin Robert. She had always gotten along with him; he was not a ninnyhammer like Agnes and Lizzie. He had always been game for a lark. The only gay times she had had as a child were with him.

Cherry wiped her eyes, ruining the handkerchief from her reticule, then went to the writing table and penned a brief note. Just as she was sanding her signature, a knock sounded at the door. "Who is it?" she called.

"It's Hetty, miss."

Cherry folded the single sheet of paper, hurriedly wrote *Robert* on it, then ran across to open the door.

"Your grandmother sent me, miss," the maid said impassively; then, at the sight of her charge's tear-ravaged face, she wailed, "Oh, Miss Cherry, you've been crying again."

"Never mind, Hetty. Take this note to Albemarle Street to Lord Hilliard's house and give it to Robert. No one else, do you understand? And don't let my grandmother know that you're going. Has Lord Varian left?"

"I think so, miss. By the by, if I'm not speaking out of place, the maids here think it's so romantic that you're marrying a war hero, Miss Cherry."

"He's not a *hero*, Hetty. *He* wasn't mentioned in the

dispatches like Papa was," she added. "I don't know how he lost his arm, and I don't care. And how did the maids know, Hetty? Did you tell them?"

Receiving an emphatic shake of Hetty's head, Cherry resumed, "Well, never mind. Just hurry, Hetty, please." She held out the sheet of paper.

Hetty looked suspiciously at her mistress's note. "What's in it?" she demanded. "Are ye up to mischief, child?"

Cherry shook her head. "It's just a note asking Robert to come to see me. Please, Hetty," she pleaded.

"Very well, miss," Hetty sighed, bobbed a brief curtsey, and left.

Dobbin and she had taken their fences together. Until he'd gone to school, they'd spent summers together, Lord Hilliard deeming it his responsibility to invite his sister-in-law for summer visits. Her female cousins were too weak-kneed to do more than stroll slowly in the shade, while she and Dobbin had climbed trees, gone fishing and shooting together. *Then* her uncle had not objected to her boyish ways, Cherry reflected as she washed her face.

She examined her face in the mirror. Her eyes were still red from weeping, but she didn't care how bad she looked. She knew she had to apologize to her grandmother. Let her see just how unhappy Cherry was.

She sighed. Best do it before luncheon.

Her appearance brought a brief smile to the Dowager's face. "Come in, child." Her glance was questioning as it rested on Cherry's face.

"I beg pardon for my behaviour, ma'am."

"Yes, yes." The Dowager waved a hand. "Until the next time," she said dryly. "Cherry, I want you to listen and heed my words. I know you don't *want* to marry Varian, but I am persuaded you are what he needs. His life was

78

shattered by the ball that destroyed his arm—his actions since his return reflect that. Your high spirits may be just what he needs to liven *his* spirits."

"And me, ma'am?" Cherry asked, disappointed that her grandmother should think of *his* needs.

"You, child, need a bit of curbing. I know you don't agree, but this episode has opened my eyes. You are much too impulsive. What would you have done had I not been in residence when you arrived, eh, miss? Furthermore, I hope you realize now what you escaped at the inn. Varian's appearance saved your honour. You should be grateful to him instead of screaming at him. Many men, finding their betrothed under such circumstances, would beg off. I find your behaviour extremely reprehensible."

Grateful to Varian? When he was the cause of all her problems? But, afraid her unruly tongue might give away her plans, Cherry did not voice her thoughts and meekly murmured, "Yes, Grandmama," and gave her an arm to escort her down to the dining room.

Nine

As the Earl of Varian took his leave of the Dowager Lady
Hilliard, only the greatest determination and his own good
breeding kept his temper in check. It would be extremely
ill-mannered of him to slam the drawing room doors behind him. Moreover, the butler who came shuffling up
with his lordship's high-crowned beaver was innocent of
any wrongdoing and did not deserve a setdown, however
tempted his lordship was to deliver one.

Automatically Varian's hand went to his pocket, selected a coin, and tossed it to the butler before accepting his
hat. This he thrust onto his head with a forceful motion,
his anger momentarily increased by a further reminder of
his handicap. A gentleman of fashion always wore gloves
in public, but it was impossible to draw on a glove single-
handed, or for that matter, to remove one. Perforce, he
was obliged to do without, or suffer the indignity of having
a servant help him.

His scowl deepening, he passed through the door held

open for him, stepped out of the house, and descended the steps to the footpath.

The urchin walking his lordship's black stallion saw the scowl and began to hurry his pace, fearing he was to be rewarded with a swift kick instead of a penny.

"Here ye be, guv'nor," he muttered, eyeing Varian apprehensively.

Varian barely glanced at him. "Give me the reins," he ordered, then threw a coin into the street before climbing into the saddle.

Too good a horseman to take out his anger on his mount, his lordship seethed inwardly as he rode down Mount Street towards Grosvenor Square.

Damnation! His plan was in ruins! He had made a grievous error in judgment. While he should have expected that Miss Hilliard would run from an undesirable situation, he had totally failed to consider that the chit would regard marriage to him as anything but desirable.

His jaw tightened. It had indeed been a blow to his pride to find her gone, and a public blow at that. He had made the effort to travel forty miles to pay a courtesy call and meet the chit. With his handicap he couldn't just drive down in his curricle and return the same day. Though a single hand was sufficient to manage the ribbons, a second hand was necessary to handle the whip. Lacking that, he must needs travel with groom and valet in attendance. By now all his servants were aware that his betrothed had run away to escape marriage to him.

Not only had he to suffer the indignity of chasing after her to London. The news that an accident had befallen the coach had forced him to make inquiries at every inn in St. Albans! Fortunately he had remembered to get a description of Miss Hilliard from her mother before he went after her.

He laughed cynically as he recalled the look on Mrs. Hilliard's face as the realization struck her that he had offered for a girl without first having seen her. "Why, my lord, Cherry has bright red hair. That's why I named her Cherry, you know. When I first saw her, her head looked just like a ripe cherry. Do please find her and return her safely to me. I blame Hilliard for her unfortunate reaction, my lord. I warned him not to spring the news too suddenly. Cherry is very impetuous, you know, not at all like the Wiltons. She takes after her father."

At least the chit had a sufficient sense of propriety not to travel unaccompanied, but even the presence of a maid had not been enough to save her from attack. Was she so impulsive as to completely disregard the dangers of traveling without masculine protection, or was she so naïve as to be unaware of those dangers?

Certainly the chit's terror had been real, proving at least that she hadn't invited that scoundrel's attentions. He'd have to give her credit for some sense, but it was more than overset by her damned impetuosity, an impetuosity that could lead to scandal. And if she were involved in the slightest scandal, he would be forced to cry off, and that definitely did not suit his purpose: Miss Hilliard must be his wife.

Lord Varian turned into the mews behind his house on Grosvenor Square and dismounted, tossing the reins to a waiting groom. Well, nothing for it now but an immediate marriage, within the week at the latest. Perhaps it was just as well, now while his anger was still hot. He had disliked Hilliard's original insistence that the marriage wait. The conventions must be observed! What a farradiddle! Hilliard had been only too willing to accept his offer, the conventions notwithstanding.

Entering his house through the back door, his lordship

strode purposefully toward his study. He'd need a special license and—damn! He stopped momentarily. He'd have to send Nicole to Varian Court immediately. Chawley would have to drive her down and return in time to bring him back with his wife.

Wife! The chit was not at all what he had expected. It had been a shock to see her. She resembled neither of her parents, and her fiery hair evidently matched her temper. Ah well, it might prove more amusing this way. There would be no satisfaction to him if the chit caved in immediately she discovered what was in store for her.

Once in his study, Varian yanked on the bell pull, then seated himself at the massive mahogany desk that occupied the entire southwest corner of the room. Would two hours be sufficient for Nicole to pack? he wondered.

He picked up a pen to direct a note to Nicole, then instantly put it down again. He had underestimated Miss Hilliard once. 'Twould be better to be prepared for future impulsive behaviour on her part.

The door opened and a liveried footman entered. "Yes, m'lord?"

"Ah, Thomas, I shall shortly have a note for you to deliver, but in the meantime send word to Chawley to have my coach in readiness in two hours. He will take a lady to Varian Court. And have my curricle ready immediately after luncheon."

As the footman bowed and withdrew, Varian sat tapping the pen. Now where does one acquire a special license? he wondered. Somerset House, or would any clergyman be able to supply one? Ah well, time for that later. The note to Nicole took precedence.

Ten

Cherry lowered the leather-bound volume of *Love's Reward,* picked it up again, read half a page, then put it aside. Usually the latest Minerva novel held her attention, but today she couldn't have given the heroine's name or told a single detail of the plot.

Her grandmother had ordered the carriage immediately after luncheon and gone out—Cherry suspected to confer with Lord Hilliard—leaving Cherry to amuse herself. Cherry's apparent acquiescence to the marriage had led the Dowager to promise a new gown. "One in half-mourning, child. Gray or lavender would be most becoming to your vivid hair. If Mme. Bernardine has kept your measurements, it should take only a day or two to make it up."

But Cherry was not interested. She *had* gowns: ball gowns of white silk, morning gowns of coloured India muslin, and walking gowns in crepe and cambric, all in the latest style. The narrow skirts, high waists, and low necklines set off her figure beautifully and gave her an elegant appearance. She had enjoyed wearing fashionable gowns after years of making do with her cousins' castoffs. But now the promise of a new gown was of no importance to her. She was wearing black in memory of her father, not wearing beautiful clothes to attract an eligible *parti*.

The novel not holding her interest, Cherry fell to day-dreaming. What kind of man did she want as a husband? As a vision of Varian's black-browed visage came to mind, she jumped up and ran to the window. Did it really make a difference what she wanted? Unless she met an eligible young man who fell in love with her, her wishes would be completely disregarded. She sighed. If only novels did reflect real life. In a romance the heroine found happiness with a man originally deemed unsuitable by her cruel guardian.

But I haven't found anyone to love, Cherry protested to herself. Except for Dobbin and her Uncle Geoffrey, of course, she did not really know any men. She had met over a score in London, all young, well mannered, and pleasant. She had chatted to all of them, danced with most of them, and gone riding with a few. And knew very little about any of them.

Bertie Avery had been nice. He seemed genuinely pleased to see her and was always paying her compliments. Edward Bennet had been extremely pleasant and kind. Both had seemed attracted to her hair. They never ceased referring to its unusual colour. But neither had appealed to her—they were far more concerned with her looks than with her inner self.

Dobbin was the only man she really liked. She smiled in recollection of the happy times they'd had together when, below, movement in the street caught her attention. A smart new curricle drawn by a pair of bays drew up to the kerb and a familiar figure descended. "Dobbin!" exclaimed Cherry with delight. She raced across the room and down the stairs, arriving at the drawing room just as the footman opened its doors for Mr. Hilliard.

When the doors closed and they were alone, Cherry threw her arms around her cousin. "Oh, Dobbin, it's so good to see you."

Never before having been greeted so exuberantly, a somewhat disconcerted Mr. Hilliard stammered, "Hey, h-hold on th-there, Cher. I got your note. It sounded mysterious. Is there anything amiss?"

Cherry pulled him down beside her on the sofa and told him everything, from Varian's offer to her grandmother's treachery. "So you see, Dobbin, there's no one else I can turn to. You must help me. I can't marry him."

"Well, what do you want me to do, Cher? I mean, I have no influence over him, or over m'father, come to that."

Cherry's disappointment was reflected in her face. She had expected Dobbin to offer immediate aid. Then she brightened as a thought struck her. "Could you challenge him?"

"Challenge? Who? Varian? Don't be a goose, Cher. No one in his right mind would challenge Varian to pistols. Haven't you heard? With *one* shot he knocked out a dozen candles lined up in a row. That takes a steady hand." The admiration in her cousin's voice was painfully evident.

"Dobbin!" she exclaimed in exasperation. "Please. You're supposed to help *me,* not admire *him.*"

"I know, I know, Cuz, but how? M'father has given his approval to the marriage."

Cherry took a deep breath. "There's only one way, Dobbin. He can't marry me if I'm already married to someone else."

"That's true, but who will you marry? Do you have someone in mind?"

"Oh, Dobbin, do I have to spell it out for you?" Cherry exclaimed in vexation at the uncomprehending look on his face. "Would you marry me, to save me from Varian?"

"Marry you?" Mr. Hilliard sounded agitated. He rose to his feet, took a few steps, then turned to face her. "You know I would, Cher, but I don't think m'father would approve."

"And why not, pray? You're of age, aren't you?"

Facing the glare of her bright green eyes, Mr. Hilliard felt distinctly uncomfortable. His cravat, which had been fitting nicely just moments before, now suddenly was uncommonly tight. He ran a finger inside its folds to loosen it a bit before admitting, "Yes . . . but," he went on to explain shamefacedly, "Papa wants me to take a wife with a larger portion than yours."

"Portion! Is that all you men think of?" Cherry threw herself at him, her arms encircling his chest, her eyes raised pleadingly. "You've got to help me, Dobbin! You're my last hope!"

Unconsciously his arms enclosed her soft body, his head bent lower, his eyes fastened on her slightly parted lips.

"Very pretty! But she's not for you, m'lad."

Robert Hilliard flushed as he raised his eyes to meet the mocking gaze of the self-possessed peer standing just inside the drawing room doors.

"Ohhhhh," Cherry screamed, beating with both fists on her cousin's chest.

"Come, come, Miss Hilliard. Why punish your would-be saviour?"

The harsh, mocking voice brought a frown to Robert's face. If this is what Varian is like, no wonder Cherry does not want him. Unconsciously his arms tightened protectively.

But his lordship's words had penetrated to Cherry's

consciousness. She stopped pounding on her dear one's chest and raised eyes full of apology. "Forgive me, Dobbin," she whispered. "I should not hurt *you.*"

Mr. Hilliard, suddenly realizing the position he was in, released his arms and stepped back, trying to regain his composure. "M-my lord," he stammered, "I-I'm R-Robert Hilliard, Ch-Cherry's cousin."

"Ah, yes. She runs first to her grandmother, then to her cousin. Have you anyone else to run to, Miss Hilliard?"

At these taunting words Cherry turned to face him. "If my father were alive, my lord, there would be no need to run."

The glare in his eyes was so fierce she expected an explosion of anger, but his voice was icy as he answered her. "Indeed? Then it's a pity he's dead, is it not? Where is the Dowager?" he asked abruptly in the silence that followed his first question.

Varian's lack of consideration for the girl he wanted to wed so appalled Robert he couldn't speak. It was Cherry who answered. "She's gone out." Her voice expressed the triumph she felt at being able to frustrate him, even though over a minor matter.

Her triumph was short-lived, however. "Then I'll wait until she returns," his lordship announced, and coolly, as if he were in his own home, he walked over and sat down in the high-backed Queen Anne chair.

Cherry bit her lip in frustration: the man was impossible. She cast a pleading look at Dobbin and received a sympathetic look in return. How much had Varian overheard? Mayhap there was still a chance to escape him, if he didn't know she wanted to elope with Dobbin, for elope they must.

She walked to the window, turning her back on Varian. Was Fate against her? Why else had he interrupted them just before she could convince her cousin to marry her? Now they couldn't plan anything with him here to overhear, and if she took Robert anywhere else, even to her bedchamber, Varian would follow. Cherry Hilliard almost stamped her foot in vexation.

Robert, too polite to sit in the presence of a standing lady, stood irresolutely in the middle of the drawing room. He wanted to help Cherry. His earlier concern for his father's approval had vanished, to be replaced by anger that his father would subject Cherry to such a cold, heartless husband. Cherry was right in not wanting to marry such a hateful person. But how could he help her? He'd marry her, if it were possible. He wished now that he had accepted her proposal and not raised objections. They could have been gone before his lordship's arrival.

However, no matter how much he wished this, the fact was that he hadn't done so. What was he to do now? He could not come to fisticuffs with his lordship. He would be no match for the strong, athletic body lounging so gracefully in the upholstered chair. It irked Robert that a one-armed peer would have no trouble in landing a facer on him. His two hands would be of no advantage. He felt helpless, frustrated, and angry and blamed his father for allowing this situation to develop. Lord Hilliard could have refused the offer, or at least temporized and advised the earl to wait for the period of mourning to end.

Robert felt he had to do something; he couldn't just stand like a statue on exhibit. He felt awkward, childish even, against the polished elegance of the earl. All he could do was afford Cherry his protection by not leaving her alone with such a cruel man. He began to pace the floor, moving first to the door and then over to the wall near the window, where, when he turned, he met the earl's mocking gaze. At this point Robert began to feel some sympathy for his father, who must not have been able to resist the open mockery of Lord Varian, blatantly playing on his handicap. No one would want to admit turning down an offer because of aversion to Varian's injury, and Varian knew it.

The silence seemed interminable to two who waited.

Cherry, standing at the window, tasted blood in her mouth. She had bit her lips until they bled to keep from crying out and railing at this horrible lord who held her fate in his hand. To him she contrasted Dobbin, sweet, kind Dobbin who wanted to help her. Hadn't Uncle Geoffrey seen how dreadful Varian was?

But she had to admit that her uncle really did not care. Were Varian the Devil himself, Lord Hilliard would not have refused an offer. He wanted her gone. He had three daughters of his own to marry off, and she was a threat to them. No one looked at Lizzie or Agnes in Cherry's presence, and their portions were not enough to outweigh their lack of beauty. Cherry could almost sympathize with her uncle, forced to choose between the conventions of Society and his daughters' futures.

Other men were guided by convention, but not Varian. She hated him! Not only had he offered before the year's mourning was up—that was improper enough—but now he asked for an early marriage!

In all honesty, however, Cherry could not entirely blame him for the latter. She knew her own actions had precipitated that request. If she hadn't run off, he would have no cause to condemn her behaviour as scandalous.

She ground her teeth together in frustration. She knew he had come today to seek help from the Dowager Lady Hilliard. Or—a sudden thought struck her. Had he come to prevent her getting help from anyone else? No matter. Whatever his reason in coming, it was unimportant now.

What was of importance was his future action. What would he do now that he had seen her in Dobbin's arms? Insist on an early marriage or cry off?

A heavy, outdated carriage rumbled over the cobbled pavement and drew up at the kerb just below Cherry, who watched dully as a footman assisted her grandmother down the steps and over the footpath.

When the door opened and the Dowager, regal in black silk, entered, Varian rose to his feet. "Your services as chaperone are no longer needed, Hilliard. I suggest you— ah—retire."

"What's this?" the Dowager asked sharply as she saw her grandson flush. "Robert, what are you doing here?"

"I came to help Cherry. M'father must have been mad to accept an offer from this—this—" Robert's voice failed. He had not sufficient courage to voice his thought that the Earl of Varian was a "monster." "Cherry's life will be hell if she marries Varian," he substituted.

"Cherry's life will be what she makes of it," the Dowager replied sharply. She, too, had doubts of her son's wisdom, but having accepted Varian's implied suggestion that Cherry was capable of more scandalous behaviour, she would not admit that she could be mistaken. "You've made your point, my boy. Now I trust you remember your manners and leave us."

His colour heightened at this pointed rebuke, Mr. Hilliard bowed to his grandmother, then walked over and took Cherry's hand in his. Tears made her eyes appear huge. He wished he had a sword to run Varian through. "Courage, Cuz," he whispered. Finally he faced the earl. "You, sir, are no gentleman." His words rang in the air as he spun around on his heels and strode from the drawing room.

"Now, what is the meaning of this?" demanded the

Dowager, angry at her son's inept handling of the affair, as she seated herself in a comfortable armchair. Why Hilliard had not insisted that the betrothal be postponed, she could only guess. He was so damned conventional in everything else!

His lordship remained standing. "I would like to suggest an immediate marriage, ma'am."

"I knew you'd say that" burst from Cherry.

The Dowager ignored her. "Why, my lord?"

"Miss Hilliard has an unfortunate tendency for—ah—impetuosity," he murmured. "When I arrived this afternoon, I believe she was in the process of convincing her cousin to elope with her."

So he had guessed!

"Is this true, miss?" The Dowager was furious. A marriage between those two would have absolutely no chance of success. Robert would have no opportunity to run his own life, and Cherry would soon tire of ordering him about.

Cherry had never seen her grandmother so angry. Cold fear filled the pit of her stomach, but she held her ground. "Yes, Grandmama, it is true." Then she lifted her chin defiantly and faced Varian. "You may have stopped us today, m'lord, but I'd liefer marry Dobbin . . . or Bertie Avery . . . or Mr. Bennet, or . . . or any other man than you."

Varian smiled complacently. He had counted on Miss Hilliard to prove his point. "A private ceremony, perhaps," he murmured.

The Dowager nodded. That would be the lesser of two evils. There was a much greater potential for scandal if Cherry eloped with some ineligible young man.

"No! Oh, no!" A low moan escaped Cherry. She had been standing to the right of her grandmother's chair.

Now, at her nod condemning Cherry to a life too horrible to contemplate, Cherry acted. Without thinking, she ran. She had to get away!

She was pulled up short, however, as the earl's arm shot out and grabbed her by the elbow. He jerked her close to him, until she was standing facing him, just inches away from his chest, her eyes level with the stickpin in his cravat.

Cherry was held tight, cruelly tight. She tried to pull away, but the more she pulled, the more his grip tightened. His fingers were biting into her arm and she feared it would snap off. He looked as if he was enjoying hurting her, too.

It was no use! She felt weak and helpless and stopped struggling. Almost it seemed as if Jack Keene were attacking her again.

But she hadn't been completely helpless then and she was not so now. He had only one arm to hold her. Her right arm was free! She could raise it!

And raise it she did. Cherry slapped her betrothed across his face as hard as she could.

"Miss Hilliard, another such display of your childish manners will meet with a similar action on my part."

He was threatening her! Her eyes widened in disbelief. "You wouldn't!" she gasped.

"Do you wish to try me?" he asked softly.

His eyes were hard. There was no pity for her helplessness, no sympathy for the pain he was inflicting. She shook her head, defeated.

He released her and addressed the Dowager. "I have a special license, my lady. It only remains to find a clergyman who can hold his tongue. It would be advisable to delay any public advertisement until after Miss Hilliard's mourning is over."

The Dowager had watched the scene with mixed emotions. It was obvious that Varian was cold. Yet he wanted the chit! Were there passions hidden within this controlled male? No matter, there was no way for her to discover his true character. Of far more immediate importance was Cherry's behaviour. She was standing quietly, as a well-bred female should.

"You have several livings at your disposal, m'lord," she reminded him.

"True, but that would cause a delay in sending a carriage."

The Dowager did not like the way Varian was making her an accomplice, insisting not only on her approval of the marriage, but on her compliance and assistance. However, no alternative was possible. There must be no scandal. She spoke reluctantly. "I have just come from Lady Dudley. Her nephew has been recently ordained."

"Just so. An hour will be sufficient for me to make arrangements. Miss Hilliard, I suggest you pack your bags. Will you send a message to Mr. Dudley?" At the Dowager's nod, Varian bowed—"Your servant, ma'am" —and walked over to the doors. "There is no need to ring. I'll let myself out."

He was gone, leaving Cherry to stare with grief-stricken eyes at her grandmother. "Grandmama, you can't do this to me."

"Hush, child." The Dowager rose and rang for a footman. "Bring me some writing paper, James. I wish you to deliver a message."

As the Dowager wrote, Cherry stood watching. She felt numb, without feeling, overwhelmed by the shock of being disposed of so swiftly to a cold, heartless man who had no consideration for her.

As the Dowager handed the note to James, she spotted Cherry. "Well, what are you waiting for, miss?"

Her sharp voice roused Cherry. "I have only two gowns to pack, ma'am. I did not realize I was to embark on a wedding trip when I came here."

"Don't be impertinent, miss. I'll send to Mme. Bernardine. She may have a gown finished that is suitable for you."

Dismissed, Cherry slowly dragged herself up the stairs and rang for Hetty. "Pack, Hetty," she directed in a listless voice.

"But, miss . . ."

"I can't talk about it, please, Hetty, or I'll cry, and I won't give him the satisfaction of seeing my tears. I swear he wants to hurt me. He has no consideration for my feelings, none at all."

Cherry stood at the window, looking out. In an hour, she would be wed. An hour . . . time enough to find Dobbin. She could walk to Albemarle Street. She'd have to chance being seen by her uncle.

She moved swiftly, past the bed, over to the door. It was locked!

Cherry fell to the floor, hands raised to her face, fighting to keep back tears that threatened to engulf her. She must not cry! Her face would be ruined and Varian would gloat!

She was pulled to her feet by Hetty and held in a tight embrace. "She locked me in, Hetty. My own grandmother locked me in!"

"Hush, Miss Cherry. Your grandmama knows what's best for you."

"No, Hetty." Cherry jerked away from her maid and ran to the window.

Hetty shrieked and quickly followed her charge.

"You'll kill yourself. Don't you try going out the window, Miss Cherry."

Cherry hesitated, her hand on the window latch. "What does it matter, Hetty? Either way, my life is over."

"Now, Miss Cherry, that's not like you, not like you at all. Mayhap it will turn out for the best," said Hetty as she led a suddenly quiescent Cherry to a chair.

Shortly before the hour was up, a footman delivered a gown. It was of lavender crepe with black velvet ribands. Cherry glanced at it disinterestedly. "Pack it, Hetty." She had no intention of changing out of her black gown. She would not dignify the occasion by wearing a new gown. It was a farce of a marriage, meaningless to her—but not to Varian, of that she was sure. For some reason he was insisting on marriage to her. Cherry was filled with foreboding. She sensed that he wanted to hurt her.

Her feelings were reinforced by his later behaviour when, following the simple ceremony in her grandmother's drawing room, she left with her husband in a hired post chaise. Varian had handed her into the chaise, then took his seat beside her, barely glancing at the bride he had taken such pains to marry.

Cherry had not spoken since she took her vows, and had no intention of doing so. She had no idea where he was taking her and didn't care. Her life was ruined!

However, she was relieved at Hetty's presence. Varian had not hired a second carriage for the servants and baggage, so both Hetty and his valet were seated across from Cherry, the valet's face blank, Hetty's showing an anxious expression.

Briefly, Cherry allowed her thoughts to dwell on the recent ceremony. If it hadn't been so tragic for her, it would almost have been amusing. The young clergyman, obviously disconcerted by her silence and Varian's coldness, had attempted to hide his inexperience by exaggerated obsequiousness. Varian's vail must have been generous, for the reverend had agreed with alacrity to his lordship's suggestion that no announcement be made.

Should I have tried to climb out the window? Cherry wondered. She could have gone to Dobbin. But in all truth, what could he have done? She might have been discovered by her uncle, who certainly would have turned her out of his house or, even worse, sent for Varian. And if they had set off for Gretna Green, Varian would have been sure to follow.

Life was so unfair to females, not giving them any rights. First, one had to obey one's father; secondly, females were not allowed to choose their husbands; and lastly, they had to spend the rest of their lives obeying their husbands!

Thoroughly depressed, Cherry sank into the corner of the seat. The chaise was not as comfortable as Varian's private carriage. Why weren't they traveling in that? It had brought them to London. Had it been only yesterday? It seemed so long ago. Well, it wasn't important where his carriage was. Cherry closed her eyes.

It seemed as if hours had passed before the chaise stopped and a postilion opened the door. Again there was the hated touch on her arm as Varian grasped it and assisted her to alight. He retained hold of it as he escorted her through the door of an inn, to be met by a beaming landlord, who assured them he had a private parlour for "your worship" and fresh linen for the beds.

Cherry allowed herself to be led to a bedchamber where she waited with resignation until a chambermaid brought hot water. Then she washed her face and hands and allowed Hetty to tidy her curls. Finally and reluctantly she descended to the parlour.

Though she had had nothing to eat since luncheon—how long ago was that?—she had no appetite and watched listlessly as the waiter, supervised by the landlord himself, brought in ham, a pigeon pie, a beef roast, and several side dishes.

Cherry could see their curious glances at Varian's empty sleeve. She herself was not curious as to how he would manage to eat single-handed. She didn't care. If he wanted her help, he could ask. She was not about to offer.

And ask he did, after dismissing the waiter. "I fear you must rouse sufficiently from your sullens, m'lady, to cut my meat."

She flashed him a glance—sullens, indeed!—but obediently picked up a knife and sliced the beef, then cut it into pieces. Cherry put a serving of the pigeon pie on his plate, sliced and cut the ham for him, then poured a glass of wine. The omelette and dish of spinach he could manage by himself, she decided.

After putting a spoonful of the pie on her plate, Cherry tried to eat, but it was difficult to swallow with his eyes on her. She poured some wine into a glass and gulped it down. It tasted vile and she almost choked, but felt better.

It must be frustrating, having only one hand. She would hate it. Did that explain Varian's actions? Was it that simple? Did he take out his frustrations and anger on others as compensation for his loss? She could understand that, but had no intention of telling him so.

The landlord brought a bottle of port, which Varian waved away after glancing at the label, and a pot of tea, which his lordship did accept. Cherry poured, then hesitated over the sugar, finally handing him the cup without any. He was much too sour to like sweet things, she decided.

She drank her tea, then sat waiting to be dismissed. She

knew if she tried to leave he would refuse to allow her to go, and she had no intention of giving him the opportunity to chastise her in a public place. He would welcome that. She would have to bide her time. She must learn to curb her impatience and learn to wait. Mayhap the opportunity would arise later when she could escape him.

Finally Varian put down his cup, rose from his chair, and walked around the table toward her. As he approached her chair, Cherry quickly got up and preceded him to the door, hoping to get away from him. In this she was foiled, however, as he escorted her to the door of her bedchamber, where Hetty was waiting. Neither spoke as Cherry was undressed, Cherry because she had nothing to say, and Hetty because she feared to upset her mistress.

After Hetty left, Cherry sprang out of bed and ran over to lock the door. She had no intention of again having an unwelcome male in her bedchamber.

Back in bed, she pulled up the sheet and blanket, then tried to compose herself for sleep, when a sudden thought struck her. Varian was her husband. He had every right to occupy her bed. He had other rights, too. What they were, she didn't know, and didn't want to know. Not with him as her husband!

Would he try to enter her bedchamber? He must have his own. His bags had not been brought into hers.

What would happen when he found the door locked? Cherry held her breath. A cold feeling began to envelop her, starting in her stomach and spreading to her limbs. She sat, shivering, clutching the blanket around her. Never before had she known such a cold fear. She had been terrified when Jack Keene had attacked her, but then her fear had been due to a feeling of helplessness that had quickly changed into a hot, fighting fear, not this teeth-chattering coldness.

Should she open the door? Cherry was too frightened to move. She didn't want him here, not in her bed. What would he do to her? Yet, if he came and the door was locked, what would happen?

Long minutes passed. Cherry waited, apprehensively shivering, for her husband to come. The candle burned down, sputtered, and went out. Cherry was left in darkness. He hadn't come! Surely if he had wanted to, he would have been here by now. Breathing easier, she finally lay down. Now that she knew Varian was not making an attempt to enter her bedchamber, she could sleep.

Eleven

The chaise turned into a tree-lined lane, the ancient elms so tall and dense they formed an overhead canopy. Cherry roused herself. They must be nearing their destination. All day they had been traveling, with only a brief stop for luncheon. It was twilight now and she was exhausted, physically and emotionally. She so dreadfully wanted to berate Varian for his lack of consideration for her, but she refused to speak to him, and her self-imposed silence was telling on her nerves. She longed for bed and a respite from his presence.

They broke out of the shade as the drive curved. To her right Cherry could see an imposing gray stone house of immense size. Its leaded windows, reflecting the rays of the setting sun, gave it a splendidly shining appearance that increased its magnificence. She had never seen a house this huge. How could she ever find her way about?

The carriage stopped. A postilion opened the door and Varian stepped down. Cherry knew she had to climb out also, but for a moment she hesitated. What would her life be like as Varian's wife? Would all her vague feelings of unease, of apprehension, of fear, be justified?

"My lady, if you please."

Cherry glanced up. Varian was standing in the open doorway, his hand held out, a frown on his face. She sighed. She had no alternative, not really. She stood up and allowed him to help her from the chaise.

Liveried footmen were pouring out of the house and lining the steps. Cherry had a momentary impression that they were surprised to see her, but if a look of surprise had been apparent on their faces, it was quickly erased, as each footman quickly resumed the mask of the perfect servant.

"Welcome, my lord." An elderly butler stood at the top of the stone steps. Yes, there was a look of surprise on his face, too. Evidently the staff had not yet been told of Varian's hasty marriage. How many servants were there? Would she have to meet them all tonight?

Cherry braced herself as Varian escorted her up the steps. "This is Ridley," he said as they reached the top. "His wife is housekeeper at Varian Court." Then he raised his voice slightly to say, "Ridley, this is Lady Varian."

Cherry smiled as she stepped through the doorway into the entrance hall and held out her hand. "How do you do, Ridley?" She was not about to make the mistake of extending her antagonism toward her husband to his servants.

No answering smile greeted her. The butler bowed his white head formally and shook her hand, merely saying, "My lady." No welcome from him!

Cherry's heart sank and she turned away, but her attention was caught by the butler. He was facing Varian and stammering, "But, b-but, m-my lord . . ."

"Escort the countess to her apartment, Ridley," Varian ordered, then strode across the hall to disappear through a door. Evidently he was not to extend her the courtesy of an introduction to the rest of the staff.

"I beg your pardon, m'lady," Ridley muttered as he started to move slowly toward a staircase that rose gracefully opposite the main door of the entrance hall. The hall itself was beautiful, with chairs and gleaming tables along its wood-paneled walls, but Cherry had no time to examine her surroundings.

"Wait." She put out a hand. "Surely one of the footmen or a maid is available to show me my rooms." A younger person would be more able to climb stairs than this white-haired, fragile-looking butler.

"Marston, ah, there you are." Ridley's voice held relief as he called to one of the footmen entering the hall with the luggage. "Escort her ladyship to her bedchamber. I'll send Mrs. Ridley along shortly," he informed Cherry.

"Come, Hetty."

She followed the footman up the wide staircase to the half-landing, then along the left branch to the first floor. There they proceeded down a long corridor. Just where the corridor turned, Marston stopped before a door, then reached out a gloved hand and opened the door. Cherry, preparing to enter, paused on the threshold, struck dumb at the sight of her bedchamber. Everything was shrouded in holland covers.

Hetty pushed past her to pull off a cover and reveal a delicate chair, its legs carved in a scroll design, its seat and back of pale green brocade. "You can at least sit down, Miss Ch—m'lady," she muttered.

Cherry shook her head. After sitting in the chaise all day, the last thing she wanted to do was sit. She wandered about examining the furniture as Hetty set about removing the remaining covers.

There was a brocaded chaise longue at the foot of the

bed. The bed curtains and the counterpane, as well as the chaise, were of the same heavy brocade. There were several rosewood tables, one next to the bed, and a writing desk along one wall. A large gilt mirror was above the dressing table and another was over the white marble mantel of the fireplace. A huge wardrobe stood in one corner. Green brocaded draperies hung at the windows, a dark green carpet covered the floor, and the walls, like the doors, were of pale ivory. Cherry stared about her with growing delight. Had the chamber been decorated with her in mind, it could not have been more flattering to her colouring. This was a room made for *her*. Her spirits, always mercurial, began to rise. Perhaps, just perhaps, she had been too pessimistic.

Mrs. Ridley proved to be a rotund matron, much younger than her husband. She was dressed in a neat black gown with a white apron and cap. "I must apologize for the condition of this room," she said as she came in. "His lordship neglected to inform us of your arrival. I'll have the maids up with clean linen and remove the covers."

Her manner, though correct and deferential, was aloof, and her voice was sharp. Cherry's spirits plummeted. Were all the servants to be hostile? It was not her fault that she had arrived unannounced.

"There is no need to apologize, Mrs. Ridley," she said, trying to be pleasant. "I see no dust."

Cherry took off her bonnet and gave her head a shake. It was such a relief to be free of its confinement. As she handed the bonnet to Hetty, she discovered that the housekeeper was staring at her hair. Impulsively, Cherry smiled. "It is an unusual colour, isn't it?"

But no answering smile came from Mrs. Ridley. Instead she tightened her lips. Cherry's smile faded. Why should the housekeeper be so unfriendly? Or was it a case of like master, like servant?

Fortunately the footman arrived then, bearing her small bag. It provided a welcome diversion as Hetty came forward to take it.

"Dinner will be ready shortly, m'lady," the housekeeper announced formally, then withdrew, following the footman.

Cherry stood irresolute as Hetty began to unpack. "Oh, miss, I mean, m'lady, it's a grand house," Hetty enthused, "with ever so many servants. I'll not be needing to do more than care for you."

"Yes, Hetty," Cherry responded absently, then walked over to the window. It was almost dark by now, but she could make out vast lawns stretching far off. This was to be her home for the rest of her life. In spite of its apparent beauty, the prospect of living here filled her with dread. It was not the house that mattered, but the people in it. So far, all she had been subjected to was veiled hostility.

Two housemaids brought brass cans of water and a hip bath. Cherry, as she thanked them, looked expectantly at them, but they, too, acted strange. After bobbing respectful curtseys, they glanced at her out of the corners of their eyes, then hurriedly gathered up the discarded holland covers and ran out.

Cherry sighed and allowed Hetty to undress her. The bath washed away the traveling grime but did little to refresh her strained nerves. She hurried, for there was no fire in the grate and the room was cooling. After considering the notion of ringing for the maids and asking for a fire, Cherry discarded it. There was no time for a leisurely bath: dinner would be ready soon.

"This gown should rightly be ironed, Miss Cherry."

Hetty was holding up the lavender gown, an anxious expression on her face.

"It doesn't matter, Hetty," Cherry murmured and began to dry herself, then gasped with pleasure. The towel was thick and luxuriantly soft on her skin, not like Mama's old, worn ones.

Reminded of her mother, Cherry stood draped in the towel, lost in thought. Would she ever see her mother again? How would she get along without either Cherry or Hetty to help her? Blinking rapidly to keep back the tears, Cherry decided she had best write to Mama. She was sure Varian would not have thought of her mother's anxiety over Cherry's failure to return home.

She allowed Hetty to dress her in the new gown, for it was the only one suitable for dining, but the sight of herself in the dressing table mirror did not raise her spirits. The style and colour were becoming, she had to admit, but it would take more than a pale lavender gown with black ribands to ease her depression. Even Hetty's enthusiasm did not lessen the feeling of listlessness that engulfed her.

"Oh, Miss Cherry, 'tis a beautiful gown! It don't look like half-mourning, neither. Course you should have a string of pearls around your neck," she added. "The neckline is a bit low."

When Cherry didn't respond, Hetty said briskly, "Well, never mind, sit down now and let me do your curls. Your hair should be washed, Miss Cherry, but no time for that today."

Cherry obediently seated herself and waited with an unusual patience for Hetty to finish brushing her hair. What difference did it make how she looked? She certainly didn't want to attract Varian's attention.

Finally Hetty had finished with her and Cherry slowly descended the stairway, unsure where to go next, but a footman was waiting at the foot of the staircase. "This way, m'lady. His lordship is in the drawing room."

As soon as she entered, Varian, who had been standing before the fireplace, glanced up, an expectant look on his face. At sight of her, however, it faded and he turned away, pointedly lifting a wineglass to his lips in dismissal.

She was left to stare at him or the room. Much preferring the latter, though he did look quietly elegant in well-fitting pantaloons, white waistcoat, and blue coat, she stood silently looking about her. The drawing room was rectangular, and large enough to stage a ball. The floor at her feet was highly polished with a mirrorlike finish, overlaid by several Persian carpets. The ceiling was completely covered with sculptures in various patterns; the walls, wainscotted below in ivory, were papered above with an ivory and blue flowered wallpaper. The draperies at the windows hung from vast cornices. They were of blue velvet, as were the seats of the many chairs and sofas arranged in groups on the carpets. The fireplace before which Varian was standing had a marble mantel. From where she was, across the width of the room from him, Cherry could see that it, too, was sculptured.

When no welcome was forthcoming from her husband, Cherry slowly moved forward. Was he going to just stand there, gazing into his wineglass? Wasn't it his place to speak first?

The door behind her opened. Cherry saw Varian's eyes lift. His gaze moved past her. Then his expression lightened and he smiled.

Cherry whirled around in amazement. What had brought about this transformation in him? She had not seen him smile before.

A woman stood for a moment on the threshold, then ran across the room, her arms held out. *"Mon cher, mon amour, je vous*—" She stopped suddenly, her eyes darting from Cherry to Varian.

Cherry felt sick. This must be his mistress. The woman was beautiful, Cherry had to admit. Her face was lovely, with huge dark eyes fringed with long lashes, a soft, pouting mouth, and a beautifully sculptured nose. Raven black ringlets fell from the crown of her head in a cascade. Her long neck and white shoulders were emphasized by the low neckline of the Venetian blue gown she wore, a gown of gauze so sheer that all the curves of her body were apparent. It was a gown to draw a man's attention, and Cherry, though wearing the product of the most fashionable modiste in London, felt dowdy alongside of this vision of loveliness.

Varian strode forward. "I missed you," he said simply, then put his arm around the woman, pulled her to him, and kissed her hungrily.

Never before having seen a man kissing a woman, Cherry at first watched curiously, then with growing anger. She knew Varian had brought this woman into his house in order to humiliate her, his wife, but she wouldn't stand for it. As Varian raised his head, his gaze still on the woman held within his arm, Cherry, her voice high, asked, "Do you expect me to entertain your Cyprian, m'lord?"

His head turned then. She could see the change in his eyes as his warm and tender expression became cold and he answered her formally, his voice harsh, "I expect you to entertain *all* my guests."

At this Cherry exploded. "No!" She stamped her foot. "Is it not enough that you force me into marrying you? You disregard my wishes entirely, bring me here"—she gestured toward the room, her nostrils flaring and her eyes sparkling as she stood facing him—"and expect me to accept your . . . your whore? I won't do it!"

His lordship waited until she had ceased speaking, then released the woman and slowly strolled across to her. He calmly raised his hand and slapped her, hard, across the face. But it was Nicole who flinched: this was a never-before-seen side of Varian. She had not thought him capable of cruelty. Her eyes narrowed. Was she to be the next recipient of his cruelty if she displeased him?

Tears sprang into Cherry's green eyes, blurring their intensity. "I hate you," she whispered.

"If you're over your hysterics, m'lady . . . ?" His voice was glacial, his expression menacing. Cherry was saved from further violence as the double doors opened and the attending footman announced, "Dinner is served, m'lord."

Varian offered his arm to Nicole and led her across the drawing room floor and through the doors. Cherry hesitated, tempted not to follow them. She wanted to run to her bedchamber and lock herself in. But fear of what Varian would do and her own hunger stayed her.

Now she knew why the servants had given her such strange looks. A wife and mistress both in residence was definitely not accepted behaviour. But it was not she who was at fault in this; they could hardly blame her for his outrageous conduct!

She took a deep breath to steady her nerves and slowly followed behind her husband and his ladybird.

Throughout the entire meal she sat silent, opposite Varian at the huge mahogany table. Nicole sat at his side, cutting his meat, leaning toward him to speak in a low, husky voice, and finding many opportunities to touch his arm. From time to time, however, her eyes roved about the dining room, resting with complacency on the various items in it.

Cherry, though trying desperately hard not to stare at

this Frenchwoman, could not help but notice her glances or the smugness of her smile. It was apparent that she was pleased to be dining in state in her lover's family home.

Cherry allowed her glance to fall on the contents of the room. There were heavy red drapes, closed now, at the windows, a brilliantly lighted chandelier overhead, many pieces of silver on the sideboard, and fine porcelain on the table. Beautiful, yes, but certainly not worth an expression of such satisfaction.

Oh, well, *her* thoughts were none of Cherry's affair. She, Cherry, had things to think about. Perhaps this situation was a blessing in disguise. If he had a mistress to occupy his time, Cherry would escape his attentions. There would be no need to fear his kissing *her*, not with that woman available and willing. Besides, why should she care what he did? He meant nothing to her.

She ate heartily, for she was hungry. Breakfast and luncheon had been hurried, and last night she had eaten nothing. The food was well cooked, the salmon tender, the roast goose crisp and succulent, the mushroom fritters especially delicious. She must remember to compliment the cook.

Cherry waited until the second course was removed, then rose from the table. "Ridley, will you please serve coffee in the drawing room?" she asked quietly, then made a dignified exit. She didn't expect that woman to follow. No doubt Varian would want *her* to share his port with him, so after the butler brought the coffee tray, Cherry did not wait. In solitude, she drank her coffee, then returned to her bedchamber and her thoughts.

This humiliation was not to be borne, yet it *must* be. Cherry had learned a great deal about correct behaviour from Lizzie, her grandmother, and from overhearing the chaperones' gossip. For a bride to share her husband with a mistress was just not done. Most men had the grace to spare their wives knowledge of their amusements, and most of them spent at least the honeymoon with their wives.

However, Cherry had to admit she didn't want *that*. She didn't want Varian touching and *kissing* her. Abruptly her thoughts veered to the scene in the drawing room. What would it feel like to be held close to a man's body—to feel his lips on hers? Tentatively Cherry raised her fingers and lightly touched her lips. She could almost imagine herself in Nicole's place, with Varian's dark head bending over hers. *No!* she shrieked silently. *I don't want him. Nicole can have him.* It was just her pride that was hurt. She should be granted the respect due her as his wife, not made a mockery of before his servants.

For some unknown reason, Varian seemed to want to hurt her. How was she to exist under such demeaning conditions? And there might be more than her pride hurt. He had already slapped her, thus showing he had no compunction against using violence. What should she do? Never before had she faced a problem of such magnitude.

Always before when she wanted something, she had acted impulsively, with no thought for consequences. Her grandmother had tried to get her to act responsibly, and to accept the restrictions surrounding a well-bred young lady, but she had not been successful.

Cherry knew that the predicament she was in was not entirely Varian's fault. She had contributed: her impulsive actions had caused him to react. She would not be here, humiliated by his mistress, if she had not run off to London.

Therefore, Cherry, think, she told herself. What would Papa do? He had been a soldier, a brave man who must have faced many dangerous situations. In the face of the

111

enemy, what does a soldier do? He tries to kill the enemy, she answered herself, but that was clearly impossible. She not only would not kill her husband, she had no desire to hurt anyone, not even *him!*

What else? Think, Cherry, what else would a soldier do? He would try to keep from being hurt! That was it!

It didn't matter, not really, that his mistress was here. It would be best to pretend that she isn't here, to ignore her completely. And as for Varian, I won't ask him for anything, she decided. That way he won't have an opportunity to hurt me by refusing. She would be dignified before the servants and, above all, not let him cause her to lose her temper again, no matter what it cost her!

Twelve

Cherry wakened and lay drowsily peering through half-closed eyes at the curtains that hung like sea green foam around her bed. She couldn't remember seeing curtains like these before, not at Hilliard House or at Berkeley Square, and certainly never at home. Confused, she sat up and pulled back the curtains. At sight of the bedchamber, memory came flooding back. She was in Varian Court, wedded to its lord. Last night's scene in the drawing room returned in its entirety: Varian's disappointment at her entrance, his pleasure at the presence of the Frenchwoman, her own tantrum, and his violent means of stopping it. Cherry shuddered. Was this what the future held for her, humiliation and beatings?

No! She jumped out of bed. Her decision of last night was reaffirmed. She would not let him hurt her, but would have to get about on her own. Cherry ran to the window. Last night there had been little to see in the darkening sky. What kind of place was she in? She had no idea of the direction they had traveled since leaving London, nor did she know in which county Varian's estate was situated. Cherry drew back the heavy drapes. Vast green lawns and parks extended off to the distance, where she could barely make out fields and small cottages. Nearer, she spotted a rider. It was Varian on a high-spirited black stallion, cantering across the lawn. He was bare-headed, his black locks gleaming in the morning sun. As she watched, she realized he was guiding his mount with his legs. There was really no need for the reins held in his one hand.

For a fleeting moment, she had the same feeling of sympathy she had experienced at first sight of him. It seemed such a horrid shame that his magnificent body should be marred by an injury. Then she shook her head. Save your sympathy, Cherry, she told herself. His lordship would not thank you for such feelings. She went back to bed to await Hetty.

It seemed hours before the maid arrived with a laden tray. After pulling back the bed curtains, she admonished, "Sit up and eat your breakfast, Miss Cherry, whilst it's still hot."

Yawning, Cherry sat up and meekly accepted the tray across her lap, but immediately after lifting off the silver cover, she protested, "Oh, Hetty, I can't eat all of this!" There was a thick slice of pink ham and a huge mound of eggs. Another plate held toast. Marmalade was in a silver-topped bowl and cream in a porcelain pitcher that matched the teapot. "I've never eaten this much food for breakfast in my whole life and you know it. Why did you bring me so much?"

Hetty paused on her way to the window. "You just eat, Miss Cherry. You're just not used to a proper breakfast."

Cherry sighed and lifted the fork. Here was another change in her life: Hetty was giving *her* orders. She was not sure she liked it. "Where is your bedchamber, Hetty?" she asked to divert Hetty's attention.

"Just down the corridor from you, Miss Cherry. Your bell pull rings in it and downstairs in the kitchen, Mrs. Ridley tells me, so's I can hear you whenever you want me." Hetty tied back the draperies and the morning sun entering the bedchamber reflected off Cherry's hair, giving it a coppery sheen.

"Well, there's little enough for you to do, except wash my clothes, Hetty."

"Oh, I won't have to do that, Miss Cherry. There's laundry maids here. They do all the washing for the house, linens and all. But that reminds me, Miss Cherry. You ought to write to your mama and ask her to send on your other clothes. I'm sure a groom could be sent for them."

Decisively Cherry shook her head. "No, Hetty. I would have to have his lordship's permission for that, and I *won't* ask him for anything. He'd only refuse, anyway." She took a sip of tea. "Is the staff friendly to you, Hetty?" she asked rather wistfully.

"Oh, yes, indeed, Miss Cherry. I take my meals with the upper staff, just Mr. Hartley and the Ridleys, seein' as how I'm your ladyship's personal maid," she answered, full of self-importance.

Momentarily, Cherry was annoyed at Hetty's pleasure, then her warm nature reasserted itself and she repented. She should not begrudge her maid an easier, more satisfying life. At home Hetty had done the cleaning and cooking as well as the washing and mending without any grumbling, and for very low wages at that. She deserved a more comfortable life.

"Where do the lower staff eat?" Cherry asked. She knew nothing about the workings of a large house. Grandmother had a small staff and Cherry, as a child at her uncle's estate, had been too occupied with outdoor fun to pay attention to servants. There must be an immense number of servants, and she, somehow, must learn to run the house.

"They have their own dining room," Hetty answered. "Here they treat their servants right, they do. There's a whole wing of the house for the staff quarters, Miss Cherry. The Ridleys have their own sitting room and bedchamber. The lower staff have a sitting room and I expect Mr. Hartley has one, too, same's I do." Hetty paused to ensure that Cherry had finished her breakfast, then resumed, "Mrs. Ridley said there's a sitting room for you, through that door." She pointed to the door to the left of the bed. "The maids will be up to tidy it this morning. It's still in holland covers."

Then Hetty moved across the room to the door opposite the bed and threw it open. "This is the dressing room." She glanced at her mistress out of the corner of her eye, hesitating whether she should repeat the housekeeper's complete phrase, "shared by his lordship, of course." Better not, she decided. If Miss Cherry knew that, no tellin' what she'd do. She substituted, "The bathtub is kept in here, so's the maids won't have to lug it up all the time. And extra wardrobes for clothing."

Cherry nodded indifferently and allowed Hetty to dress her. Hours stretched before her. She would have to find some way to occupy herself until luncheon, and as far as the afternoon was concerned, she wouldn't even think that far ahead. She knew she would have to fall back on her own resources; *he* would be occupied with that woman, whose name, Cherry had gathered from last night's conversation, was Nicole.

She wouldn't stay hiding in her bedchamber all day, so after Hetty left, Cherry decided to explore the grounds.

116

They looked extensive enough. She took up her shawl and went downstairs.

No footmen were in the hall, so Cherry did not feel embarrassed to pause and look about her as she descended the steps. The entrance hall was two stories tall, completely paneled in dark wood. Its somberness was relieved by a white marble floor covered in a brightly flowered carpet and by white-painted doors. Along the walls were several satinwood tables flanked by chairs with needlework cushions. Above each table was either a mirror or a scenic picture. And on each table was a huge vase of flowers.

Cherry ran down to look closer. One alabaster vase held a huge bouquet of red roses. She loved flowers, especially roses. At home she had had a small garden of lilies, primroses, and violets: Mama could not afford roses. Were these grown on the estate? she wondered.

With increased enthusiasm she pushed open the heavy front door and went out.

Ahead of her was the driveway. She could see now that it curved in a great circle before the house, enclosing a central grass plot containing a fountain and bordered by a low hedge. Connecting roads led off to the right and left. Cherry followed the right one to the corner of the house, turned along its width, and discovered that the house was built in the shape of a vast I, though the parts corresponding to the top and bottom of the I were much longer than the connection across the width. She passed many windows and several doors. Later she would have to discover where they led.

Eventually she came to the back of the house. Its size frightened her. It was easily four times larger than Hilliard House, large enough to get lost in. And large enough to keep away from a husband in! Oh, well, she decided, time enough later to explore the house.

The road continued on to several other buildings, the stables perhaps. Behind the house itself were the gardens. Cherry hurried along the garden path, past a small herb garden that held no interest for her, past the larger vegetable garden with its long rows of greens where several small boys were industriously weeding, to the flower garden beyond.

In the midst of this garden Cherry stopped, struck with wonder. Never had she seen so many roses! There were rows and rows of them, all in bloom. Slowly she strolled along, savouring their beauty: brilliant reds, snowy whites, sun yellows, and soft pinks. Soon she came to colours she had not seen before: white roses with red edges. "Oh!" she exclaimed, "are you real?" She reached out a finger and tentatively touched a fragile petal.

So enraptured was she, she failed to hear the approaching footsteps. A voice startled her. "Ye like my roses?"

"Oh!" Cherry jumped and pulled away her hand. Should she have touched the blossom?

Facing her was a man whose bent back, wrinkled face, and white hair attested to his age. He removed his cap respectfully.

"Oh, yes!" she exclaimed. "I've never seen such beautiful flowers!"

Her response seemed to please him, for he smiled. "Aye," he agreed, "no but here do ye find such like," and pointed to the red and white blooms. "Or these." He shuffled off, with Cherry following, to point out coral shades, both pale and deep, and several bushes with flame-coloured roses. An exclamation of wonder escaped Cherry.

The gardener laughed gleefully. "This one's for ye, m'lady."

It was a flower of living flame. Her eyes wide with

amazement, Cherry stared, speechless. The colour matched her hair! She looked up to find the gardener watching her. "You know who I am?" she asked then, for he had addressed her correctly.

"Aye. Mrs. Ridley sent down word last night, late, saying as how his lordship had arrived wi' his lidy. Says I was to hurry and send up some greens. I sent out the boys to cut the spinach. They can do that. Don't let 'em touch my roses, though."

Cherry smiled and held out her hand. "What is your name?" she asked bluntly.

"Jed Frame, m'lady." He carefully wiped his hand on his breeches before shaking her hand. "Would ye like some o'these?"

"Could I?" Cherry blurted out. They seemed too beautiful to cut.

He nodded. "Aye. I'll send Will up later. For your sittin' room. It'll be like old times," he added. "T'old countess, she liked my roses, too. Always had a boo-kay in her room."

"Thank you, Frame, I'd like that." Cherry smiled warmly and continued on her walk, past the lilies and other flowers she didn't recognize. She would have to ask Frame what they were. She felt considerably heartened at the gardener's friendliness, for she knew she would need friends to counter Varian's enmity.

Beyond the gardens were the stables and paddocks, but there was no reason for her to go there. If she saw many more horses as beautiful as the one Varian had been riding, she might be tempted to forget her resolution and ask to ride. She had always had to make do with plodding old Molly. Just once she wanted a high-spirited horse under her!

Silly, she told herself. You can't ride, you don't have a habit with you. Now forget about the horses!

Resolutely Cherry set off across the lawns toward a group of shrubs and trees. As she neared it, she discovered it was a topiary garden and amused herself for a time trying to discover what each tree represented. However, beyond deciding that this one looked like an animal's head, and that square one could be a building, she had no success: was that one a bear or a cat?

Continuing on, she next came upon a vast area of shrubbery, wild and untrimmed. At first she tried to walk around it, but soon gave that up as a lost cause. Defeated, she was ready to return to the house, when the sight of something white caught her eye. She pushed straight into the center. Branches hit at her; her skirt had to be released time after time from clutching twigs, but she persisted.

A cry of delight escaped her lips as she saw, hidden in the midst of the shrubs, a white-painted wooden rotunda. The paint was peeling off the columns and the latticework between, it was dusty and cobwebby inside, and the path leading away from it was overgrown with twining vines, but it could be cleaned and repainted. She would have to ask Frame about it. This would be a perfect retreat for her, safe from prying eyes and safe from Varian.

Cherry returned for luncheon, rapidly washed her hands and face, and tidied her curls. She had enjoyed her morning's expedition and ran down the stairs to the dining room. There she spoke pleasantly to the footmen and ate a hearty meal. She ignored both her husband and Nicole and several times had the pleasure of noticing that Varian was watching her with a puzzled expression on his face.

Mrs. Ridley approached her as she was leaving the dining room. "Do you wish to approve the menu for dinner, m'lady?" she asked. "I did go up earlier, but you weren't in your sitting room."

"No, Mrs. Ridley. I went out walking and met Frame in the gardens. He has such lovely roses," she enthused, smiling. Were the servants coming round and accepting her as mistress of the house? "He promised to send some of his fiery orange ones for my rooms," she confided.

The housekeeper nodded. "Your sitting room is all ready for your use, m'lady."

"Thank you, Mrs. Ridley. Then I'll go up now. Will you be along shortly?"

"At once, m'lady." And the housekeeper moved off just as the door behind Cherry opened. Varian and Nicole came out. Cherry could tell without looking, for Nicole's perfume was overpowering.

Cherry gave no indication of their presence but started up the stairway unconcernedly. *He* had brought her here —let him acknowledge her presence!

She opened the door to her sitting room. Like the bed-chamber, it was done in green, but a deeper shade. There were a writing desk and three walnut tables, a settee and several chairs, upholstered in velvet. On the table between the windows was a bouquet of Frame's roses. Cherry clapped her hands at sight of them. She must remember to thank Frame.

Cherry had just seated herself when Mrs. Ridley arrived, a correctly neutral expression on her face. As she handed over the menu card, she said hesitantly, "You will notice, m'lady, that there is only one course. We could have another, if your ladyship wishes, but seein' as how there was a great many leftovers last night, and Mrs. Thatcher ain't cookin' for a house party . . ."

While Mrs. Ridley was speaking, Cherry glanced at the long list: trout with lemon sauce, fricassee of veal, chicken pie, roasted partridge, and a salmagundi, plus several side dishes. It seemed like a great deal of food to her! "I have no objection, Mrs. Ridley," she began; then her eye was caught by the last item and she looked up. "Could we have an apple tart instead of currant tarts, Mrs. Ridley?" she asked. "I dislike currants. They always make my mouth pucker."

Cherry knew her approval was just a formality, but it signified her acceptance as mistress of the house. Her spirits began to rise. After the housekeeper's murmured "Of course, m'lady," Cherry said impulsively, "The cook appears to be excellent, Mrs. Ridley, if the meals I've already had are any indication."

Mrs. Ridley's face softened. "Yes, m'lady. Mrs. Thatcher is one of the best. We are fortunate to have her."

"I have no experience in running a house of this size, Mrs. Ridley," Cherry confided, deciding that in this case honesty was indeed the best policy, for it would be impossible to hide her ignorance.

"You'll learn, m'lady," the housekeeper assured her. "We have an excellent staff, if I may be permitted to say so. If everyone does his job, it almost runs itself." She paused momentarily; then, speaking rapidly as if she were nervous, Mrs. Ridley said, "We haven't wanted to bother his lordship, what with him being sick and all, but the footmen need a new set of livery and the maids need new gowns."

Helplessly, Cherry stared at the housekeeper. For one moment she was tempted to tell Mrs. Ridley to seek his lordship's help. What did she know about the needs of footmen? But the vision of Varian's mocking face asking, "Are you unable to cope, my lady?" stayed her. She would have to cope!

"What did you do before, Mrs. Ridley? Surely the foot-men had their livery replaced at some earlier time?"

"Oh, yes, m'lady. The late countess sent to Grantham. There's a tailor there who does satisfactory work. Mr. Grimes would have the name."

"Mr. Grimes?"

"His lordship's man of business, m'lady."

"Very well, Mrs. Ridley," said Cherry, thinking rapidly. "If Mr. Grimes has the name, I suggest you speak to him. Ask him to write to this tailor. I suppose he will either have to come here, or measurements will have to be sent. Does he do the maids' gowns also?"

"No, m'lady. A seamstress from the village can come in."

"But cloth will have to be ordered. Mr. Grimes should have the name of the supplier, a merchant in Grantham, perhaps. He can order the fabric, Mrs. Ridley."

For a moment the housekeeper looked apprehensive. The late countess had always spoken to Mr. Grimes herself, but perhaps under the circumstances of that woman's being here and his lordship neglecting his duty, he had failed to present Mr. Grimes to her ladyship. Perhaps 'twere better to follow her ladyship's orders. "Do you wish to see over the house, m'lady?" she asked. *She* at least would do her duty!

Receiving Cherry's assent, Mrs. Ridley led the way down the corridor. "The first floor is given over to bed-chambers and accompanying sitting rooms, m'lady, except for the ballroom," she explained, "and the chambers for personal servants." She opened a door. "This is your Hetty's room."

Cherry could see an ample bedchamber, clean and obviously well cared for. She was pleased that Hetty had not been put in a cupboard.

123

She soon lost count of the number of rooms and their location as she followed the housekeeper about, but she was impressed by their beauty. Cherry liked the graceful lines and elegant simplicity of the furnishings much better than the ornate modern style Aunt Hilliard had favoured in redecorating Hilliard House. All the bedchambers and sitting rooms were large and well tended, their dark furniture highly polished and dust free. She spoke of this to the housekeeper. "His lordship is fortunate in his servants, Mrs. Ridley. All the rooms look as if they are tended with loving care."

The housekeeper beamed. "Thank you, m'lady. Most of the staff was here under the late earl. This is our home, too. We try to keep up all the rooms, even if they are not in use. In the old days, you understand, under the late countess, there was a great deal of entertaining, with many house parties during the winter, and his late lordship had hunting parties. Most of the rooms were occupied. The only rooms we had closed off were those of your ladyship's, after the late countess's death."

They had reached the gallery, which occupied one side of the central span of the house. It was a long, narrow room lined above on both sides with portraits and below with many sofas, tables, and chairs in two formal rows. After pointing out several past Mallorys, including the first Baron Mallory created by Queen Bess, Mrs. Ridley paused at a portrait to the right of the fireplace. "This is the late earl and his countess, m'lady, and Viscount Kellyn and Master Damon."

Cherry barely glanced at the adults in the portrait. Her eyes fastened on the two boys, one sitting, one standing. "Which is which, Mrs. Ridley?"

"Master Damon is standing, m'lady. His brother—God rest his soul—was never very strong."

"I didn't know his lordship was a second son," Cherry murmured, adding to herself, There's a great deal I don't know about his lordship.

"Oh, yes, m'lady. That's why he was in the army. The late earl would never have allowed his heir to join the army and fight, but Master David, Viscount Kellyn, that is, died just over a year ago, and his lordship followed soon after. A message was sent to Master Damon asking him to sell out, but he didn't." The housekeeper shook her head sadly. "Mayhap he'd not been hurt if he had come right home."

Cherry hardly heard the housekeeper's words. Her eyes were drawn to the young boy, no more than ten years old, standing proud, one hand on his brother's chair, the other on his hip. She stared at his face, an open, frank countenance, with no trace of bitterness or mockery in his handsome features. What had happened to change him?

They moved on from the gallery down the staircase to the ground floor. Cherry was already familiar with the drawing room and dining room. Mrs. Ridley indicated the corridor leading off from these rooms. "His lordship's study and library are along this corridor," she said and led the way to the opposite door and the kitchen wing.

Here Cherry was introduced to the household staff: Mrs. Thatcher, the cook; Marston, the first footman; Robert, the second footman; Ned, the third footman; the housemaids, Taylor, Cummins, and Waylow; the kitchen maids, Mary, Jane, and Betty; the scullery maids, Annie, Meg, and Sally; Jim, the boots, and Jack, the yard boy; Mrs. Farley, the head laundress; Rose and Jess, her assistants. For each, Cherry had a warm smile and a handshake. As she came round the line of servants, she ended with Ridley, who reminded her, "There's still the grooms, gardeners, and stableboys, m'lady."

125

"I know, Ridley, but I've already met Frame and he can introduce the others." To the staff, she said, "I hope you will all bear with me if I forget your names at first."

Cherry had tea in her sitting room. Mrs. Ridley had told her that his lordship preferred a late dinner, at eight o'clock. "He holds to town ways, not the early country hours, you understand, m'lady, so you'll be wanting tea to tide you over."

Later she wrote a brief letter to her mother, saying only that she was married to Varian and living at Varian Court. It would only upset her mother to be told more. She folded the heavy sheet of paper embossed with Varian's crest, sealed it with a drop of wax after writing its direction, then carefully imprinted his crest on the wax. This missive she entrusted to a footman, telling him to see that it was sent. She had no intention of asking Varian for a frank. Ridley could do that.

A few minutes before eight Cherry was ready to go down to dinner. She had deliberately waited after Hetty left her, for she had no intention of joining Varian and Nicole in the drawing room before dinner. When the hands on the mantel clock pointed to seven fifty-five she opened the door, then drew back hurriedly. Varian had just stepped into the corridor. Had he come from his bedchamber? So close to hers?

Cherry silently closed the door, then quickly moved across the floor to the dressing room door and opened it. Another door, slightly ajar, gave onto another room. Stepping softly, she crossed the dressing room to the open door and peeked in.

His lordship's valet was moving about. She saw him pick up a discarded cravat, and withdrew hurriedly. Varian's bedchamber was just across the dressing room from

126

hers! What was she to do? Lock the door? But Hetty had said the hip bath was kept in the dressing room.

There was no time to think. Cherry gathered her skirts and sped down the corridor, fearing Varian's censure should she be late. She had to go down to dinner, but perhaps during the meal she could solve this problem. She had to keep Varian from coming into her bedchamber!

But her fears were groundless, Cherry realized as dinner progressed. Varian never once glanced her way. His eyes rested exclusively on Nicole throughout the entire meal. He even kept his eyes on her as he drank his wine! Surely under these circumstances, so absorbed in his mistress, he would not want to invade his wife's bedchamber!

Yet Cherry found her relief strangely tinged with resentment. She was his wife. He certainly should acknowledge her existence, shouldn't he? Couldn't he spare her one glance? But she didn't want him to treat her the way he did Nicole. She would be embarrassed to have a man look at her like that in public.

Cherry sighed. It was all so confusing, much too confusing by far. Don't think about that, she admonished herself, just remember your resolution of last night. That's what's important!

Thirteen

A footman was waiting as Cherry came down the stairs the next morning. "M'lady, his lordship requests your presence in his study," he announced.

"Thank you . . . Marston?" There was a questioning lilt to her voice as she was unsure of his name. "Would you direct me, please?"

As she followed behind the footman, Cherry took the opportunity to look closely at his clothing. The cuffs were frayed, patches were evident. So Mrs. Ridley had not been mistaken. But her concern for the staff livery was overshadowed by a growing apprehension. Why should Varian want to see her? She had done nothing wrong. Then, realizing that she was attributing to him only a desire to criticize her, she shook herself mentally. Don't be silly, she told herself. It's probably nothing. Yet the sinking feeling in her stomach did not go away. On the contrary, by the time Marston opened the study door, it had grown. And one glance at Varian's stormy face as he sat behind the imposing desk confirmed her fears.

He waited to speak until she had walked across the floor and was approaching the desk, his frown getting blacker and more threatening. "Grimes tells me you ordered livery for the footmen."

Surprised at the harshness of his voice, at first Cherry just stared at him. How could he possibly object to that? She almost blurted out this thought, but caught herself in time, biting back the words. Instead, she forced herself to answer quietly, "Mrs. Ridley told me the footmen needed new livery. I suggested she speak to your man of business." By now Cherry had seen a pleasant-faced man, neatly attired in a brown coat and breeches, standing to Varian's right. Mr. Grimes, she surmised.

"*You* suggested!" Varian rose from his chair to stand glaring at her. "May I remind you, madam, this is *my* home, and I need no interference from you."

Cherry raised her chin. This was going too far! "Interference, my lord? Is it interference to spare you minor household details?"

Mr. Grimes stepped forward. "I beg your pardon, m'lord, but the late countess—"

He was not allowed to finish. "When I want your advice, Grimes, I will request it. And as for you, m'lady, stay out of my affairs!"

Cherry was trying desperately to hold her temper in check, for clearly the man was impossible. But when he turned his cold, contemptuous eyes on her, she could no longer contain herself. "If you did not wish me to oversee your household, m'lord, you should not have made me your wife. It is my responsibility—"

Varian broke in. "Your responsibility, m'lady, is to obey me."

"And how am I to do that," Cherry asked, her eyes

blazing, by now uncaring that her ill-mannered behaviour was witnessed, "when you never even speak to me?"

Varian moved forward, his face set, his hand raised threateningly. "Don't tempt me, madam!" he growled.

"Tempt you?" Cherry was so angry she let her voice fully express all the scorn she felt. "You need no tempting, my lord."

"That is correct, m'lady. And 'twould be better for you to remember it."

"Ohhhhh!" Cherry shook from anger, her hands clenched at her sides. How she wanted to slap that overbearing, arrogant, hateful face. Instead, she whirled around and ran out of the study. If she'd stayed she would have burst into tears, and she would not give him the satisfaction of seeing her cry.

She sped across the hall and through the front door, along the front of the house, slowing only as she came to its corner. She had to get away from *him*. By the time she reached the gardens she was gasping and she sank down on a stone marker to catch her breath. Her anger had disappeared, to be replaced by self-contempt. She had lost her temper! After promising herself that under no circumstances would she allow Varian to provoke her, she had forgotten her resolution on the very first occasion he spoke to her! This would not do! She had barely escaped another slap in the face. Perhaps the presence of Mr. Grimes had stayed Varian's hand, for he had wanted to chastise her; she had seen it in his face. Why, why, why could she not learn to contain her anger?

The sound of approaching footsteps made her look up. "Oh, Frame," she called to the gardener, "there is a rotunda—" Then abruptly Cherry stopped speaking. Would Varian object to her asking to have it repaired and refuse to allow it?

"Aye, m'lady. T'were built for t'late countess. An' whin she died, there was no one to keep it up, his lordship not wanting to be reminded of her, so to speak."

"Would you need his lordship's permission to start work on it? There's weeding to be done and it needs repainting."

Frame's glance from under his bushy eyebrows was sharp. Cherry nervously waited his response to her question, but his words were mild. "When I finds work to be done, m'lady, I sends m'boys t'do it."

"Thank you, Frame," she whispered and turned away so he would not see tears in her eyes. If Varian continued to be unreasonable, she would desperately need the sanctuary of the rotunda.

On her return to the house, having discovered a path leading from the shrubbery to a wooded area that she briefly explored, Cherry met Mr. Grimes in the hall. Reminded of the painful scene in Varian's study, she would have preferred to ignore him, but his voice stopped her as she began to ascend the stairway.

"I beg your pardon, m'lady."

"Yes?" Cherry sighed. She could not display ill manners to this man who had not harmed her in any way.

There was a troubled expression on his face as he said, "I wish to apologize, m'lady. I spoke inadvertently to his lordship about the livery. In the past her ladyship made arrangements with me, the late earl not wanting to bother with household matters. Had I continued this tradition his lordship would have remained in ignorance of the matter."

"Yes, well, thank you, Mr. Grimes. I suppose it doesn't much matter who orders the clothing, just so long as the footmen and maids get it. The staff seems to be excellent,

Mr. Grimes, and I should hate to deny anyone what is rightfully his."

"I'll see to it, m'lady," he promised.

At luncheon Varian did not refer to her "interference." In point of fact he did not at all acknowledge her presence, not even by a frown, and as the days passed, Cherry, perforce, became accustomed to such cavalier treatment. Her hours were spent much as they had been on her first day in residence as Lady Varian.

Every morning she was awakened early by faint noises coming from the adjoining dressing room. Occasionally she could hear murmurs of voices, but never any words. And every morning she felt drawn to the window to watch wistfully as Varian rode off. She'd be willing to put up with his mockery and high-handedness to ride with him, but dared not ask.

Her morning walks continued, through the gardens, across the lawns to the rotunda in the shrubbery, where she could see evidence of work being done. A crew of gardeners had trimmed the shrubs and weeded the path. They were followed by scullery maids with buckets and finally painters with brushes. By the end of a week her sanctuary was gleaming white and accessible.

Every afternoon, after briefly meeting with Mrs. Ridley to discuss the day's menus and other household matters, she took another walk, but in a different direction. The estate was vast and she was determined to explore it.

The housekeeper offered a parasol. "You really should carry one, m'lady, or wear a hat to protect your complexion. I'm sure there's one of her ladyship's old ones in the boxes in the attics."

"Thank you, Mrs. Ridley, but I prefer not to." Cherry could hardly admit that she feared Varian's reaction if he caught her with one of his mother's possessions. She would most certainly be accused of interfering with *his* home again. As for her own bonnet, it was uncomfortably tight in the warm summer sun.

Every day just before tea she explored the house on her own, wishing to learn the location of the various rooms and doors.

A highly embarrassing moment occurred one afternoon in the corridor near the ballroom. A black-clad middle-aged female emerged from a doorway. Cherry was sure she'd not been introduced to this servant, who reluctantly bobbed a curtsey.

Cherry stopped. "Who are you?" she asked.

"I am Marie, milady." She did not expand her brief statement, but there was no real need for further explanation. She spoke with a French accent. Cherry realized the woman must be Nicole's maid.

Feeling slightly flustered, for Cherry would not acknowledge Nicole's presence and Marie must know this by now, Cherry inclined her head slightly and moved on.

Later she spoke to Hetty about it. "What else could I do, Hetty? I felt so dreadful, not speaking to the woman. It's not really her fault that her mistress is a . . ." Under the glare of Hetty's eyes, Cherry could not speak the word trembling on her tongue, a word which a properly brought-up female should be in ignorance of. She discovered it was one thing to speak vulgarly to Varian, another matter altogether to use such words to Hetty but then, she cared for Hetty's opinion of her.

An embarrassing moment for her, but at least she had learned the location of Nicole's apartment and could stay away from that part of the house in the future.

After tea she spent an hour working on the needlework Mrs. Ridley had brought her. "Her late ladyship started it, m'lady. As you can see, it's a design of the house and the fountain. She had planned it as a surprise for the late earl, but death took her before she was able to finish it. All the yarns are here."

"I thought you hated sewing," Hetty commented, after catching Cherry industriously stitching.

"I do, Hetty. I detest it. But there's nothing else to do. Mrs. Ridley runs the house and I can't make any changes, not obvious ones, anyway. There are no books up here, and I won't ask his lordship for any. I can't walk *all* day," she wailed.

Hetty set her lips. It was not her place to comment on the behaviour of her betters or to encourage Miss Cherry in her willfulness. She kept silent.

Cherry's original enjoyment of the garden remained. Each morning Frame would take her with him on an inspection tour among the rose bushes. He spoke knowledgeably of black spot, white spiders, and throwbacks, and Cherry, though mystified, tried to show her interest.

"Have t'watch every day for theys spiders, m'lady. They's awful bad. Why, they could ruin all my roses!" he would exclaim in horror.

By the end of the week Cherry had discovered that the servants were outraged by Nicole's presence. She didn't really need to have Hetty tell her so. "Mr. and Mrs. Ridley, now, they don't say nothin', but when the bell from her room rings and the maids is slow about goin' up, Mrs. Ridley don't scold 'em," she reported. "And that French . . . woman, she can't drink morning tea like a body should, but must have her chocolate. But it seems it's not hot enough for her, the maids not bringing it fast enough, so's she's had to send *her* maid for it. You should hear the talk in the kitchen, Miss Cherry, everyone saying how it's a shame his lordship keeps her here. No one on the staff wants her here."

Cherry had personal experience of their dislike. Marston, bringing in a tureen of soup one evening, had broken step as he neared Nicole's chair. Fortunately, Cherry had glanced up and shaken her head slightly. Instinctively she had sensed that he intended "falling" and jumping the contents over Nicole. She had to prevent it, not because she wanted to allow Nicole to escape the hot liquid, but because she was afraid Varian would turn him out. Already she had overheard his lordship speaking to Ridley about the poor service.

The support of the servants was her only compensation as the days passed. She was becoming bored, restless, and more and more unhappy. There was nothing to do but needlework and walking, no one to speak to but Hetty. One did not discuss personal affairs with servants. Only with Hetty, who was more a friend than a servant, could she be free with her thoughts. She kept up her walks only because they took her out of the house and away from Varian.

Cherry felt driven from the house, as if it were somehow safer to be away from him. Within doors, near him, she was experiencing a growing sense of unease that she could not define. Moreover, it was getting harder and harder to sit through luncheon and dinner: her eyes felt drawn, against her will, to Varian. It was proving impossible to ignore him. He was *her* husband. He should speak to *her,* smile at *her,* not Nicole.

As she watched him with the Frenchwoman, there was a strange feeling in the pit of her stomach—a longing, for *what* she did not know. Probably it was apprehension, worry of the future, but it frightened her.

Each day so much like the preceding day, Cherry was

losing track of time. Each day dragged on and on. She never knew what time it was. Only the position of the sun overhead told her it was time to return for luncheon.

One afternoon she found a small stream deep in a forest of beech and chestnut trees. Its banks were thickly covered with ferns, under which mosses grew and a few late violets bloomed. She walked slowly, looking for fish, anything to pass the hours. Ahead of her was a large stone. She sat down on it, dipping her hand in the cool water, wondering how painful it would be to drown. She had been taught that suicide was a heinous sin, not to be contemplated, but surely there were circumstances . . . ? What had she to look forward to but more humiliation and more and more unhappiness? She had been married for over a week and her husband had not spoken to her since that horrid day in his study. She started back reluctantly, her steps dragging.

Marston was waiting for her in the hall. "There are guests in the drawing room, m'lady. His lordship requests your presence."

"Thank you, Marston," she murmured, pausing before a mirror to assess her appearance. Her curls were disheveled. She probably was late now. Should she take time to run upstairs?

Cherry shrugged. What difference did it make? *He* didn't care. She shook her head, but that didn't help. Next she ran her fingers through the bright red mass. That would have to do. She nodded to the waiting footman, who held open the doors.

"Don't you find Lincolnshire more comfortable than London, my lord? I know Brinsley does, and if he is typical of his sex, then gentlemen like their comforts. Brinsley refuses to spend the Season in London. He says it's much too formal, but then he never wears aught but his riding gear. I'm sure I don't know what I'll do. Amelia must be brought out, but Brinsley seems not to care."

Cherry had paused in the doorway, thinking it ill mannered to interrupt the speaker, but as the words continued to pour forth, she judged it wiser to appear. How long had his lordship been waiting?

Varian was seated in a high-backed wing chair, a bored expression on his face. Facing him, seated side by side on a settee, were two females. Cherry could see only backs covered by Paisley shawls and their bonnets, from one of which golden curls peeped. Was this Amelia? she wondered.

In the slight pause as the speaker seemed to catch her breath, Cherry spoke. "My lord, I must apologize for my lateness, but I was just now informed of guests."

She could have been mistaken, but she had the impression that a look of relief appeared briefly on Varian's face, to be replaced by a frown. However, she could not mistake either the look of apprehension on the young female's face or the frown on the older one's.

Reluctantly, Varian rose. His voice was frigidly formal. "My lady, allow me to present Lady Brinsley and Miss Brinsley." He paused and then added, as if it were an afterthought, "Lady Varian."

There was a distinct gasp from Lady Brinsley, but her ladyship pulled herself together, rose from the settee, and curtsied.

Miss Brinsley gave Cherry a shy smile as she curtsied. There was now a distinct look of relief on her face, in contrast to the hostile expression on her mother's.

Cherry offered her hand. "How do you do, Lady Brinsley? I collect you are a neighbour. Miss Brinsley, I am

137

pleased to make your acquaintance." Cherry spoke with sincerity. She needed a friend.

Lady Brinsley's greeting was cool. "How do you do?" she murmured, barely touching Cherry's hand before pulling her own away. "You must forgive my surprise, m'lady, for you must know Miss Brinsley and I had been in the habit of calling on his lordship this past winter, while he was recovering from his wounds, you know, and I doubt I speak falsely if I say we became great friends. Hence my surprise at your appearance, my lady. I did not know you were contemplating marriage, my lord."

Cherry remained silent. What, after all, could she say to this? Instead she moved to seat herself in a nearby chair.

"Are you suggesting I must account to you for all my actions, Lady Brinsley?"

Cherry was shocked at Varian's tone of voice. He need not be so rude. Granted Lady Brinsley had an ulterior motive—it was easy to see she had hoped for marriage between Varian and Amelia, taking advantage perhaps of his weakened condition—but her calls could not have been entirely negative. Miss Amelia Brinsley was a pleasant-looking, pretty child whose mild manner reminded Cherry of her cousins Lizzie and Agnes.

Lady Brinsley laughed. "To be sure, my lord, that was not what I was suggesting. However, there was no notice in either the *Morning Post* or *The Times*." She turned to confide in Cherry, "Brinsley must keep abreast of all the news, though he refuses to visit London."

Then, as her sharp gaze rested on Cherry, she blurted out, "You're in black gloves, my lady. That explains the lack of an advertisement, to be sure. But really, my lord" —and she turned to address Varian—"the conventions ought to be upheld, don't you agree?"

Varian, who had remained standing after Cherry seated herself, now bowed. "Of which conventions do you speak, my lady?"

Somewhat taken aback, Lady Brinsley sputtered, "Why, all of them, my lord. What would Society be like if everyone chose to act as he pleased?"

"Society, ma'am, would be very much as it is, I imagine," Varian replied in a bored voice.

"I shan't stay to argue with you, my lord. Come, Amelia, we must go." Lady Brinsley rose and offered her hand to Cherry. "You must come calling, my lady," she said politely, but the insincerity in her voice belied her words.

Cherry, after seeing their guests to their carriage, stood hesitating in the hall. Should she return to the drawing room? Varian had seemed angry that she was late in arriving, but at least he had spared her a scolding in front of the guests, and she realized, with relief, he had spared her the humiliation of Nicole's presence. She took a step toward the stairs, then, looking up, saw Varian standing in the doorway. As her eyebrows rose questioningly, he gestured curtly. Meekly she entered the open doorway.

"You wanted to speak to me, my lord?" she asked.

Ignoring her question, not even giving her the courtesy of a reply, he announced, "It is your duty to be present to entertain guests. Surely it does not take a quarter of an hour to primp?"

"I was out walking, my lord," Cherry protested. "I came as soon as I was informed of guests."

It was as if she hadn't spoken. "In future, you will be available, my lady." His words were icy, his tone commanding. Cherry knew any protests she might make would not only be overlooked, but disregarded. Didn't he care for any excuse? Was this the way he had been in the army? Were orders to be obeyed with no possible excuse for disobedience? *But I'm not one of his soldiers, I'm his wife!*

Her protest was silent, however. Varian had turned away from her in dismissal, and slowly, defeated, Cherry left the drawing room to climb the stairs.

Fourteen

The blackness was receding . . . Slowly, oh, so slowly, it was lifting . . . bit by bit, it was growing lighter. But as the darkness went, the pain increased. He became aware of extreme discomfort, which grew and grew into sharp pain . . . There was a fire in his chest . . . every breath he took was an agony . . . his mouth was dry . . . he couldn't swallow . . . his tongue felt enormous, it filled his mouth . . . his lips were parched. . . . He must have water. Where was his flask?

The sun was beating down, impaling him on its hot rays. He began to feel like a piece of meat roasting on a turnspit. Why did he just lie here and let it cook him?

Where was his mount? He had been riding . . . He had to get back to his regiment. There were enemy movements to report. . . .

He tried to lift his head, but it was much too heavy. He gave up and reached out his left arm for the water flask. Fiery pains shot up his arm and the intense torment almost brought on the blackness again. He lay gasping

. . . then desperately tried to control his breathing as the agony in his chest became unbearable. He felt enveloped in hot blazing fire, his only relief the slight coolness on his brow as his sweat evaporated.

He must have water. His breathing steadied, he reached out with his right arm. It touched warm, living flesh.

Damon Mallory, Earl of Varian, opened his eyes and saw not the hot, burning sun of Spain, but the dimness of a bedchamber. He shuddered and sat up in bed. Next to him, Nicole stirred in her sleep but didn't waken.

Gad! When would these nightmares end? The actual experience had been torment enough. Must he constantly relive that hell?

Every night the same dream, and every night Nicole's warm body brought him back to sanity. If she weren't with him to waken him by her presence, would he have to reexperience the whole bloody mess, culminating in the excruciating pain of the saw as the surgeon took his arm? Was not one drawn-out fiery hell enough suffering?

His lordship threw off the bed covers, got out of bed, and walked over to the window. The sun was just over the horizon—early for a ride, true, but too late to try for more sleep.

Varian picked up his dressing gown, draped it over his left shoulder, then slipped his right arm through the sleeve. I'm becoming quite adept at this, he thought bitterly, as he quietly left Nicole's bedchamber.

Once in his own quarters, he rang for Hartley. He disliked waking his valet at such an ungodly hour, but it had to be done. He could not pull on his boots.

A sleepy valet, still clad in dressing gown and nightcap, appeared at the door. "You rang, m'lord?"

"Yes," Varian answered curtly. "I've decided on an early morning ride, Hartley."

"Yes, m'lord. Do you wish to shave before your ride?"

"I will shave when I return." He spoke patiently, as if to a child, and the valet, recognizing signs of his lordship's anger, moved quickly.

Hartley pulled out a pair of buckskin breeches, stockings, and top boots, then took out a fine lawn shirt. Silently he assisted the earl in donning the latter, then fastened the buttons. Next he held the breeches for his lordship to step into, pulled them up carefully, easing the leather over his lordship's muscular thighs, and smoothing down the shirt tails. After fastening the breeches, he knelt down and pulled on the stockings, buckling the breeches around Varian's calves. The boots came next. Then, as Varian stood, Hartley held first the waistcoat, then the blue frock coat, assisted him into them in turn, and after buttoning the coat, pinned the left sleeve to it.

Before offering a cravat, he stole a glance at his lordship's face and decided against it. That, like the shave, could wait his lordship's return. He held out the high-crowned hat. Varian shook his head.

"Go back to bed, Hartley," he advised as he left the room. "I may be gone for hours."

An equally sleepy groom had to be roused to saddle his horse, while Varian fumed. In the past he could have been up and gone with no one the wiser. Now all his movements had to be tended by servants. He had no privacy! His lordship swung into the saddle and rode off.

Fifteen

He wants me to sit waiting for guests to arrive, but I won't do it, Cherry decided. Lady Brinsley was the first caller we had in a whole week. I can't just sit in my bedchamber waiting for other neighbours to call.

So with determination renewed by Varian's opposition, Cherry continued her outdoor expeditions. Her visits with Frame were one of the few compensations in a life filled with boredom and increasing depression.

The stream seemed to draw her. Every afternoon she followed its length for a greater distance before turning back. The darkened woods and the quietly murmuring stream lulled her low spirits. There was a gentle solace in the outdoors that strengthened her for the ordeal of each day's dinner when she had to sit, ignored, at the same table as her husband's mistress.

Several days after Lady Brinsley's call, Cherry was returning home along the stream when she saw a young man, clad in a farmer's smock, carefully and stealthily moving amidst the willows bordering the stream. His intent expression changed at sight of her, but Cherry overlooked his blushes and the furtive glance he gave her. If he wished to poach from Varian's streams, that was Varian's business, not hers. She smiled. "Good afternoon. It's a most pleasant day to be walking, is it not?"

He touched his cap respectfully. "Aye," he agreed. "Be ye t'lady?"

"I am Lady Varian," Cherry admitted, and when he showed no indication of introducing himself, she asked, "Do you work for his lordship?"

"Aye, I be Jock," he answered reluctantly.

"I saw some men haying yesterday."

"Aye, t'hay be in."

Cherry tried again. "Do you grow wheat here in Lincolnshire?"

"Aye."

Rapidly reviewing what little she knew of farming, Cherry next asked, "Do you grow turnips, or do you allow the land to lie fallow?" That should get some response from him!

But again Jock defeated her. "Some does an' some don't."

"What about sheep?" she asked. "Do you raise sheep?"

"Aye." He nodded his head, then brightened. "T'shearin's done."

Really, it was most difficult to get him to say anything, Cherry thought in exasperation, then almost giggled as she realized that she, too, was very carefully skirting the subject of fishing. So with a smile and a "Carry on," she continued on home, wishing she could learn if he was successful in his quest. She entered the back door of the kitchen wing, a slight smile on her lips.

A scullery maid, catching sight of her, hurriedly wiped

her hands and bobbed a respectful curtsey. "Mrs. Ridley be wantin' ye, m'lady," she reported.

"Thank you, Annie." Cherry hurried into the kitchen to find the housekeeper.

Mrs. Thatcher was busily stirring the contents of a large kettle, almost stepping on the boy turning the spit at the cavernous fireplace. At the center table a kitchen maid was rolling pastry. Another was cutting bread into thin slices. On a side table there was a great silver tray, with Ridley standing guard.

"Hurry, m'lady," he called. "There are guests in the drawing room. M'lord has been asking for you. I'll delay serving tea for a bit."

"Thank you, Ridley," Cherry murmured. With a sinking heart she passed through the door held open by Betty. Late again. Varian would be furious.

Quickly she ran her fingers through her tangled ringlets, grateful that fashion favoured a short hairstyle. There would never be sufficient time to tidy long curls. When she passed a hall mirror, she sought a quick glimpse of herself and almost gasped. With her unruly curls and the prominent band of freckles across her nose, she looked like a street urchin. Fortunately her skin was still fair. The summer sun had not tanned it, but *that* was small consolation as she passed through the doorway into the drawing room.

"I tell you, Damon, things are coming to a pretty pass when a man is not safe on the King's Highway." The hearty voice broke off at her entrance and a portly man with a flushed, open face rose to greet her.

Varian was sitting in a chair opposite his guest, his elbow resting on its upholstered arm. He was the picture of languid ease, but his eyes when they met hers were dark with anger.

Cherry broke into hurried speech before he could castigate her. "You must forgive me, my lord, but I was occupied and just now learned of our guests." She came forward, her hand outstretched and a smile on her face. "How do you do? I am Lady Varian."

The gentleman bowed, then shook hands heartily. "Francis Warrick, m'lady. And this"—he indicated a pleasant-faced woman in pale mauve—"is Lady Warrick."

Lady Warrick curtsied, then shook hands. Cherry, still slightly flustered from the deference being paid her, having forgotten that a countess outranks a baroness, looked helplessly at Varian.

Her husband had risen reluctantly at her entrance. Now he demanded, "Was your business of such great importance that you neglect our guests? Sir Francis and Lady Warrick have been here some time."

"I was making the acquaintance of your tenants, my lord," she said quietly, then sat down on the chair next to Lady Warrick, who gave her a nervous smile.

Sir Francis looked uncomfortable and sought a neutral topic of conversation. "As I was saying, Damon, it's outrageous that nothing has been done to stop them, though Burleigh has sent for the Runners."

Cherry breathed a sigh of relief when Varian sat down and directed his attention to his guest, not to his wife.

"I fear the Bow Street Runners will be of little help, Francis."

"Just what I told Burleigh. Can't expect 'em to know the county. But one can't blame Burleigh. B'Gad, he was angry, fit to be tied he was. Lost most of his wife's jewels and five hundred pounds."

Cherry, after almost two weeks of entertaining herself, was overjoyed to have guests. Lady Brinsley she didn't count as a guest, since her ladyship had seen fit to leave

147

immediately. Now she listened avidly. Sir Francis's conversation interested her, but she knew better than to interrupt him: Varian would be sure to criticize her. Instead she leaned closer to Lady Warrick and whispered, "What has happened, my lady?"

"Highwaymen!" she was informed in a low voice.

"No!" Cherry's eyes widened. "How dreadful." Her attention was again caught by Sir Francis, who in response to a murmured comment by Varian was expounding again.

"I say we comb all the woods and forested areas and arm the servants. Any strangers caught should be detained and investigated." He broke off at the entrance of Ridley bearing the tea tray.

The butler placed the tray on a low table next to Cherry, then removed a decanter and two glasses, which he took over to place on a tripod table at Varian's right hand.

Cherry poured tea for Lady Warrick and herself as Varian poured the wine.

"This Madeira is excellent," Sir Francis said after taking a sip. "You have an excellent cellar, Damon. I must compliment you on your taste, in wine, and in women." He raised his glass to Cherry, who blushed faintly.

Her attempt to thank him was aborted, however, by her husband's "The cellar was laid down by m'father."

The earl's words were left hanging in the air. Cherry had the distinct impression that he would also like to deny his taste in women and began to wish she were elsewhere.

This time it was Lady Warrick who entered the breach. In the silence following Varian's words, her voice rang out. "You are in mourning, m'lady?"

Grateful for a new topic of conversation, even such a painful one as her own grief, she answered, "Yes, my father was killed in Spain."

Her guest took a sip of tea, then murmured, "A sad business, that."

Sir Francis took up the gambit. "I fear we're losing a great many of our young men, but not as many as the Frogs, I'm glad to say. What regiment was your father in, m'lady?"

"He was a major in the Fourth Dragoons."

"Would I know him?" he probed.

Cherry smiled faintly. "Major John Hilliard, Sir Francis."

Sir Francis shook his head. "No, I can't say I do. Know your uncle," he added.

Varian, whose lips had been held tightly together during this part of the conversation, now broke in. "To return to your earlier suggestion, Francis, I fear that arming the servants would result in a great many unnecessary killings. No cattle or horses would be safe, nor would any larking farmboy. Servants with a pistol in hand would be too apt to shoot at any sound or movement."

Sir Francis considered this suggestion while swirling the wine in his glass. "Perhaps you're right, my boy." (Cherry almost choked on her tea. If there was anything Varian wasn't, it was boyish.) "But something has to be done. Three holdups last week, and two more this week. It's not to be borne! What is the world coming to, I ask you?"

Not waiting for an answer, he put down his glass. "Missed you at Newmarket, Damon."

Varian shrugged, then gestured toward the wine decanter. "Help yourself, Francis." As his guest promptly followed this directive, the earl inquired, "Was there any special reason for me to attend?"

Sir Francis paused in the act of pouring the Madeira. "Well, dammit, Damon, I had a prime 'un running. He took the first heat, too. I'm thinking of running him again

149

this fall. Has plenty of bottom, but"—here he paused to stopper the decanter and resume his seat—"he seems to run better in cooler weather. I'm even considering a few side bets on 'im."

Varian's lips lifted slightly. "Then you must have a winner, Francis. Remind me, please, to enter a bet."

"Will you be hunting this fall, m'lord?" Lady Warrick asked. To Cherry, she confided, "The Belvoir Hunt, you know."

Varian's face, which up to now had held a carefully neutral expression as he chatted, now became aloof. He turned away and deliberately removed the stopper from the cut-glass decanter, picked up the decanter, and filled his glass.

Sir Francis, looking as if he would burst from indignation, nevertheless waited to speak until Varian held his glass to his lips. "Well, Damon, are you? And don't try to gammon me by claiming you can't ride. Blindfolded and with both hands tied behind your back, you're a better rider than any man I know. You've got the seat and legs, man, you don't need your hands!"

This was plain speaking indeed! Cherry held her breath, fearing an explosion of wrath. She knew Sir Francis was correct, but would Varian?

"My compliments, Francis. After that encomium how can I refuse?"

A beaming smile broke out on Warrick's face, to be quickly replaced by an apprehensive look. "You do have some hunters left, I hope. Leastways, your father wouldn't have been such a fool as to send his best ones with you for cannon fodder."

"No, Francis"—Varian bowed his head slightly—"you can rest assured your judgment of my father is correct."

Again Sir Francis smiled, then rose from his chair.

150

"Time to go, Sarah. Thought I'd warn you, Damon. On your honeymoon and all, you wouldn't be hearing about highwaymen. Just remember to carry a brace of pistols with you if you travel."

Cherry, who had rung for the footman at the first indication that the Warricks were leaving, now shook hands with both guests.

"We are pleased to welcome you to Lincolnshire, m'lady,' Sir Francis said, and his wife murmured, "Please feel free to call at any time, my lady. We keep open house all year."

Cherry had hoped that Varian would see the Warricks to their carriage, thus giving her an opportunity to escape him, but he allowed the footman to perform that chore. He did, however, have the courtesy to wait until the door closed on their departing guests before rounding on her.

"It is an insult to me and to our guests that you were not here to greet them. When I sent Marston to inform you of their arrival, I was told you were not in. Henceforth, madam, you will be available."

Cherry's resolution to keep calm and not provoke Varian left her at this order. "I went for a walk. There's nothing else to do here. And I met one of your tenants. Was I supposed to snub him and rush back on the odd chance that you might want me, when you've ignored me ever since our arrival? For someone who was in such a hurry to marry me, my lord, your subsequent actions have been . . . inconsistent, to say the least. You haven't even introduced me to your servants and tenants, and I was under the impression that such was your responsibility."

"Hold your tongue!" he said sharply. "That's enough of your tantrums. Your place is here, my lady, in this house, do you hear? Next time I have occasion to send for you I wish your immediate presence."

Cherry seethed. Was she to sit waiting until he deigned to summon her? He ignores her for two weeks, then is angry that she doesn't come running. Oh! It was so unfair!

"You want a servant, not a wife, my lord," she informed him.

"Is there any difference?" he asked coldly.

Cherry felt as if a knife had entered her heart. He could sit and smile at Nicole. He was always touching her, his face soft, his smile warm. With his mistress he was a different person, but Cherry he treated as if she were an enemy. She couldn't understand him, not after he had insisted on their immediate marriage.

At meals she had to watch them together. The French-woman could not resist throwing gloating glances at Cherry. She seemed to go out of her way to show Cherry that she, Nicole, was loved by Varian. She spoke French exclusively, trying to make Cherry feel an outsider, not realizing that Cherry had an excellent understanding of that language. However, Cherry much preferred to ignore the low, seductive voice drawling, *"mon amour, mon cher"* or *"chéri."*

The lovers had become more brazen. It seemed as if they were acting a part, trying to get Cherry to react. Varian would kiss Nicole's hand, then lean over as he seated her at the dining table and kiss her neck. His lips would linger for a long moment, before traveling down her throat to rest just above the neckline of her gown.

And Cherry would have to stand by and watch them until Ridley and the footmen entered with dinner. She kept telling herself she didn't care. *She* didn't want his attentions: she didn't want him fondling her or kissing her. She just wished he would be kinder to her, smile just once at her. He was handsome when he smiled.

Her thoughts were interrupted as Varian turned away

in dismissal. Cherry was annoyed that he did not even have the courtesy to tell her she could go, but decided it was wiser not to provoke him further. She did not want another slap in the face. Gladly she escaped to her sitting room. For a few hours she would be free of his presence.

Cherry had just picked up the needle to begin her hour's stint on the hated needlework when Varian entered. She looked up in surprise. Never before had he come here. Was he coming to apologize for his bad manners? She waited hopefully.

"My lady," he began, when his eyes fell on the needlework.

It was a shock to Cherry to see the change in his face. From coldly formal he became furiously angry.

"How dare you?" he shouted. "That was my mother's. How dare *you* contaminate her work?"

He grabbed the frame and spun it out of her hands. Cherry sat with her mouth open, staring at him, too shocked to move or protest. She had never before seen anyone so angry, not even Uncle Geoffrey at his worst.

Varian rang for the footman. "Take this and burn it," he ordered, shoving the frame at Marston.

The footman stood speechless, holding the wooden frame helplessly.

"Well, what are you waiting for, Marston?" Varian snapped. "You heard me," his lordship commanded, then spoke to Cherry, "As for you, madam, keep your hands off things that do not belong to you," and stormed out.

Sixteen

At first Cherry sat, too stunned to move after Marston left her sitting room carrying the offending needlework. She couldn't understand such hatred, for hatred it was. Hatred so intense it impaired his judgment, hatred so great an inanimate object must be destroyed merely because she had touched it. Why did he hate her so?

Then she jumped up. Why waste time asking herself hypothetical questions? She sped down the stairs after Varian, not even bothering to consider that he might be going to Nicole. She must discover the cause of his feelings toward her.

Robert was on duty in the hall and informed her that his lordship had just entered the library. "Shall I announce you, m'lady?"

"Thank you, no," Cherry murmured and forced herself to walk slowly down the corridor. She must be calm, for it was imperative that she not lose her temper.

She entered the library quietly and watched as Varian, his back to her, walked over to a mahogany side table and

poured a glass of wine for himself. He had to remove the
stopper and place it on the table, pick up the decanter, fill
the glass, then put down the decanter before replacing the
stopper, just as he had done before during the Warricks'
call. Her heart turned over. Even a simple task was made
difficult by lack of a hand.

But she was not here to feel sympathy for a man who
wanted none, she reminded herself. "Varian," she called.

He started at the sound of her voice, then looked up.

"You hate me. It shows in everything you say to me, in
everything you do. Why? What have I done to deserve
such hatred?"

He eyed her over the rim of the wineglass, then deliberately raised the glass to his lips. His eyes were icy black.

When he did not speak, Cherry tried again. "I never
spoke to you, I had never even met you before you offered
for me. How could I have hurt you enough to cause such
bitter hatred?"

The earl set down the empty glass. "Yes, perhaps you
should know. Sit down, my lady." He gestured with elabo-
rate courtesy.

Cherry lowered herself into one of the leather chairs
before the fireplace, her eyes fixed apprehensively on his
face. What was she to learn?

Varian seated himself in the opposite chair, then began
speaking in a toneless voice. "We were before Salamanca.
Hooky had been hoping the French would attack, for we
were in a strong position, but Marmont was too cautious.
He withdrew up the Douro and we followed. Then Marmont caught us off balance and we were forced to retreat
back to Salamanca." Varian paused in his recitation, his
eyes staring ahead of him. Cherry wondered whether he
was able to visualize the events he was describing.

Then his lips curled in a grimace. "We must have been

a pretty sight, the English and French armies marching parallel to each other, only a few hundred yards apart." Again he was silent.

Cherry was listening quietly, hardly daring to breathe. She knew nothing of military strategy, but had no trouble following his lordship's words: Hooky must be Lord Wellington and Marmont must be the French general.

"Harry Lorimer and I had been sent on ahead to discover the best place to ford the Tormes River. We had the fastest horses, and could easily outrun any French cattle. We were returning from our reconnaissance when we met Major Hilliard." He seemed to spit out her father's name. "He claimed he was lost." Again he paused, and Cherry held her breath. She sensed the climax was near.

"We were following a slight trail through the hills, the guide leading, then Lorimer, myself, and Hilliard bringing up the rear, when we were attacked by a company of French. I took a ball in my arm—it shattered the bone. My horse was also hit and threw me. I was lying in the dust, stunned, but I could see Lorimer fall, ahead of me. The guide was dead, and I turned my head, expecting to see Hilliard suffer the same fate. But instead"—and Varian turned to look directly at Cherry—"I saw Hilliard turn tail and run. The last I saw of him he was slashing his mount as he sped away and left us to the mercy of the French."

"No, no, it can't be," Cherry whispered, her eyes bright with shock and tears.

"No? Oh, the French were merciful. I received a sword thrust that should have been enough to kill me, but unfortunately, it missed my heart and lungs. I survived, if you can call it that. For two days I lay there with the Spanish sun beating down on me. Do you know what it's like to be in hell, madam? To pray for death, but be unable to voice your prayers because your mouth is too dry, your tongue swollen, and your lips parched and cracked? With a fire in your chest that makes breathing excruciating?

"Hilliard hadn't even bothered notifying the camp of the attack. I was found, by accident, by our own troops returning after the battle of Salamanca, too late to save my arm. It was cut off, madam, with a saw." He spat out these words.

"War, at best, is a messy business. You learn to accept death, even though convinced that somehow you will escape. I could even accept this"—he gestured toward his empty sleeve—"if I had earned it honourably in battle. But to lose a hand as the result of an English soldier's cowardice? No! I feel dirtied and part of his shame. And there's no end to it. Each time I am forced to depend on others for my private needs I am reminded of this dishonourable act."

His voice was bitter as he continued, "I spent months recuperating, vowing I'd find Hilliard and shoot him down like the dog he was. But unfortunately for you, the French had already done that."

From somewhere Cherry found the courage to speak. "You must be mistaken, my lord. My father would not, he could not, do such a cowardly act."

His lips curled in a sneer. "No? I beg to differ with you. I saw him, running away, leaving us." The look he gave her was one of intense loathing.

By now tears were streaming down Cherry's face, in sympathy for Varian's loss and in sorrow that he blamed her father. "Perhaps he went for help," she suggested.

"Then why did not help come, my lady? No, there are no excuses. I learned later that Hilliard rejoined his regiment that day and never said a word about the attack on us."

"It can't be. My father was not a coward."

"Of course, you know him well, my lady."

That stopped her. What did she know of her father? She could not remember him: she had been a child when she had seen him last. He had never written to her mother. In truth, he existed, if he existed at all for her, in her imagination.

"And now," she breathed, "you hate my father . . . and me."

"Exactly. John Hilliard's cowardice ruined my life. I vowed vengeance for the hell he'd made me suffer." Varian shrugged. "As I said, it's unfortunate for you that he died."

"Now I pay," Cherry whispered.

He nodded. "Of course. I intend making you suffer, Cherry Hilliard, as I did."

"Have you no pity? No mercy?" she asked.

"Was there any shown me?"

"I'm not my father," she protested.

"You show the same tendency to run away."

She stared at him. "I ran for help."

"You ran to escape, Cherry Hilliard, just as your father did."

She buried her face in her hands again. There was no hope for her now. He truly believed she was a coward as he believed her father had been. But it wasn't true—it couldn't be! There must be some other explanation! What it was she didn't know, but she had to find it. She must prove him wrong!

"I dislike tears, m'lady."

She choked. "Then I shall leave you, m'lord." Cherry

rose, unsteady on her feet. Almost blinded by her tears, she lurched across the floor and through the doorway. Once in the corridor, she sank to the floor, sobbing soundlessly, until fear that Varian would find her thus made her rise and seek the sanctuary of her bedchamber.

Seventeen

Jack Keene came riding down the High Street in Corby at a fast trot. He'd been in the saddle all day, the past two hours seeking those two footpads he'd been forced to hire as his cronies, and he was in a black mood. Damn! He'd have their bloody hides if they'd blown his cover. It had taken him no small amount of thought to arrive at a plausible tale to spin for a nosy landlord. Strangers who remained in a second-class inn in a small village, especially strangers who were out all day, were suspect. After discarding several possibilities, mainly because his companions, though clad in sober middle-class attire, could pass for nothing but London scoundrels, he'd finally hit on the very thing: they'd been sent by the Turnpike Trust to investigate the conditions of the Great North Road. It had touched his sense of humor, for they were indeed inspecting conditions, the conditions of coach passengers' purses, and if those stupid oafs had jeopardized his plans, he'd dress their hides!

Too angry to slow his pace, he barely missed an urchin

who had to dodge quickly to escape the chestnut's hooves. With no thought given to his mount's mouth, Jack jerked hard on the reins before the White Hart Inn, tossed them to a waiting ostler, and stalked into the low-beamed taproom.

The sight of his two companions placidly dicing with the locals did nothing to lessen his anger. With his hands on his hips, he stood glaring at them, until Ben Newton, throwing a pair of treys, chanced to glance up and caught his eye. Jack jerked his head toward the corner and strode over to the table that he'd made his own since their arrival.

Ben shrugged and raised his glass to his lips. After emptying it he wiped his mouth on his sleeve and only then tried to get his comrade's attention. He pawed at Jasper's arm, whispered a word in his ear, then spoke up. "Time t'quit, mates. Me friend wants a word wi' us."

Both Ben and Jasper Suggs wore uneasy expressions as they seated themselves at the corner table, for Jack was scowling.

"I thought I said to keep together," he growled.

"We was, guv'nor, wasn't us, Jas?"

His partner nodded.

Jack's eyes narrowed. "Don't expect me to laugh at your witticism, for it won't fadge. You know very well I meant all three of us *together.*"

"Orl right, Jack, orl right. You don't have to get your back up. No 'arm's done."

"I can't handle a coach by myself," Keene said softly, his eyes hard as he looked from one to the other of his companions. It went against the grain for him to work with a gang; he much preferred to work alone, but as he had just said, a coach and four could not be held up by a lone man. "Next time stay with me," he ordered.

Ben shrugged. "You've made your point, Jack."

"I hope so," Jack responded, then his hand reached out and caught Ben's wrist. "Have you been using fulhams on these yokels?"

"Aw, Jack, 'tis only for a pint or two." Jasper leaned forward conspiratorially.

"Only for a pint or two," Jack mocked, his voice vicious. Then he slammed his fist on the table. "Damn blast you! We have a good thing going here and you two risk it for a measly pint of beer."

"But, Jack," Ben intervened, "we just wantit to wet our whistles, didn't we, Jas? And asides"—he lowered his voice—"all t'coves here is gudgeons. They'll never catch on."

"You heard me. No fulhams. You play with honest bones or none at all. There'll be no cheating here, no bubbling the local bumpkins, you hear? If you're caught"—he paused to look first at Ben, then at Jasper—"that will be the end of our game, our very profitable game, I might add. And these yokels might even call the harman and then the fat would really be in the fire. Some of these country chaw bacons don't like being diddled, especially by cits. They might even resent it enough to blame us for *everything* that happens round here. And that could mean Newgate."

"Orl right, Jack," Ben muttered, while Jasper, feeling enough had been said on the subject, spoke up. "Let's ha' done wi' your jawin', Jack, you don't ha' t'harp on it. We get the point."

"Just see that you do! I told you when I invited you along on this caper, we're here to do a *job,* so don't queer it!"

Ben glanced over at Jasper, caught his eye, then asked hesitantly, "How come we're stuck in this hick spot, guv'-

162

nor? We're Lunnon fok, Jas and me. Ain't there better spots for the rum pad?"

"I've a score to settle," Keene muttered, his voice low. "Do I hear any complaints?" His hard gaze raked his companions, passing over Ben's stocky form, topped by a pockmocked face, to Jasper's slight frame, his face marred by a gashed cheek.

Ben spoke up. "Aw, Jack, you get no jawin' from us. It's not every day we kin lay our hands on yellow boys. It's jist that we're not high tobymen. And asides," he muttered, "there's naught to do here but shake an elbow."

Jasper nodded agreement. "T'biddies here ain't willin' t'oblige a cove."

"Stow it," Jack muttered.

The landlord's daughter, a bright smile on her face, was approaching. A fresh-faced, buxom wench, she had welcomed the arrival of strangers two weeks ago as a break in the monotony of serving the regular local customers. However, the two who kept eyeing her were beneath her notice, and the older man, who seemed more of a gent, had ignored her. She spoke directly to him. "Be ye wantin' your dinner now?"

Ben turned in his chair. "Wot you got?" he leered, reaching out a hand.

She sniffed, "Mutton, onions, and biscuits," and slapped his hand away from her thigh.

At their collective nods she went off, watched by both Ben and Jasper. "Now that's a prime article," Ben muttered.

"Aye, a fine biddy she is. I'd like to sample her wares, I wud."

Jack Keene, though ready to take what was so obviously offered, had his thoughts on another prime piece of flesh. That red-haired baggage he'd met on the coach was a fetching wench. Real class she was. Gave herself airs, though, but he could take her down a piece.

Why a wench like that wasted her life as a governess was beyond his understanding. She could be the mistress of any man she chose, no matter how high. That combination of innocence and fiery hair would attract any man!

His lips tightened as he recalled their previous encounter. He could have had her, too—a guinea or two would have kept the maid away—if my lord Varian hadn't intervened. Keene's brow furrowed; he began to drum his fingers on the table in anger.

Fate was against him! It had been Varian who had happened upon him before, just when he was to be paid, too. The only bit of luck he'd had then was that Varian had had his hands full with the French agents and he'd escaped. But he'd blown his cover and had to desert. He couldn't take a chance on not being recognized, and his word would be useless compared to that of a *gentleman.*

The army just didn't pay enough, leastways not enough to cover his expenses. A cove had to earn his living some way, didn't he? And the information he'd sold to the French had been worthless to them. But trust an Englishman to shoot first. . . .

And now for the second time Varian had cheated him out of a chance for some ready money. He could have kept the chit as his ladybird for a time and, when he tired of her, sold her to the highest bidder. She'd easily have brought a hundred guineas.

Keene's eyes narrowed. Yes, he definitely had a score to settle. His share of the holdups did not begin to make up for what he'd lost: the French were very generous.

Well, Varian couldn't stay in his house all summer. He was bound to come out, and when he did, Jack Keene would be waiting.

Eighteen

There was consternation in the servants' wing of Varian Court. Marston's appearance with the late countess's needlework and his lordship's order to burn it, coupled with Robert's report of her ladyship's tears following a meeting with his lordship in the library, had thoroughly upset the staff.

The needlework was easily disposed of. "Give it to me," Mrs. Ridley instructed the footman. She took it to her quarters. It would be ridiculous to obey his lordship's order. When he came to his senses, he would want this memento of a mother he had loved.

But his lordship's behaviour was another matter. It was not the place of proper servants to question their master, as Mrs. Ridley informed the staff, but his lordship's present behaviour went beyond the bounds of propriety. They had a clear duty to the family to protect its interests.

"I'm not sayin' he shouldn't have a lightskirt. All gentlemen, includin' his late lordship, keep a bit of muslin." The housekeeper looked around as if defying her listeners to disagree with her. The upper staff was gathered around the table in their dining room following luncheon a fortnight after Lady Varian's arrival. "But a gentleman keeps his amusements private, not flaunting them for all to see, especially his lady," she added emphatically.

"Aye," Ridley agreed, as the others nodded.

Mrs. Ridley turned her still indignant face to the valet. "Mr. Hartley, can ye not speak to his lordship? You're closest to him."

"Beggin' your pardon, Mrs. Ridley, but I *was* closest. Since his lordship returned from the fightin' in Spain, he's not been the same man. He hates bein' helpless, hates it somethin' awful. O'course, he don't mind not bein' able to shave himself, that I must admit, but he's never satisfied with *my* cravats. And when I remembers the perfection of *his* past efforts, I don't rightly blame him. He's taken to cursin' somethin' awful. And he . . . well," he finished lamely, "he'd rather not have me around *all* the time." Hartley's vague suspicion that his lordship was having difficulty in sleeping he kept to himself. One did not discuss *such* matters with the staff.

"We've all felt the lash of his tongue, Hartley, but that was when he was first home, and weak and all, but he's recovered his health now," Ridley objected.

The valet shook his head. "It'd be all my position is worth, Mr. Ridley, if I was to speak out against that Frenchie."

Somewhat reluctantly Ridley nodded his head, but Mrs. Ridley was not to be denied. "Even if he hates bein' helpless, as you say, Mr. Hartley, that's no call to take it out on her ladyship. She had nothin' to do with the loss of his arm."

Beyond murmurs of agreement, no one offered a suggestion.

166

"Well"—Mrs. Ridley looked about her—"we can't just sit back and do nothing. Both Ridley and I have warned the entire staff to hold their tongues and under no circumstances to breathe a word of that jade's presence, but that's not enough! No tellin' wot a man in his cups will say."

"But who can speak to his lordship if Hartley can't?" her husband asked.

Marston had been sitting quietly listening. As first footman his place was in the lower servants' hall, but he had been included in this conference because of his long years of service to the family and because Mrs. Ridley felt it inappropriate to ask her ladyship's abigail to attend. Now he said hesitantly in the silence that followed the butler's question, "Beggin' your pardon, Mr. Ridley. I hope I'm not speakin' out of turn, but I think we should be askin', who would his lordship listen to?"

As Mrs. Ridley and the valet both nodded their heads in agreement, the butler muttered, "The only person who could calm Master Damon when he was in a temper was Nanny."

"Nanny!" Mrs. Ridley exclaimed. "The very person! Ridley, you send Ned off now. He can reach Westmacott afore dark and bring Nanny back tomorrow." She rose hurriedly and moved toward the door. "I'll have the girls pack a hamper. Nanny always did have a weakness for Mrs. Thatcher's pasties."

Nanny—no one remembered her by any other name— was still a spry woman in her late sixties. Tiny, thin, and bony, she had ruled the nursery by strength of character, not body. Briefed by Mrs. Ridley the next day in the housekeeper's sitting room, she shook her head sadly. "It's not like Master Damon, not one bit. He's never held a grudge in his life, never resented being second to Master David neither. Course I haven't seen him since he went off

167

to the wars. He didn't come visiting me like he ought when he returned. You say he lost his arm?"

Mrs. Ridley nodded. "Cut off at the elbow, it was, Nanny."

"Poor lamb. He always was a proud young 'un, always ready, and *able* to do anything. Not like Master David. Now *he* wouldn't have minded losing an arm. Just give him a book and he'd be happy for hours. The ways of Providence are strange, Mrs. Ridley. Ah, well," Nanny sighed, "ours not to question. If you think I can help, Mrs. Ridley, I'll be glad to talk to him."

"We don't know what else to do, Nanny. Ridley reported that her ladyship looked like death last night at dinner, eyes all red from weeping. She never ate a bit neither, just sat at the table, all the time he was carryin' on with that ladybird of his. And let me tell you, Nanny, that Frenchie gives herself such airs! Why she thinks herself better'n her la'ship, and *her* just a common whore, not to mince words."

Nanny stood up. "Where's his lordship now?"

Directed to the study, Nanny entered quietly. Her former charge was sitting at the desk, pen in hand, absorbed in some papers. His face was harder, not as open as Nanny remembered it had been. It was leaner, too, and there was a particularly set appearance to his mouth that disturbed her.

Varian looked up. "Nanny!" he exclaimed, more in surprise, it seemed to her, than pleasure.

"You didn't come to see me when you got back from Spain, Master Damon, so I came instead," she temporized, hesitating, in view of that mouth, to state her real objective.

"But . . . how? . . . I thought . . ." his lordship stammered, frowning.

168

"Yes, I'm still at m'sisters in Westmacott, not three hours from here. You could have come to visit me, Master Damon!"

"Why? To show off my war souvenir?" His voice was bitter as he gestured toward his left arm, and Nanny's hopes of being able to reach him lessened. "How did you get here?"

"Ned Burney brought me up."

"Ned?" Varian's face darkened. Then his eyes narrowed suspiciously and Nanny's hopes plummeted.

"Iffen you're thinking that sweet young wife of yours sent for me," she said sharply, "you're wrong. There's others concerned with your behaviour. Now, do I get asked to sit down or not?"

"Forgive me, Nanny. Of course." Varian rose and pulled a chair forward for her.

Nanny folded her hands in her lap. The interview was not going as she had planned. She had thought it best to lead up to the subject of his wife's unhappiness, but Varian's suspicions had ruined such an indirect approach. Best to attack then. "I never thought I'd see the day when one of my boys was deliberately cruel. Shame on you, Master Damon. There's some things a gentleman doesn't do."

"Nanny, you know nothing of this matter."

"No? I know there's someone in this house who don't belong here."

His lordship had returned to the chair behind the desk, his fingers playing idly with the pen he had put down at Nanny's entrance. At her words his fingers tightened. The pen broke and Varian looked up, his face that of a stranger. "Whom I invite as a guest is not the concern of the servants," he said icily.

"Your mother would turn over in her grave iffen she heard you. A gentleman's diversions are always kept pri-

169

vate, my lord, never dignified by public appearances. Why, your mother never knew of your father's doxies."

"Nicole is not a diversion," he snapped. "Nanny, I refuse to hear any more of this. If you care to converse on other matters, I'll be glad to hear you, but not on this topic."

His face was adamant, his voice cold, hard, and implacable. She had never before seen him like this. How could the warm and loving boy she had raised have changed so much? Did he resent the loss of his arm to such an extent that he punished everyone for it?

Not satisfied with such a simplistic explanation, yet knowing she could get no further with his lordship, Nanny rose. "Very well, Master Damon." She walked to the door, then turned to face him. "I feel sorry for you, my lord. You're making your own hell, you know."

Nineteen

An extremely low-spirited Nanny left the study and slowly walked up the stairs to the countess's apartment. She had failed in her mission, his lordship refusing even to listen to her. The staff would be so disappointed; they had counted on her. And she had felt confident of success. After all, her Master Damon had never before refused to listen to her advice. But he was different now. She was appalled at the extent of the change in him, a change that could not be due solely to the loss of an arm! Perhaps a visit with the countess would give her a better perspective. She knocked on the door to the sitting room. Receiving no answer, she opened the door and entered.

The room, as bright and beautiful as it had been just after the late countess had it redecorated so many years ago, was empty. Nanny paused, giving silent credit to the staff, for no sign was apparent that the sitting room had been shut up for years. Even the orange roses, so loved by the late countess, were in place. The years fell away and Nanny half expected to see her young charges chatting excitedly to their mama. But her own slow steps reminded her of her age and the changes that had taken place. No time now for memories!

In the bedchamber she found a forlorn-looking figure lying on the huge four-poster bed. Only her hair, shining like autumn fire against the sea green counterpane, provided a contrast to the gloom of her black gown and her pitiful face, made red and blotchy from weeping.

"Who are you?" Cherry roused herself sufficiently to ask, but her eyes remained dull and listless.

"Master Damon's nanny."

Cherry was puzzled. Mrs. Ridley hadn't spoken of a nanny. She sat up. "Why are you here?"

"Well, child, there's people concerned over the change in Master Damon."

Cherry giggled. "Master *Demon,* you mean, don't you, Nanny?" she asked, then burst into tears. The warmth in the elderly woman's voice had proved her undoing.

She was soon cradled in arms that rocked her gently. "There, there, child. Tell Nanny all about it."

Soothed by the rhythmic rocking, Cherry, brokenly at first, told her story: Varian's insistence on marriage; her attempts to escape him; Varian's coldness and heartlessness; the presence of Nicole; and finally, his revelation of the reason for his actions.

"He means it, Nanny, I know he does. He blames my father for the loss of his arm and thinks I'm a coward, too. How can I prove him wrong? He won't listen to anything I say . . . and everything I do is wrong and just proves him right in his judgment." She buried her head in Nanny's bony shoulder and wept silently.

Nanny shook her head. It was much worse than she had feared. The girl was beautiful and if she, Nanny, was any judge of character, a warm, sensitive person. How any

172

man in his right senses could resist such a wife, she didn't know. But Varian was not in his right senses. He was blinded by hate and thoughts of revenge. Couldn't he see that her ladyship was no coward? She had faced him, stood up to him, hadn't she? What fools men were!

After a few minutes Cherry pulled away from Nanny's comforting arms and raised a tear-ravaged face. "What was he like, Nanny, as a boy? I've seen the portrait—Mrs. Ridley showed it to me—and he looked kind, not like a *devil.*"

Nanny was silent for a long moment, then spoke hesitantly, "Ye ken I had two boys?"

At Cherry's nod she continued, "Master David was the heir. Viscount Kellyn he was, but nobody called him that, mayhap 'cause he seemed too gentle. If t'old lord was disappointed in his heir, he never let on. But Master David was not at all like his father. He took after his mother—God rest her soul!—the most gentle creature, and kind! No one in the parish went hungry, not if her ladyship knew about it.

"Master Damon, now, he went everywhere with his father. Whatever he saw t'old lord do, that Master Damon must do. He took many a tumble, he did, but ride he would. The same thing wi' drivin'. The more mettlesome the team, the more determined he was to master it.

"But, mind now, he never resented that Master David was the heir and would be lord some day. He had his horses, he used to say. 'Course his lordship had property, not entailed ye ken, which would go to Master Damon and provide him wi' a good livin', but 'twas nothing like the estates goin' to Master David. Right protective of his brother, he was, too. Never a word said against 'im."

"What happened to David?" whispered Cherry. "Mrs. Ridley just said he died."

"He took the pox, grown man that he was, his lordship not believin' in this newfangled vaccination. And just after his lordship sent a letter off to Spain, to recall Master Damon, he got thrown takin' a fence. Broke his neck, he did."

"How horrible!"

"Aye. T'family's had a streak of bad luck, it has. That's one reason t'staff was so happy at Master Damon's return. No one wanted his cousin as next lord. Master Damon, now, would be a good master. But I don't want you to think he had no faults, my lady. He had a temper, he had. And I'm not sayin' I never swatted his breeches."

Cherry giggled. It was hard to imagine this tiny woman taking a switch to Damon. But then she sobered. The Damon Nanny was describing was not the man *she* knew. "What can I do, Nanny? How can I make him *like* me?" Cherry knew she'd settle for that. The thought that couldn't be admitted, even to herself, she pushed to the back of her mind.

"Do, child? You can do nothing." But there's something I can do, Nanny reflected. Her reminiscences had brought to mind a certain event that held promise for helping the present situation.

"But, Nanny," Cherry protested.

"Hush now and listen, child. If what you tell me is true, his lordship not only wants to hurt you to revenge himself on you, but he wants to know he's hurtin' you. You'll have to overlook his cruelty and pretend it doesn't exist."

"I've tried that, Nanny, truly I have. I ignore *her* and their" —her lips tightened as she sought for the proper word— "carrying-on before the servants."

"You'll have to continue, m'lady."

"I'll try, Nanny, but . . . will it work?" Cherry pleaded.

"I don't know, child, I don't know. He'll either tire of hurting you or . . ."

"Or get worse," Cherry supplied as Nanny's voice faded. She felt heartened by Nanny's sympathy and warmth, though she doubted her wisdom. Varian would never tire of hurting her!

"The staff is behind you, m'lady. They remember Master Damon the way he was. They know how sweet he can be. Never before has be behaved so badly." After more words of consolation, Nanny left the countess to seek the herb garden.

Twenty

Nicole Claude stretched languidly, her eyes dwelling complacently on her luxurious surroundings. The house in London was comfortable, but it could not compare to the sheer richness of Varian Court. Even the sheets seemed finer!

She wished she could live here permanently. But to do that, she would have to be Damon's wife. The status of mistress was much too uncertain, for men's passions were totally unreliable, being too ephemeral by far. Other men married their mistresses. Why not Damon? But no. Though he said he loved *her,* he had married that . . . that child. For an heir, he'd said. Hah! There was little chance of that happening. He hated his wife, that was obvious, and Lady Varian was looking most unhappy.

Was Damon trying to drive her to suicide? She shrugged. He really had no reason for such a drastic course. He was rich; he didn't need his wife's dowry. Besides, he already had control of her money, and there was little indication she was an heiress. Lady Varian had only two day gowns of the plainest black fabric, although one had to admit her lavender gown had been made by a master seamstress—French, no doubt.

What was Varian up to? He had admitted to not having met the chit before he offered for her. There was no indication he had been forced into marriage. Why would he marry a woman and then try to get rid of her?

Nicole smiled. She didn't understand Damon's motives, but she did like his actions. *She,* not that fire-headed child, should be Lady Varian. If it hadn't been for the Revolution, which forced her mother to flee to England, she would have been the wife of a French peer, instead of being forced to earn her own living in the only profession open to her. Was she not the daughter of M. le Comte de Guissemont? By virtue of her birth and beauty she was more fit to be the Countess of Varian than that chit.

Nicole rolled over in bed, smiling as she caught sight of the mussed bed sheets and pillow. Damon was a most agreeable lover. He could arouse her to exquisite heights of passion. And while her feelings were not important— she was quite able to pretend passion, if necessary—still, it was much more pleasant this way. And Damon loved her. She just might be able to profit from that, to obtain the security missing from her life.

She hated this life, living with one man until he tired of her, then being forced to find another lover to keep her. All men were not generous. Some even begrudged her living expenses. She hated having to entice clothes and jewels out of men who thought nothing of losing thousands of pounds at hazard, faro, or *vingt-et-un,* but refused her a few guineas. She was no longer young, though no older than Damon, but one had to think of one's future, *n'est-ce pas?*

Diable! Her skin was still smooth. Nicole ran her hands

177

over her face, shoulders, and arms. She didn't really have to search every morning for telltale signs of age. There were none to be seen. She was just feeling old, compared to that child Damon had married.

She sat up as her maid brought her morning chocolate. "Hand me a negligee, Marie."

As she slipped her arms into the wide lace sleeves, Nicole caught a glimpse of her body in the mirror atop the dressing table. Yes, she still had soft skin, round breasts, and a firm belly. She still looked like a young girl. With her disheveled ringlets, she could easily pass for sixteen. She smiled complacently as she sipped her chocolate.

These were days of infinite pleasure. She would rise late and lunch with Damon, pretending the two of them were alone. After all, his wife was of no consequence, and one could overlook the servants. She smiled now as she remembered her original fear at Damon's announcement of his marriage. It was she who had profited from that. In the afternoon they would ride together and in the evening she would dine in state in the family dining room, wearing his jewels. She enjoyed that, the fine porcelain, the heavy silver, the old family furniture, only wishing she had the right to sit opposite him as his wife.

All this as prelude to their nights of passion. She almost purred with satisfaction.

There was only one problem. Should she urge him to divorce his wife? There was something not right about his marriage. Perhaps the contract had been made between their parents. That happened often in France. But surely, had he not wanted to marry her, he could have gotten out of it. But if she suggested divorce, would it make her appear too pushing, too interfering? Better not, she decided. Let that decision come from him.

Nicole finished her chocolate and handed the cup to

Marie. Leaning back against the pillow, she was ready to discuss the selection of her day's gown when she felt a sharp pain in her stomach. She moved quickly, but there was barely time for her to lean over the edge of the bed before she began retching on the rug.

"Madame, qu'est-ce que c'est? Is it that you are with child?"

Nicole lifted her head. "Of course not," she denied. "Now, hurry, ring for a maid to clean up this mess. It offends me." But as she lay back, exhausted, the thought persisted. Was she increasing? It was a possibility, certainly; but no, Marie must be wrong. A child now would be a problem. It was much too early to bear Damon's child. It would not be legitimate. He needed an heir, yes, but he wouldn't be able to obtain a divorce and marry her before its birth.

Should she tell him? Would he be pleased? It was hard to know what to do. Besides, maybe it was just indigestion. These English cooks were incredibly bad.

By evening, as she waited for Damon, Nicole had forgotten her morning's upset. Another delightful day with nothing to mar its perfection had been spent in his company. The only jarring note had been the countess, who earlier had looked like the wrath of God. Tonight she had spoken pleasantly to the servants and eaten a hearty meal. So much for her visions of Lady Varian's suicide!

Forget her, Nicole advised herself, she is not important.

The door opened and Varian entered, his dark looks set off by a bright red dressing gown.

"Mon cher, you look like the Devil himself." Nicole smiled lazily.

Varian raised his eyebrows but didn't respond to her sally. He seemed preoccupied.

179

Immediately she felt jealous: his thoughts should be on her.

Nicole rose from the daybed on which she'd been reclining and removed her ivory negligee to reveal a bedgown so sheer all her curves were visible and so close in colour to her ivory skin that she appeared unclothed.

She walked slowly over to him and twined her arms about his neck. "You like, *mon amour?*"

Varian looked down into her face, seeing inviting eyes and moist red lips, then, as his gaze traveled lower, her ripe breasts. Gad, she was delicious! Everything he'd ever wanted in a woman: beautiful, clinging, passionate, and wanting only him!

Then, unbidden, an image of fiery curls, green eyes bright with tears, and a chin raised in defiance came to him. He shook his head to clear it. Why spoil his evening with thoughts of *her?*

"You don't like my gown, *mon cher?*" Nicole laughed deep in her throat. "Then I'll remove it from your sight."

Swiftly twisting away from him, she lifted her arms down, then up over her head, to stand naked before him. "Is this better?"

"Much better," he answered. "Much, much better, my sweet." His gaze roved over her alluring body, then he moved forward quickly and caught her to him, crushing her lips under his.

Nicole sighed with satisfaction as she surrendered herself to him. Her charms were still sufficient to entice Damon to her. Hurriedly her hands reached out to untie his dressing gown and push it from his shoulders. "Come to bed, *mon cher,*" she whispered.

Damon's lovemaking soon removed all desire for thought as she gave herself up to his caresses, but the next morning brought a recurrence of the pain and retching.

She lay back against the pillow, eyes narrowed. The problem must be faced. Was she indeed with child? Or—a new thought struck her—were the servants trying to poison her? She'd not put it past them. Their disapproval of her was quite apparent. Not content with being proper servants who do not dare to judge their betters, Damon's staff was taking advantage of their long tenure at Varian Court to provide her with poor service.

She could do little about it now, for she was just a guest in his house, and she didn't quite dare to ask Damon to dismiss his servants, but wait . . . wait until she was its mistress. First to go would be both Ridleys, to be replaced by servants who knew their place. She was tired of raised eyebrows and supercilious expressions on the faces of servants! Next to go would be the cook. She was tired of English food. Only a French chef knew how to cook.

Nicole hurried her bath, then went to walk in the garden while a housemaid scrubbed her bedchamber, but her thoughts were not on the beauties of nature. Was she increasing? Always she'd been careful: she didn't want her body disfigured by an unwanted child. However, more important than the question of her possible pregnancy was Damon's attitude. If she told Damon and he didn't want it either, would he hold it against her?

Twenty-one

Cherry, coming out the back door that morning, was surprised to see Nicole strolling toward the rose garden. She would have to postpone her regular visit with Frame, for she couldn't take a chance on meeting Nicole face-to-face. Instead, Cherry turned in the opposite direction, toward the stables.

As she passed the open door, a groom came hurrying out. "Do ye wish to ride, m'lady?" he asked, touching his cap respectfully. "I have just the mount for you, a fine mare, she is."

"No, thank you, Dalton. As you can see, I am not dressed for riding." Cherry smiled and continued past the stables. The servants all liked her; why couldn't Damon?

But she knew that was too much to ask. Now that she had learned the truth, she realized there was no hope. He would never change his mind. Every time he was forced to rely on someone to assist him, every time he was reminded of his lack of a forearm, he would blame her father, and her.

He was deliberately humiliating her before the servants by keeping his mistress in his own home, by showing a marked preference for that bit of muslin, and by treating his wife like a servant. He thought nothing of ignoring her for days, then expecting instant response to his slightest request.

He had threatened to make her suffer. What else lay in store for her? Would her words to Nanny prove prophetic? Would Varian's mistreatment of her worsen? He had already slapped her. Would he begin to beat her as well?

Cherry sat down on the bank of the stream, her head in her hands. Nanny had counseled patience, but how long must she wait? And Nanny herself had admitted she could not predict Damon's reaction, for he was no longer the boy she had known.

What was she to do? Continue on in this farce of a marriage? Or should she end it all? If she threw herself into the stream, she could rob Damon of his revenge and deny him the satisfaction of hating her. He'd be free then, free from any taint of the hated Hilliards . . . free to marry his Cyprian.

Nicole wanted that, instinct told Cherry. The Frenchwoman would not be content with forever being a plaything. Cherry could tell from the way her eyes lingered on the family silver, the way her fingers played with her jewels and smoothed her gown, that possessions were important to Nicole. Not that Cherry spent much time looking at Damon's mistress. She was much too embarrassed by Nicole's blatant display of her feminine charms: she always wore muslin evening gowns so fine that it was apparent she wore neither petticoat nor camisole under them. The footmen had difficulties in keeping their eyes off her as they served the evening meal.

No, killing herself would only reward Nicole. There must be another solution! If only she had someone to turn to, someone to help her. She felt so alone. Nanny had provided some comfort, but she had returned to her home. Lady Warrick had seemed friendly, but how could she get to the Warrick home? It was too far to walk. Cherry, in all her daily walks, had not yet succeeded in traversing Damon's estate, and Warrick must lie beyond Varian.

She could no longer ask Dobbin for help, for she couldn't run off with him now. Where would they go? England was at war with France; they couldn't go to the continent. War had been declared between England and her former colonies, so they couldn't go to the United States. Ireland and Scotland were much too close. Varian would surely follow them and Dobbin's life would be in danger.

She couldn't divorce him. Only a man could be granted a divorce and then only if he petitioned Parliament. Besides, Varian would never divorce her. He would never release her from captivity.

The sound of a branch breaking roused her. Fearfully Cherry looked around. Varian? Had he come after her?

The wood was silent, save for the chirping of birds. No movement caught her eyes. All was serene: calm and peaceful. An almost churchlike atmosphere prevailed. Cherry glanced up at the green canopy above her head, a canopy effectively blocking out the sun's light, and vaguely wondered what time it was. She had no idea how long she'd been sitting by the stream. Was it time for luncheon? If she was late again, Damon would be angry. But could he be any angrier than he had been? She didn't want to go back to the house; she wanted to stay here, where there were no frowns, no anger, no punishment. What was she to do?

Nanny had known Damon far longer than Cherry had. Was it wiser to follow her advice and wait, to hope for him to change? But Cherry knew, deep down inside her, where a secret thought nestled, too fragile to be exposed, that there was no hope for her, not really. There was nothing to look forward to, she was deluding herself if she continued to hope.

Apathetically, Cherry started her return trip, groping her way through the wood more by instinct than by conscious will. She walked across the vast grass-covered lawns as if in a trance. In a hopeless situation, was it not wiser to recognize the truth? Damon would continue to punish her, and she must suffer for her father's sin. That was the way it was and the way it would continue to be, forever and ever. She was trapped!

Cherry passed, unseeing, the gardeners at work trimming the hedges, scything the grass, and weeding the borders of the walks. Ordinarily she would stop to speak to them, their friendly faces her only consolation in a life of misery. Now she walked by without any consciousness of their existence, all her thoughts drawn inward, concentrated on one question: what was she to do?

She entered the house and mounted the back stairs, dragging her feet. When she reached her bedchamber, Cherry fell into the nearest chair. She felt exhausted, both physically and mentally: there was no more fight in her. Most of her energies had been spent, her few remaining resources were drawn inward to keep her alive.

Cherry was sitting, staring ahead of her, when Hetty entered. "Oh, Miss Cherry, there you are. We've been looking all over for you. His lordship said to hold luncheon until you returned."

Hetty broke off as she realized her mistress was not heeding her words. She moved to stand directly in front of her ladyship, but Cherry's eyes gave no indication that she saw her maid. Suddenly frightened, Hetty closed the door softly, then ran down the corridor to the back stairs. She had to find help.

Breathing heavily, Hetty burst into the kitchen. "Mrs. Ridley, please . . . please come. Miss Ch—her ladyship—"

"What's happened?" "Where is she?" "Has she been hurt?" All the occupants of the kitchen, from Mrs. Thatcher to the lowliest scullery maid, dropped the various utensils they were holding and, without pretending to work, crowded around Hetty, who was wringing her hands.

"I don't know what's wrong," Hetty whispered, her eyes wide with fright. "She's just sitting there. Her eyes are open, but she didn't see me or hear me. It was awful—to see her like that."

Mrs. Ridley took charge. "Back to work now, all of you. Luncheon is ready to be served. Ridley, inform his lordship that her ladyship is indisposed and begs to be excused. Come, Hetty," she directed and led the way upstairs.

But once inside the countess's bedchamber, the housekeeper was as much at a loss as Hetty had been as to how to proceed. Her ladyship just sat there; she gave no response to their presence. Hetty, tears falling down her cheeks, tried chafing her hands, to no avail.

"Do you have a vinaigrette?" queried Mrs. Ridley.

Hetty shook her head. "Miss Cherry has never been ill, never had the vapours, not like her mother." She hesitated, then suggested, "We could burn feathers, or send for a doctor."

"No, that won't do. All a doctor would do would be to bleed her, and she's pale enough."

The door was thrust open. Momentarily Varian stood

186

on the threshold, then he strode in, frowning. "Where's Lady Varian?" he demanded.

Hetty hurriedly got up from her knees and Mrs. Ridley stepped back respectfully. Varian saw his wife and checked his stride.

"She doesn't respond, m'lord," Mrs. Ridley whispered.

Cherry's eyes looked vacant: great green empty globes in a face so pale the freckles stood out like soot on snow. There was no animation, no awareness, just blankness. If her eyes hadn't been open, she would have appeared dead.

His lordship stood for a moment, considering. Was she drunk? Had she tried to escape him by drinking?

He walked up to her, but her eyes remained unchanged, staring before her as if she saw nothing. She showed absolutely no consciousness of his presence!

Varian became angry. He knew she was blocking him out of her mind, and very effectively, too. How he wished he had two hands, to reach out and shake some life into her!

He lightly slapped her face. Her head rolled sideways against the green velvet, but her face remained unchanged.

"My lord" burst from Mrs. Ridley in protest.

"Hold your tongue," he ordered, and slapped Cherry again, somewhat harder, and then again.

Each time her head rolled, but there was no livening of her features.

"Get some brandy."

The housekeeper nodded and hurried from the room. In her agitation she descended the front staircase. The nearest brandy was in his lordship's study and the fastest way there was by the family stairway. She snatched up the decanter and a glass and reentered the hall, where she met her husband, closing the doors of the dining room behind him.

"That tart is calmly eating lunch," he whispered. "She ordered me to serve her after his lordship went up to fetch her ladyship."

Mrs. Ridley smiled. "Put in some of Nanny's elixir," she directed.

Ridley stared at his wife for a moment, then his eyes crinkled in glee. "Not now," he said. "I'll wait until I hear his lordship's foot on the steps. She's always stuffing herself with plum tarts and won't notice a little extra flavour."

They smiled conspiratorially at each other, then Mrs. Ridley, not even bothering to stop for a tray, hurried back to the countess's bedchamber.

Hetty, in tears, was on the floor, holding her mistress's hands. Lady Varian was sitting, limp, in the chair, her head leaning against its back, her cheeks bright from repeated blows. His lordship was standing over her, his face "as black as thunder," as Mrs. Ridley later reported to Ridley. She quickly poured a glass of brandy and held it to Cherry's lips.

"It's no use, m'lord, she won't drink."

"Damn." Varian grabbed the glass from the housekeeper's hand and tried to force it between Cherry's lips.

Her mouth opened, but the brandy dribbled down her chin and onto her gown.

There had to be a way of reaching her! Varian handed the glass to Mrs. Ridley, then encircled Cherry's waist with his arm and lifted her to her feet. B'gad, she was light!

With the help of Mrs. Ridley and Hetty, he got her onto the bed. There he sat down next to his wife and cradled her against his chest. Using his left upper arm, he held her against him, then motioned to Mrs. Ridley to give him the brandy glass.

Again he held the glass to Cherry's lips.

"She's swallowing, m'lord. Thank God!"

Varian threw a sharp glance at Mrs. Ridley but refrained from comment.

Cherry's eyelids fluttered after she had swallowed the entire contents of the glass.

"Oh, it tastes awful. What is it? What's happened?" There was a strange warmth in her stomach, a stranger warmth against her back. Then, as the realization struck her that Varian was holding her, Cherry struggled to rise.

Varian dropped his arm, his face set. He stood up. "Now, my lady, if you please, luncheon is waiting."

Once on her feet, Cherry felt light-headed. The warmth had spread from her stomach to the rest of her body, dispelling her earlier coldness, but her head felt as if it were way above her body.

She faced Varian accusingly. "What did you give me to drink?" Cherry swayed slightly, her words slightly slurred.

"All that brandy on an empty stomach, m'lord," Mrs. Ridley whispered. "She needs food."

Varian took Cherry by the arm. "Come along."

She eyed him suspiciously. "Where are you taking me?" she asked, but went willingly, holding onto the railing as Varian guided her down the stairs.

They reached the doors of the dining room just as a shriek resounded through the ground floor. The footman opened the doors, his face impassive. There was Nicole, retching, in the middle of the floor.

Shocked sober, Cherry stared. "What's wrong?"

Nicole turned on her, a napkin clutched in her hand. "Food poisoning, that's what's wrong. Your precious servants, Damon, are trying to kill me."

"Nonsense." Varian's eyes were on Nicole and missed the glance that passed between the two footmen, but Cherry caught it. Could Nicole's accusation be true? But they surely would not try to kill her. Maybe they were just trying to make her sick. She would have to speak to Mrs. Ridley.

"Your condition, madame, is probably due to your own —ah—overindulgence," Varian said dryly, then turned to the butler. "Ridley, have this mess cleaned and the room aired. And serve luncheon in my study."

He pulled Cherry down the hall and, once in his study, pushed her into a chair.

Her mind was in a whirl. Still dazed from the brandy and shocked at Nicole's sickness, she found it hard to think. What had Damon meant by "overindulgence"? Overeating? Hardly. Then a slow blush invaded her cheeks as she grasped his meaning. Could Nicole be increasing? She didn't dare look at him until he spoke.

"I believe some females do react thusly to impending motherhood."

He had been watching her. Her embarrassment seemed to amuse him. For the first time since he'd come into her life, his face had lightened and softened.

"I wouldn't know," she whispered, hurriedly lowering her eyes, then hastily looked up again as a great burst of laughter sounded. He was handsome when he laughed, but his amusement angered her.

"So you think that's funny, do you, my lord? Will you please tell me, pray, how I am supposed to have learned 'such matters'? Young ladies are shielded—" Cherry broke off as Ridley and the footmen appeared, bearing trays.

Luncheon was served on a small table, then Damon dismissed the servants. Cherry realized that for the first time there was no enmity between them. She was afraid to break the silence, to say the wrong thing and bring on his anger again. A small sigh of relief broke from her lips at the sight of the veal pie. Damon would need no assistance with that, and there would be no consequent reminder of his loss.

Varian's thoughts as he ate were on Nicole. He, too, was wondering whether she was increasing. His child, but not his heir. For that his wife would have to be the mother. Had he been foolish, marrying for revenge? He could have wed Nicole. Then this occasion would be one of joy in anticipation of the birth of Viscount Kellyn, the future Earl of Varian.

Twenty-two

"I wish to go to London, *mon cher*," Nicole announced defiantly, angry that Varian had not been more solicitous when she was ill. He should have been more concerned for her health, escorting her to her chamber and insisting on immediate rest, instead of first lunching with his wife. "To consult a physician," she added.

Varian frowned as he sat down next to her on the bed. "We are not without physicians, Nicole. There's one in Corby, a good man, and another in Bourne. Or if you wish, I can send to Grantham."

She was surprised at his mild response, expecting he'd be vehemently against her going anywhere without him. But too experienced in her profession to reveal her true feelings, she merely raised her eyebrows as she replied scornfully, "Country doctors! You may trust them, *mon cher*, but not I. I will see Dr. Jamieson, or no one."

Idly Varian wondered whether she would insist on an abortion if she was with child. He didn't know her feelings concerning children; the occasion to speak of them had never before arisen in their relationship. Would she welcome them or consider children a nuisance?

Somewhat unnerved by his silence and his hooded stare, Nicole raised her head from the pillow. "Well?"

He shrugged. "If that is what you want, my love, of course you may go. Chawley can take you in the carriage. When do you wish to leave?"

His acquiescence staggered her. He could offer some argument to her going, or insist on accompanying her! You'd think, from his reaction, that he was glad to see the last of her!

"Immediately, I think. Before any more poison attempts "

His eyes hardened. "There have been no attempts to poison you, Nicole. You are probably with child."

She shook her head decisively. It would be best to dissuade him from that idea. "No, no, *mon cher,*" she smiled, "I have been most careful. I doubt you would like me with the big belly, *hein?*"

Her response had answered his unspoken question. Had she been his wife, Nicole would have undertaken motherhood reluctantly, if at all.

He kissed her lightly on the cheek and rose from the bed. "I'll order the carriage for you, *ma chérie.*"

After the door closed, Nicole sprang from the bed and violently pulled the bell cord. When Marie came running, she found her mistress stark naked in the middle of the room, pulling gowns from the wardrobe and tossing them to the floor. "We go to London. Where are my trunks?"

Two housemaids were called to help with the packing and were soon busy folding the innumerable gowns Nicole had deemed necessary for a visit to the country. Their attention was alternately claimed by the delicate fabrics and beautiful colours of the gowns and the sight of the

Frenchwoman being dressed in a jonquil crepe traveling gown with matching gloves and bonnet and a fur-trimmed pelisse of golden velvet.

Footmen carried down the two trunks. "You take this case," Nicole instructed Marie and handed over the locked jewel case. Varian had been most generous, and if his lack of enthusiasm over her departure meant a lack of interest in her, she would need to pawn her jewels for living expenses, until her next lover, of course.

Twenty-three

"Where's Jack?"

"He said he was goin' t'keep his glimms on t'pike from t'other side of this here woods," Ben snorted, "an' he's t'cove who says we have to keep together. Seems to me it's only when it suits him."

"I don't ken why Mr. High an' Mighty wants to lay around *here*. T'city is t'place for the likes of us, Ben Newton. There be more marks there, an' more coves wi' blunt. T'High Toby 'tis no place for us'n. We're footpads. Why, this tit could take it into 'is 'ead to run an' I cudn't stop it," Jasper whined, tightening his grip on the reins.

"We hit six rattlers, didn't we? We got some rum bawbles, too. The likes o'them'll fetch a pretty bundle, an' we'll get our regulars from that, don't you forget. An' we got more blunt than we'd cadge in a week of Sundays in Lunnon. Lissen to me, Jasper Suggs. Lunnon may have more marks, but it's got more Runners, too, an' more coves t'cry beef on us an' more coves t'stop us afore we kin run off. There's nobody here but us." Ben gestured widely, taking in their entire surroundings.

They were in a clearing in a forested area to the west of the Great North Road between Grantham and Stamford in southwest Lincolnshire. The forest of ancient oaks and tall elms was situated on a slight rise, giving a clear view of the turnpike for several miles. It also provided more than adequate cover for the highwaymen, for its dense shade and heavily leaved branches effectively prevented their being seen by any passersby.

"Well," Jasper grumbled, not quite convinced by Ben's argument. "There's still somethin' havey-cavey about Jack's wantin' t'be here. Why here, for Gawd's sakes? There's nothin' t'do in Corby, exceptin' t'shake an elbow, which Jack don't like, or drink a pint or two, which Jack don't like neither. That there Betty, whose wares I'd be glad to sample"—he smacked his lips appreciatively—"has her peepers on Jack an' no time for the likes of us. Orl we do is sit out here an' wait for a rattler wot don't have more'n one guard. He *says* he's a score to settle, but—"

"Mum's the word, mate, he's comin'," Ben warned.

Jack Keene rode into the clearing, his frock coat open, showing the brace of pistols that was stuck into the top of his breeches. He pulled his mount to a halt by a vicious jerk on the reins. "See anything?" he asked.

"Naw, nothin's movin', Jack," Ben answered.

"Can't we call it quits? We bin here for hours," whined Jasper.

Keene threw a contemptuous look at his two companions, then pointed off in the distance. "What's that?" he asked.

That was a coach, drawn by four Yorkshire bays. It was moving along smartly, with only two men visible, a coachman and a groom. More importantly, there were no outriders in attendance, nor were there other vehicles close by to witness or possibly interfere with a holdup.

Ben, Jasper, and Jack Keene turned their mounts and rode south. There was no need for verbal directions. All three knew there was only one place for a holdup: just before the tollgate, where all vehicles had to stop.

Chawley pulled up on the ribbons, slowing the team. This was the first tollgate since entering the pike. He disliked tollgates. Just when a team had settled down into a steady pace, it had to be stopped for a gate, then started up again, losing time. He also disliked the late start to their present journey, but he consoled himself with the thought that the Frenchwoman was returning to London without his lordship. Mayhap Master Damon had come to his senses at last. It defied understanding, it did, that he should prefer a Frog to his own wife, when everyone knew Frenchies weren't to be trusted. Wasn't England at war with France? And her ladyship was a right pretty woman, she was. How his lordship could resist a female with such hair—why, it was like fire, that it was.

Chawley didn't understand his lordship, not anymore. There'd been enough death on the estate in recent years, what with his late lordship going soon after Master David bin took by the pox. And Master Damon hisself, escaping death by inches, he should thank the Lord he was alive, instead of bemoaning his lost arm. So he couldn't drive a team without a groom to handle the whip—he was alive, wasn't he? Howsomever, it was a bloody shame. A nonpareil, he'd been, too, Chawley knew. After all, hadn't he taught his lordship? Best pair of hands he'd seen; had a real feel for a horse's mouth, too.

A shot over his head broke up the coachman's reverie.

He pulled the team to a stop as Dalton yelled, "Oh my Gawd, Mr. Chawley, highwaymen."

"Well, don't just 'oh my Gawd' me, Dalton, get out the pistols," Chawley yelled. *He* could do nothing. Both of his hands were needed to stop the plunging horses.

But the opportunity for an effective defense was lost. Before Dalton could gather his wits and reach for the pistols in the pockets of his greatcoat, three horsemen, their faces covered with kerchiefs, rode up. Both coachman and groom found themselves facing three pistols, held in steady hands.

"Stand and deliver," one of the highwaymen yelled.

Nicole, thrown about by the sudden stop, was momentarily panic-stricken to hear these words. Her jewels must be saved at any cost. She fumbled with the clasp at her neck. Perhaps if they saw no jewelry they would expect none. "Marie," she whispered, "put your skirts over the jewel case. Hurry!"

The door was jerked open and a man's head and shoulders were thrust in. Marie shrieked and cowered in the seat at sight of his pistol. Then the opposite door was also opened and a second highwayman appeared. So far Jack hadn't cheated them, but there was no sense giving him the opportunity to do so, thought Jasper Suggs, just before eyeing Nicole. "Coo, what a rum mort! I'd like to sample her wares, I wud," he exclaimed, staring at the beauty.

"I'll trouble you for your jewels, my lady." Jack Keene had spotted Varian's crest on the door of the coach. This beauty must be Lady Varian. Jack's eyes glittered. He appreciated his lordship's taste in women.

"Never," Nicole said crisply. She released the catch on her pearls and calmly let them slide into the bodice of her gown. Now that she faced the highwaymen, she was no longer panicky. They were only men, and she'd always been able to twist men to do her bidding. She smiled archly. "I earned the right to wear them. Would you deprive me of my earnings?"

"We, too, must earn our way, my lady." Jack gestured with his pistol. They couldn't remain all day talking; the alarm could be raised at any moment by the gatekeeper.

This time Nicole heard his use of the title. She smiled. So he thought her the Countess of Varian. Well, why not? She looked more like a countess than that red-headed chit he married.

Jasper, seeing Jack occupied with the beautiful passenger, turned his attention to her maid, who was still cowering in fear, her arms raised protectively across her chest.

"Jack, t'other mort's hidin' sum'un." Jasper gestured toward the maid's skirt. Her cowering posture had raised her skirt above the carriage floor, revealing a hidden object. When Jack didn't immediately respond, Jasper transferred his pistol to his left hand, and reached forward with his right hand toward Marie's feet.

Nicole screamed, "No!" and threw herself on the jewel case. "No, you shan't have it."

Her sudden movement jarred Jasper's arm. The pistol went off, the ball searing a path across Nicole's shoulder, along her collarbone and across her left breast. At the unexpectedly agonizing pain she began to scream, a great peal of sound that reverberated within the confines of the carriage. Then, as she comprehended the full horror of her torn and lacerated flesh, she lost consciousness, sinking in a heap at Marie's feet.

In the silence, Marie could be heard whimpering.

"You fool! Now you've done it!" Keene shouted. While he had no aversion to killing and actually liked the idea of punishing Varian by shooting his wife, he was very

199

much concerned for his own neck. "Grab that box and let's be off!"

"She hit me hand, she did," Jasper said stupidly. "I didn't mean t'pop a gentry mort." Quickly he stuffed the pistol into the pocket of his coat, then reached for the jewel box, shoving Nicole aside in his haste.

"Hurry, you numbskull. Let's be off, or it'll be Newgate for sure."

Chawley and Dalton, too stunned at the rapid turn of events to move, sat immobile, watching the three highwaymen ride off, one clutching a small box. Was the Frenchwoman dead?

"Better take a look, Jimmy me boy," Chawley said kindly. He suspected a most unpleasant sight. Hadn't they heard the scream and the highwaymen's words?

"T'whore's not dead, but she's bleeding like a butchered hog," Dalton reported as he climbed back to sit next to Chawley on the box. "What do we do now, Mr. Chawley?"

"We'll have to go back to Varian," the coachman said resignedly. "Iffen we go on to London and she dies on us, his lordship will have our heads." He began to turn the team.

Twenty-four

Following luncheon Cherry returned to her apartment and immediately rang for Hetty. She could not remember what had happened to her that morning. One moment she had been in the wood by the stream, the next she was being held against Varian's chest while he forced brandy down her throat. And that, of course, was impossible. Time must have passed and distance traversed between these two separate events.

"What happened, Hetty?" she asked on her maid's arrival. "Why was his lordship here?"

"Oh, Miss Cherry, I was so feared. I knew it wasn't the vapours, not like your mama has, leastways. You was just sittin' there"—and Hetty pointed to the upholstered chair. "You didn't know me, me, that's taken care of you all your life," she exclaimed indignantly.

"I don't blame you for being upset, Hetty, if I did that, but truly, I don't remember," Cherry whispered. "I was in the wood . . . thinking . . . and then . . . and then, I was here."

"Well, that's as may be," Hetty sniffed, slightly mollified. "Leastways, I ran to get Mrs. Ridley, but she warn't no help at all. Then his lordship came, and . . . and . . ." Hetty stammered uncertainly. She knew how much Cherry disliked the earl and hesitated to, as she expressed it, "add fuel to the fire."

"And what, Hetty?" Cherry asked sharply.

"He slapped you, Miss Cherry. But that didn't help neither. You was just like a body sleepin'. Then he sent Mrs. Ridley for some brandy, and that woke you up."

"I see, Hetty, thank you," Cherry murmured, but she really didn't understand. Earlier she would not have believed it possible to be so deep in thought as to be totally unaware of one's surroundings.

After Hetty's departure Cherry remained indoors. If she went out again, would she suffer another loss of memory, another withdrawal? For that truly was what she had done, withdrawn totally from her surroundings, from *Varian*.

Yet that didn't make sense. Why should she withdraw from him? If she didn't care for him, if she were truly indifferent to him, she couldn't be hurt by him, could she? Cherry sighed—it was all so confusing—and began to pace the floor. Did any other bride have such problems in the first weeks of marriage? she wondered. It was not enough that she had to worry about her husband's mistreatment of her; but now, she had the additional worry of her own reaction to him.

Think of something pleasant, she advised herself. Varian *had* been kind to her, he had held her close to him, helped her down the stairs. He could have just walked away and left her. And when Nicole was sick, he hadn't gone to *her*. He had lunched with Cherry!

And he hadn't looked as if he hated it! He had laughed,

too. Even if his laughter had been at her, he didn't have to laugh, did he? He had seemed at ease, too, for the first time since they met.

Could she begin to hope?

The hours passed slowly, with Cherry's thoughts alternating between Varian's many misdeeds and this one brief moment of harmony.

Shortly before teatime, Hetty burst into Cherry's sitting room, then collected herself sufficiently to bob slightly. "Beggin' your pardon, Miss Cherry, but the Frenchwoman has gone. Cummins and Waylow just now came to the kitchen. They bin up packin' for her. Two trunks full of clothes, t'was, most of them gowns so thin a body could see through 'em. I don't know what the world's comin' to, that I don't, with females bein' so disgraceful."

"Never mind, Hetty."

Nicole had been sick, and now she was leaving. Should a minor bout of indigestion drive her away? Then Cherry remembered the strange glance between Marston and Robert and Nicole's accusation of poisoning. "Will you please ask Mrs. Ridley to join me here, Hetty?" Something was going on, and the servants were involved in it.

Cherry began to pace the floor again, waiting for the housekeeper. It was a delicate matter. She didn't want to antagonize the servants, but a suspected poisoning was a serious matter. In addition, for servants to take matters into their own hands, to act without the permission of their employers, was just not done. How could she condone it?

"Mrs. Ridley, the Frenchwoman claimed she'd been poisoned," Cherry stated bluntly as soon as the housekeeper closed the door behind her.

"Never!" Mrs. Ridley exclaimed, then asked apprehensively, "You don't believe the word of that lightskirt, do you, m'lady?"

"Not unless I see guilty looks on footmen's faces," Cherry retorted. She was taking a chance in attributing to the servants more than she had actually seen, but felt justified if she could arrive at the truth.

"That was just your imagination, my lady," said the housekeeper, but there was an apparent lack of assurance in her voice.

Cherry stood up and, using her sternest voice, asked, "What did you put in her food, Mrs. Ridley? If I don't have the truth, I will have to tell his lordship. We can't have the servants poisoning guests, you know. The magistrate might have to be called."

The threat of discovery by both his lordship and a magistrate was too much for the housekeeper. Her shoulders sagged. "It wasn't poison," she wailed, twisting her hands in anguish.

"What was it then?"

"Just some simples. White hellebore, it was. Nanny said it'd . . . ah" —she hesitated, trying to find a delicate phrase, but gave up and finished lamely— "make a body cast up its accounts."

Cherry sank down again in her chair, considerably relieved. "That was all? You're sure?"

"Yes'm. Nanny said there'd be no harm done. It's been used as a remedy if someone did swallow poison by mistake, m'lady. Nanny knows all about herbs and simples, you know. And we didn't want to hurt that Frenchie, just get her to leave." The housekeeper seemed eager now to rid herself of any guilt.

Nanny! She had counseled patience, had told Cherry to do nothing, while plotting to rid the house of that woman. And all the servants probably knew of it.

"You won't tell his lordship?" Mrs. Ridley begged.

"I don't know, Mrs. Ridley, truly I don't," Cherry admitted.

"No harm's been done, m'lady."

"I doubt his lordship would agree with you, Mrs. Ridley," Cherry said dryly, then added, "I must think about this. It is not a light matter."

Then, as the housekeeper stood waiting, an apprehensive expression on her face, Cherry said, "Very well, thank you, Mrs. Ridley."

She was grateful to the servants for their concern and their success in getting rid of Nicole, but she couldn't overlook their highly improper behaviour, could she? But if she told Varian, he'd blame Nanny. He'd be furious with her and with the other servants. He might even dismiss them, and he'd be sure to bring Nicole back.

It had been pleasant having lunch alone with him in the study, even though there'd been little conversation. With Nicole gone, could he accept Cherry? Would his hatred for her lessen as time passed?

Then, as the full implication of her thoughts struck her, an appalled Cherry jumped up from her chair and began to pace the floor. She wanted Varian to *love* her!

She wanted him to accept her as his wife!

How could she?

He had mistreated her from the first. He'd had no consideration for her. He'd humiliated her! He hated her! Had she so little pride that she would not only accept a man who treated her so shamefully, but actually want him?

This was far worse than questions of servants' misbehaviour. This involved her entire life. So far she herself had not really been hurt by Varian. Her pride had suffered, for she had been humiliated, but her innermost feelings had not been hurt, for she had been indifferent to him as a man.

However, if she wanted him, if she . . . yes, admit it, if she loved him and he hated her, what then?

The trend of her thoughts frightened her. What was love? All she knew of it was her mother's references and what she had read in romances. But in novels the heroine's heart would beat rapidly at sight of her beloved, or she would feel faint, neither of which Cherry had experienced. However, her parents had cared enough for each other to risk parental displeasure. They had wanted to be together above all things. And she was beginning to care for Varian's acceptance of her.

Cherry threw herself on her knees and began to pray: "Dear God, please, please, don't let me fall in love with him. I can't love him, I can't!"

The door burst open. "Miss Cherry, hurry! Somethin' dreadful's happened." It was Hetty, her eyes big with fright.

"What is it, Hetty?" Cherry jumped up and ran across to take Hetty's hand.

"The coach has returned. Highwaymen," Hetty gasped, then followed Cherry, who was running down the corridor.

The entrance hall was empty. Cherry sped down the stairs and pushed open the front door, to find the traveling coach pulled up in the driveway, surrounded by a silent group of servants. The absolute stillness was frightening. What had happened?

She pushed her way through the mass of servants. Chawley and Dalton were holding the horses. The coach door was open. Then she saw Varian. He was kneeling on the driveway, supporting Nicole. There was blood on the white ermine collar of her pelisse and all over the bodice of her yellow gown.

Cherry moved forward reluctantly. Was Nicole dead? She had never before seen a dead person, and this limp, bloody form was horrifying.

"Tell me again," Varian commanded, his voice icy.

Chawley cleared his throat and looked at Dalton, who shrugged.

"There was three of 'em, m'lord. They had kerchiefs over their faces and each had a pistol. They came at us just afore the tollgate, just as I was slowin' the team. They came out of that stretch of woods near the gate."

"Why didn't you shoot, blast you?" demanded Varian savagely. "You had pistols."

"Dalton had a pair, my lord," Chawley explained patiently. "He could have gotten off two shots, and there were three of 'em. They were better shots, too, I warrant. An' iffen us had been killed, t'team would ha' bolted an' no tellin' *what* would ha' happened."

"Go on."

"Well, one of 'em, the tall 'un, opened t'door of the coach. An' another 'un, a small 'un he was, opened t'other door. They asked for jewels. But"—he stared at Varian, his face impassive—"the Frenchwoman wouldn't give him her jewels, m'lord."

Varian's voice was vicious as he exclaimed, "So he shot her!"

"*Non,* milord."

Everyone's attention had been centered on Varian and Chawley. The voice of Marie took them by surprise as she stepped down out of the coach. "Madame had me hide the jewel case under my skirts, but that *canaille* found it. She tried to stop him from taking it and the pistol went off. I'm sure it was not intentional."

207

"That's right," Chawley agreed readily. "They was arguin' about it."

While Marie was talking, Cherry had kept her eyes fixed on her husband. His reaction to the shooting was one of anger, and it puzzled her. Surely he should be grieving at the loss of his loved one?

Suddenly her breath caught in her throat. It seemed as if her heart stopped beating. Involuntarily her hands flew to press against her lips, and Cherry shuddered. Then, not understanding her extreme reaction to the tragedy, she glanced away from Varian and saw Nicole's eyelids flutter.

Impulsively, Cherry moved forward. "M'lord."

As he raised a face still retaining a look of fury, Cherry gasped, "She's not dead. I saw her eyes move."

A strange expression appeared on his face. For a moment as her eyes met his, Cherry had the astonishing impression that they were communicating without words, but the moment passed as Nicole stirred again, claiming his attention.

"Dalton, ride to Corby for Dr. Hughes. Marston, you and Robert carry Madame to her bedchamber."

The footmen hesitated at the earl's orders and Cherry laid a hand on Varian's shoulder. "My lord, would it not be better to make a stretcher from a blanket?"

Again his eyes met hers briefly in what appeared to be a searching glance. However, she was probably mistaken, for he turned away abruptly to give orders to the footmen.

Feeling dismissed, Cherry approached the housekeeper and whispered, "No more of Nanny's simples." Then she raised her voice slightly. "We will have dinner at the usual hour, Mrs. Ridley."

Her calm demeanor and quiet words seemed to rouse the remaining servants. They all scurried off, not without a few backward glances at his lordship.

Cherry felt awkward waiting with Marie for the footmen to appear, but she didn't want to leave Varian alone with Nicole. He was probably growing tired from supporting her, but Cherry knew it would be useless to suggest he lay her head down on the driveway.

Marston appeared with a blanket, Robert with two poles, and shortly a stretcher was made up and Nicole lifted onto it. Cherry went ahead to ensure that the door was held open, then waited in the hall.

Varian entered the house behind the stretcher but, to Cherry's surprise, did not follow the footmen up the stairs. Instead, he headed directly toward his study.

Thus it was left to Cherry to send up the maids with hot water and to welcome Dr. Hughes.

Twenty-five

A totally confused Cherry sat in the drawing room with the door open, waiting for the physician to return. Marston had taken him up to Nicole's bedchamber, and fortunately she had nothing to do. At this moment she doubted she could function in a rational manner.

Her world had changed drastically. It was no longer a simple world in which Varian was the harsh and punishing master and she the suffering and humiliated victim. It was a chaotic tangle!

Today for the first time since they'd met she had perceived Varian as a fellow person, not just her abuser. And for the first time she had apprehended that *he* could suffer. Of course, she should have realized that from the loss of his arm—one doesn't have his arm cut off without pain, agonizing pain—but earlier she had been too busy trying to defend her father to think of Varian.

But now when she saw him as a man suffering a loss, he wasn't suffering! Instead he was angry! It didn't make sense. But then nothing made sense anymore!

She had wanted to comfort him—and he didn't want comforting, certainly not from her.

And those astonishing moments when his eyes had met hers . . . had they really happened or had she imagined them?

Her feelings seemed to be in some kind of a horribly mixed-up jumble. She was no longer sure of how she felt about anything!

And Varian was not acting in character either.

She should be afraid, and she wasn't.

She should be depressed at Nicole's return, and she wasn't.

Instead she was experiencing a strange kind of excitement that thoroughly disconcerted her.

Cherry's first reaction when Ridley announced Dr. Hughes was one of thankfulness that she had other matters to attend to and could forget her muddled emotions. "Will you inform his lordship of Dr. Hughes's presence, Ridley?" she asked, rising to greet the physician.

"Come in, doctor, and sit down," she invited.

"Thank you, m'lady."

The middle-aged physician had a calm, reassuring manner and Cherry felt drawn to him. "It was most kind of you to arrive so quickly," she murmured. "May I offer you a glass of wine?" she asked next, spying the cut glass decanter on the tripod table.

"I can't refuse his lordship's fine Madeira."

Cherry was startled. "Was his lordship your patient, Dr. Hughes?"

"Not really, m'lady. By the time he returned from Spain he was almost recovered. It was more my job to see that he didn't overdo. A combination of wounds such as he suffered can leave one remarkably weak, and his lordship is not one for half measures."

The door opened just as Cherry was handing the wineglass to the doctor. She glanced up, expecting to see Varian. Instead, Ridley stood there, shaking his head.

Cherry interpreted this to mean Varian did not intend speaking to the physician. She took a deep breath, nodded to Ridley, then sat down. "How is madame?" she asked reluctantly. Nicole was Varian's responsibility, not hers!

"She's a very fortunate woman. The ball missed her vital organs. It traveled along the collarbone, opening a long and fairly deep gash, but she should recover. There will be a scar, of course, but her clothing will cover that."

As he paused, Cherry wondered briefly if Nicole would consider herself fortunate. A scar such as Dr. Hughes described might be visible through the sheer gowns Nicole wore.

Dr. Hughes put down his glass to warn her, "There is a possibility of fever, of course, but that will only delay matters. Within a fortnight the wound should be healed. She will need complete rest, of course," he added.

Cherry was not surprised that her reaction to the doctor's statement should be mixed: she didn't know whether she should be sad that Nicole must remain for another two weeks or relieved that she wasn't dead. She sighed in resignation. What was one more confused reaction?

Deciding she would have to sort out her feelings at some later time, Cherry murmured, "Thank you," as Dr. Hughes took his leave.

"Just remember, m'lady, if any relapse occurs, feel free to call me. I've given the maid directions on changing the bandages. And I'll return in three days."

Marston appeared after showing Dr. Hughes to his carriage to announce, "Dinner is served, m'lady."

Cherry glanced down at her black gown. It would have to do. It was much too late to change now. Besides, Varian wouldn't notice what she wore, if he even bothered to come to dinner.

However, he was there, standing behind his chair when she entered the dining room. She expected to be castigated for being late again, but Varian said nothing as he seated himself.

Her relief, however, began to give way to unease as the meal progressed, for Varian refused to eat. He sat drinking steadily, one glass of wine after another. Cherry lost count of the number he consumed. After the covers were removed and Ridley brought in the port with an apologetic glance at her, she rose and excused herself. If Varian was not drunk by now, he soon would be, and she had no desire to see him in his cups.

It was evident he missed Nicole, and Cherry retired to her bedchamber with the disquieting knowledge that her presence did not make up for Nicole's absence.

Hetty was waiting for her. "I thought we was rid of that baggage, Miss Cherry. It's not right that the staff has to do extra duty to keep the likes of *her* alive."

"Ouch! Don't brush so hard!" Cherry remonstrated. "Hetty, please, you're hurting my head."

"I'm sorry, Miss Cherry, but it galls me, it does. Why couldn't the coach have gone on to Lunnon? Then she'd be gone."

"I imagine she would have been permanently gone, Hetty, if they had done so, and I suspect Chawley feared his lordship's anger if she died."

"Everybody'd be much better off if she did." Hetty's response was so low Cherry could not be sure of her words, but decided it would be wiser to ignore them.

"Your hair is growin' longer, Miss Cherry. It should be cropped again, if you wish to remain in fashion."

Cherry smiled bitterly. "For what, Hetty? There is no need to be fashionable in the country."

Silently she added, "And no need to be fashionable for a husband who ignores you."

Cherry had just climbed into bed when the door opposite the huge four-poster was pushed open. Varian stood there in his dressing gown, a glass in his hand.

Her eyes widened in alarm.

"Aren't you going to welcome me, wife?" His words were thick.

"You're drunk," she accused.

"Of course." He waved his glass. His steps were unsteady as he approached the bed. "Only in my cups would I want the daughter of Jack Hilliard." He laughed harshly. "The way I feel now, any woman will do, even you."

She cringed as if struck. His brutal words hurt. "Go away," Cherry whispered. "You don't know what you're doing."

"No? Nicole is not . . . available. Who'll take her place in my bed?"

She waited tensely until he came up to the bedside, then she rolled to the other side and slid out of bed. She tried to reach the door but he had guessed her intention. Even as her feet touched the floor, he was moving around the foot of the bed. A long arm stretched out, caught her, and pulled her back. "No, you don't," he growled as he spun her around to face him.

Cherry, suddenly terrified, fought for her life. She tried to pull away from his tight grasp, to kick at him. This was too much like the earlier attack in the inn and to her terror-stricken mind, Varian was Jack Keene.

She had the satisfaction of slapping his cheek, but before she could hit him again, he released her. She fell to her knees, sobbing from mingled pain, frustration, and terror.

214

"A wife is supposed to welcome her husband's attentions," he stated as he pulled her to her feet.

Then he stared at her. "You're not Nicole," he muttered, shaking his head.

"No, I'm not." Cherry blinked back tears. "Damon, please. Tomorrow you'll regret this and hate yourself."

He shook his head. "Can't hate myself, only you." His voice was ugly. He lifted his hand, and Cherry, expecting him to strike her, was unprepared as he grabbed the neckline of her bedgown and ripped it down the entire front, then jerked the gown off her.

"It's about time I see my wife's charms," he muttered.

Her face burning, Cherry turned away, but Varian grabbed her around the waist and threw her onto the bed. As he snuffed out the candle, he muttered, "In the dark, all women are alike."

Twenty-six

As an awakening Cherry turned drowsily in bed, her hand touched warm flesh. A scream rose to her lips but was immediately stifled as she remembered the events of the past night.

She turned her head on the pillow. Damon was asleep, his head facing her. In repose the customary harsh lines of his face were not apparent, and his lips were no longer tight with anger, but soft and full. She remembered them on her body and blushed.

Cherry had feared for her life last night when Damon had tossed her naked onto the bed, shed his dressing gown, and joined her under the sheet; but his hand, touching her, moving possessively over her, had been warm and soft and surprisingly delicate.

She had lain quiet and passive, not knowing what to expect and fearing to anger him further by a show of defiance.

His hand had caressed her, her arms, her neck, her breasts. She scarcely breathed. Never before had she been touched so intimately. Then his lips began moving over her cheek, up to her ear, where he nibbled her earlobe gently, and down her neck. Then they, too, found her breasts.

Her immediate fear was giving way, for his touch was gentle and pleasant. He was not hurting her. On the contrary, he was arousing physical sensations in her, feelings so new to her she couldn't begin to describe them. She lay in wonder that she could experience such pleasurable sensations in her body.

Then the wonder, too, gave way, as her body began to respond to his caresses. She was no longer able to fear, or to wonder, only to feel.

His hand was on her thigh . . . then it moved higher to the most private part of her. She began to move in protest, but his lips, softly murmuring, gentled her, and she offered no more resistance—nor wanted to as she began to be carried away on a rising tide of passion.

When he spread her legs and entered her, she welcomed his hardness as he swept her up to undreamed of heights.

Now she stared anxiously at him, wondering what Damon's reaction would be when he awoke in her bed. She had never before noticed his long lashes, curled at the ends. As she was idly speculating on the unfairness of Providence in giving such lashes to a man, his eyes opened. They were warm and dark until he became aware of her. Then he frowned, sat up in bed, winced, and clasped his hand to his head.

Cherry hurriedly pulled up the sheet, which his movement had disarranged. Though Damon's lips and hand had thoroughly explored her body, that had been at night in the dark. She was still too shy to expose herself voluntarily to him.

"I must have been in my cups," he muttered and got out

of bed with one swift motion. Cherry had an impression of wide shoulders, lean hips, and muscular thighs, before her attention was caught by his left arm. It was unnatural, the arm's ending so bluntly at the elbow. She knew she was staring, but couldn't pull her eyes away. How painful it must have been for him!

"Does it offend your sensibilities, my lady?" Varian's voice was ugly as he grabbed up his dressing gown and strode toward the connecting door.

There he turned. "I assure you, m'lady, this won't happen again," he said coldly and formally before closing the door behind him.

"Ohhhhhh!" Cherry pounded on the pillow in complete frustration. The only way he'd make love to her was when he was drunk! It was humiliating, and made doubly so by the knowledge that she wanted him to love her.

Last night she had become his wife, discovering what it really meant to be a wife. He had awakened her to delights she couldn't possibly have imagined in her virginal purity, and then after arousing her passions, after making her want him, he refused to approach her again. Varian could find no better way to make her suffer.

Cherry sprang out of bed and began to pace, trying to calm herself. Some of the desires and emotions bedeviling her she could comprehend: she wanted Damon to love her, to care for her, to be kind and gentle to her; she wanted him to smile at her and be happy with her. Such desires for peace and harmony were reasonable. She could understand them.

But as she paced back and forth, trying to soothe nerves that felt lacerated, Cherry realized that she truly didn't understand herself. Never in her life had she been under such emotional strain. She was vaguely conscious of a longing, a need for something she couldn't define. Her entire body was reacting, both physically and mentally. She felt keyed up and excited, and at the same time, apprehensive. She felt caught up in a tangled, tumultuous, jumbled *mess* and she didn't understand any of it.

When she finally came downstairs, after spending hours pacing the floor, the house was in an uproar. The maids were standing around in the hall, the footmen talking excitedly among themselves. No one was working. Cherry hurried her steps. Had another holdup occurred? Had Nicole died?

"Is there aught amiss, Mrs. Ridley?" she inquired breathlessly of the housekeeper.

"Aye, m'lady, you might say that." Mrs. Ridley straightened her cap and apron, both of which had become awry. "His lordship has sent for all the neighbours: Sir Francis, Lord Franklyn, Squire Allerton, Lord Brinsley, Mr. Burleigh, and the local farmers. He wants them to help scour the countryside." She paused at Cherry's blank look, then explained, "The highwaymen must be found, m'lady. Next time it might be a *proper* woman who gets shot, mayhap killed. Why Providence didn't see fit to kill *her* off, I won't pretend to understand."

Cherry was shocked. "Surely you don't mean that, Mrs. Ridley?"

"And why not? That Frenchie has disrupted the entire household. It ain't right that housemaids have to act as nursemaids. Taylor stayed up all night with her and now she's no good for her regular tasks."

"We'll just have to make do, Mrs. Ridley," Cherry soothed.

"That's what it will be, m'lady, makin' do," Mrs. Ridley sniffed, then added, "I beg your pardon, m'lady. I shouldn't be complainin' to you, seein' as how it's not your fault—" The housekeeper broke off, tightening her lips, then said, "It would be better not to go walking today, m'lady. There's no tellin' who might mistake you for a highwayman and shoot first."

Cherry had a lonely luncheon in her sitting room, then wandered down to the library. Surely Varian would not notice if a few volumes were missing among the hundreds in the bookcases lining the walls. There were no novels, but there were several travel books. Carefully opening a tall glass door, she selected a leather-bound volume on Spain, a country her father had died trying to defend.

She returned to her sitting room to read, but the hours passed slowly, much more slowly than usual. She would read a page, then reread it, for she couldn't remember a single word she had just read. Each time she turned a page, she would glance at the clock on the mantel, willing it to move faster and faster. Finally giving up, she went to the window to peer out. She was waiting for Damon. She wanted to see him again. She didn't understand why this should be so, she just knew that it was.

When Cherry entered the drawing room before dinner, it was difficult to keep from smiling. She had to bite her lips. She couldn't let him see that she was glad to see him. He would only use this knowledge to hurt her further.

He handed her a glass of wine. Being careful to hide her surprise at this consideration, she asked, "Did you find them?"

"No."

Her heart plummeted at this bald answer, but Varian, after seating himself in the wing chair before the fireplace, continued, "We went back to the wood, to the spot where the gatekeeper had seen them enter. There we found tracks leading to a clearing, but lost them again. The ground was too dry."

He was actually conversing with her! Her voice was breathless as she asked, "What did you do then?"

His glance was level as he replied, "We combed that wood, then went on to the next stretch. In all we searched every strip of wood between the tollgate and Folkingham. But there was no sign of highwaymen."

"Could they have gone to London? I mean," Cherry began to explain when he glanced quizzically at her, the words tumbling out, "if they did not intend to kill, they might have run—" She stopped suddenly as she realized what she was saying.

Cherry could have screamed. Why did she have to remind Damon of her father's supposed cowardice? His face, which had been showing only fatigue, had now become cold and remote. He bowed his head. "Perhaps you're right, my lady. You would have intimate knowledge of such actions."

Cherry sighed. Her unruly tongue had spoiled any rapport between them. When would she learn to think before she spoke?

An uneasy silence reigned during dinner, but at least Damon was eating. Much better than last night, she thought. Or was he just insuring that he would not become drunk and come to her again?

Twenty-seven

Cherry wandered disconsolately down the wide corridors and into the many rooms of Varian Court. For the third day Damon had gone out searching for the highwaymen, and for the third time it was Mrs. Ridley who had told her of his whereabouts, her husband not having had the courtesy to inform his wife. She had given up making a pretense of reading the travel book. It was much too difficult to concentrate on written words when her mind kept asking, "Where is he? When will he return?" Moreover, with every reference to Spain's hot climate, she had visions of Damon lying suffering under the pitiless sun.

She couldn't understand herself: he seemed to have become an obsession with her. Finally, in desperation, she had thrown down the book and sought release in activity, wandering from room to room.

She was drawn almost against her will toward the wing where Nicole was lying feverish. Both Mrs. Ridley and Hetty had taken pains to keep her informed of Nicole's progress, Hetty to report, "Waylow says she's been tossin' about in bed somethin' awful and gabblin' in that heathen tongue of hers," and Mrs. Ridley to complain that yet another maid had to be freed from household duties for the sickroom.

As she drew near to Nicole's bedchamber, Cherry refused to admit to herself that she might want to see Damon's disfigured mistress—it was unworthy of her. When she came to the ballroom, therefore, she made herself enter it, pretending it had been her goal.

The heavy gold brocade draperies were drawn. In the dim light she could barely make out the gleaming floor and the three chandeliers, each capable of holding a myriad of candles. Her imagination could people this room with many guests, some dancing gaily under the blazing lights, others conversing on the settees and chairs lining the walls. For a wistful moment her thoughts took her back to the London balls where she had whirled in the arms of a waltz partner or skipped through various country dances. Then all her dreams faded before the reality of chairs and settees ensconced under holland covers. There would never be balls at Varian Court! Damon had too much pride even to attempt the awkwardness of waltzing one-armed. Besides, he would not want to hold *her* that close.

Cherry whirled about and ran to escape from these thoughts. Swiftly closing the ballroom door behind her, she hurried down the corridor, past the closed door of Nicole's chamber. At the end of the corridor she paused. To the left lay the gallery and Damon's portrait. She couldn't face that, not now—it would hurt too much to see him as he could be—and turned to the right.

She was in a part of the house that was strange to her. Mrs. Ridley had neglected to show her this section. Slower now, she walked past the closed doors. More bedchambers?

One door caught her attention. It was separated from the other doors by a great expanse of wall. It must be a large room. Another ballroom?

Ready to grasp at anything new to redirect her thoughts, Cherry opened the door and, entering, discovered she was in the day nursery.

She moved forward slowly, her eyes moving over the contents of the room. The large windows were hung with gaily patterned curtains; the tables and chairs were child-size; before the fireplace was a rocking chair for nurse; in one corner stood a cradle; in another, a wooden rocking horse with a real horsehair mane and tail. In the wall to her left was a door. She opened it to find a row of small cots.

Cherry stood staring at them. Cots . . . for children. And visions of infants with black ringlets and long, black lashes framing warm, dark eyes came to her. Damon's children: little boys with two whole arms. Children she wanted to give to him.

Cherry closed the door softly and sank into the rocking chair, completely overwhelmed with these new thoughts. She wanted to help him, to care for him, to be part of his life. Damon was important to her—his happiness was important to her.

She leaned forward and covered her face with her hands at the full meaning of her newfound understanding. She had been against marriage to Damon because her pride had been hurt that he had not courted her. She had been thinking only of herself. But wasn't that what she always had done? Weren't her impetuous, unthinking actions only for what she wanted? She had been selfish. Her wishes alone had been foremost.

Cherry shook her head and began to rock back and forth. She knew now why her eyes had felt drawn to Damon, why it hurt to see him caress Nicole, why her emotions were all muddled up and her senses in a tumult. She loved Damon!

She stopped rocking, amazed at the direction of her thoughts. How it could be, she didn't know, but he had become the center of her existence. She cared only for him. She wanted to be with him, help him, be part *of* him. And she wanted him to love her.

Cherry stood up and slowly started back to her bedchamber. That Damon would love her was an impossibility. She would have to settle for second best: wanting him to stop hating her.

However, at dinner that evening she again realized that there was small chance of Damon's ever forgetting his hatred. He had returned late, exhausted from another day spent in the saddle. He entered the dining room just as Marston carried in a huge roast.

Cherry glanced helplessly, first at it, then at Ridley, who was standing just behind his lordship's chair. Should she offer to help Damon? She dared not risk offending him further. There always seemed to be some kind of reminder of his handicap. So many ordinary daily tasks required the use of two hands. And Damon resented his awkwardness or sheer inability to perform them single-handed and blamed her.

"My compliments to the cook, Ridley, but what am I supposed to do with that roast?" Damon's voice was cool and neutral when he addressed the butler, but when he turned to her, his voice became harsh. "Your housekeeping is inadequate, my lady. You have neglected to inform the cook that only milk sops are fit food for invalids."

"Stop it, Damon," Cherry burst out. "You're not an

225

invalid. Handicapped, yes, but still capable of living a full life."

"Indeed." A sardonic eyebrow rose. "Now Lady Varian has become a physician. I trust she is more accomplished at that occupation than she is at housekeeping."

Cherry opened her mouth to retort, but Varian hadn't yet finished. There was a glowering look on his face as he said, "You know nothing of my abilities, my lady, so I trust you will keep out of my affairs."

"With your permission, my lord." Ridley, with a soft murmur, moved forward and began to carve the roast.

Cherry forced herself to sit down and pick up a fork. Was every meal to be such an ordeal now that Nicole was unable to be here to please him? And to think that she had wanted to be with him, had waited for his return, had hoped that they could live amicably together. How silly of her. All he wanted was to rail at her, blaming her for his inabilities.

To the relief of the servants, the rest of the meal was eaten in silence. After a few mouthfuls, which she forced herself to swallow, Cherry pushed at her food. She had no appetite. She kept her eyes lowered, only glancing up a time or two to notice that Damon was eating heartily. When the footmen removed the covers she took the opportunity to leave, Marston taking the liberty of giving her a reproachful look. Damon, however, barely glanced up as she rose and did not acknowledge her murmured "If his lordship will excuse me?"

In the hall she met Mrs. Ridley. "I must apologize, my lady. Mrs. Thatcher was just not thinking, to send in a whole joint like that."

"It doesn't matter." Cherry bit her lip. Then, the threatening tears overpowering her determination not to cry, she brushed past the housekeeper and ran upstairs.

226

Mrs. Ridley was left alone, shaking her head. Things were worse now that his lightskirt was not able to entertain him. It was almost as if his lordship blamed her ladyship for everything that went wrong. She sighed. What had happened to the merry boy who used to laugh off cuts and scrapes, who thought nothing of a skinned knee or two, who had not allowed a broken arm to hinder him?

Twenty-eight

Sir Francis and Lady Warrick came to call the next morning. Cherry had just entered her sitting room when Marston announced the callers.

"Thank you," she replied, then mechanically instructed the footman to serve tea for Lady Warrick and wine for Sir Francis. "Madeira, I think, Marston."

"Very good, m'lady." The footman bowed and withdrew.

Cherry's first thought—that the Warricks were calling much too early—was dismissed when she glanced at the clock. It was past eleven! Hetty hadn't mentioned the late hour when she came in answer to Cherry's ring, and Cherry, not wanting to admit to a near sleepless night, had not asked the time. She had not been able to sleep: her constantly churning thoughts had kept her awake until near dawn. During these long hours she had finally faced and accepted the realization that her relationship with Damon had not been altered by her change of feelings. She may have grown to love him, but he still hated her and would continue to do so.

Her pale face reflecting the lack of sleep, Cherry reluctantly descended to meet her guests, wishing she were ill-mannered enough to refuse them, for she did not feel up to facing the Warricks.

"Damon not in?" Sir Francis asked after greeting her. "Still out trying to find those highwaymen, eh? Well, if he does, there won't be anything left of them to hang, I warrant. I rode with him for two days, you know, m'lady, but we couldn't find 'em—must have left. I told Damon it was useless to hunt anymore."

"It's scandalous that he makes so much effort to find the men who shot *that* woman," Lady Warrick murmured.

"Now, now, m'dear. I told you." Sir Francis shot a warning glance at his wife. "If a . . . ah . . . person in a peer's coach is not safe from attack, then any lady traveling about is in danger. Before it was only a matter of losing one's valuables to the highwaymen; now that we know they won't hesitate to shoot, it's a matter of life and death. Besides, she was a guest, was she not?"

Cherry, who at Lady Warrick's words had begun to wonder how much the neighbours knew of Damon's mistress, was grateful to her caller for publicly putting the best face on the matter. "Perhaps they did not intend shooting her, Sir Francis. They may have run away." To Sir Francis she could speak these words without fear, but then, he did not have bitter memories of her father's supposed cowardice.

Sir Francis had not been content to sit, as the ladies did, on the comfortable drawing room chairs, but had been pacing up and down before the fireplace. "The entire countryside has been searched, north to Grantham and south to Stamford. I told Damon there was no point doing more. They must have given us the slip or gone into hiding."

"You don't look well, m'lady," Lady Warrick whispered, wondering whether her ladyship was already increasing. Of course, Lady Varian's nerves could be overset by Varian's *affaire*, but then, most well-bred females learned to ignore their husbands' peccadilloes.

She had spoken in a low voice, but her husband picked up her words. "You do look a trifle peaked, m'lady. You're not worrying that *you* might have been the one to be shot, are you?"

As Sir Francis's hearty voice boomed out this question, the doors opened and Varian entered, followed by Marston bearing a tray. Cherry, who had indeed thought her husband was out searching again, struggled to conceal her surprise from her guests. The shooting of Nicole would provide enough grist for the gossip mill.

"Ah, Varian, there you are. Just trying to reassure your lady. You realize the whole of Kesteven is upset, don't you?"

Varian's eyebrows rose as he strode forward to greet the baronet. "By my efforts or by the shooting?" he asked coolly.

"No, no, you misunderstand me. Everyone realizes that no one's life is safe now."

Cherry felt sick. The immediate countryside must be gossiping about Nicole. Everyone must know by now that Varian had kept his mistress in the same house as his new bride. How could she possibly hold up her head?

Grateful for the opportunity to occupy her hands, Cherry busied herself with pouring tea as Sir Francis resumed the conversation.

"I just came to suggest that you let the squire and the constable handle the affair."

"Oh, come now, Francis." The earl replaced the stopper of the decanter and, as he handed a brimming glass to his guest, said, "A parish constable accustomed to such flagrant crimes as poaching and a local magistrate whose head has been turned by a female?"

Sir Francis looked uncomfortable. "Well, yes, there is that. But, damn, Damon, we're not used to *crime* hereabouts! Kesteven has the best record in the whole of Lincolnshire. It's because we take care of our people better." He leaned back in his chair and crossed his legs. "They at least have more experience in apprehending criminals than the lot of us. The countryside has been searched. It won't do any good to do more. Let it be, Damon."

"Perhaps you're right, Francis." Varian swirled the wine in his glass, then glanced up. "But there's more than one way to skin a cat, wouldn't you say?"

A frown appeared on the face of the baronet. "You're not thinking of going out alone, are you, Damon?"

Cherry held her breath, waiting apprehensively for Damon's answer. He would be no match for three armed highwaymen!

"Hardly. I'm not that foolhardy. No, no, Francis, I was just thinking that if action doesn't work, perhaps a bit of thought might turn the trick."

Both skepticism and hope were apparent on the baronet's face as he rose. "Well, I hope that you do, Damon, but I don't see how *thought* will apprehend highwaymen. We'll have to be going. Come, Sarah."

Damon accompanied the Warricks to their carriage, a courtesy on his part that surprised Cherry, as did his continued amiability during luncheon. Although he did not converse with her—indeed, she didn't really expect that of him—she was grateful for a quiet meal with no cruel words.

She had no sooner returned to her sitting room when Marston announced more visitors. Cherry descended the stairs wondering whether they were calling to satisfy their curiosity about Nicole: certainly no one had called before the attack on Damon's mistress. However, all thoughts about their neighbours' motives left her as she reached the bottom step, for Damon joined her there.

As she raised questioning eyes—was he annoyed that she was late?—Damon grasped her arm and started to lead her toward the drawing room. Cherry almost gasped aloud when he touched her, for her entire body began to tingle. Momentarily her new response to Damon threatened to overwhelm her and she hesitated. Then, steadied by her fear of his reaction should he learn of her feelings, she allowed him to guide her. As it was, she felt as if she were existing in a dream world.

Damon must have presented their callers to her and she must have spoken to them, but Cherry had no later recollection of any conversation. She was conscious only of Damon, a conciliating and pleasant Damon. She watched wistfully, wishing he would always be like this.

At first she had been surprised at his affability, but then she realized that it was just a mark of his good breeding. A well-bred gentleman is always civil. Moreover, he may have wanted to give a good impression to his neighbours.

In any case, his civility continued when she joined him in the dining room for dinner. Again there was no conversation, just soft words directed to the servants, for which Cherry felt a great sense of relief. The strain she was under had intensified. Not only were her emotions raw from the ordeal of the past weeks, but they had been made doubly sensitive by the realization that all their neighbours were aware of Nicole's presence at Varian Court. In addition, she was very much afraid that she would be unable to keep her love a secret from Damon.

With all these thoughts turning about in her mind and fearing that Damon could read her glance if she looked at him, Cherry determinedly kept her gaze fastened on her plate during the meal. Thus, she missed the glances directed at her.

She passed a restless night, her dreams filled with callers all whispering about Nicole. Near dawn she was awakened by a sound. To her drowsy mind it seemed to be a scream of someone in extreme pain, but it must have been her imagination, for immediately after she heard the sounds of Hartley's arrival at Damon's door. If the screams had been real, Damon surely would have investigated.

Cherry remained in her sitting room that morning, holding the travel book and trying to read, but her thoughts were on Damon and their marriage. Somehow it didn't seem important anymore that he wished to revenge himself on her. Even the thought of her father's cowardice no longer disturbed her. All that mattered to her was Damon. She wanted him to be happy and she wished with all her heart that she could bring joy to his life.

Marston interrupted her thoughts with the announcement of more callers. She thanked him, hoping that the reluctance she felt was not apparent to the footman.

As she slowly descended the staircase, she saw Damon waiting at the bottom and hurried her steps, fearing his anger at her tardiness. He raised his eyes as she neared him and Cherry was shocked as she met his gaze. There was a haunted look in his eyes.

She realized then how greatly he missed Nicole, but he said nothing to her. Again he led her forward to greet their callers, Cherry walking beside him as if in a daze.

The rest of that day passed like the previous one, in

amiable civility and no recollection on Cherry's part of their visitors' names or faces. The only face she was conscious of was Damon's. As he chatted, his attention centered elsewhere, she was free to watch him with yearning eyes.

That night her dreams were filled with Damon: a smiling, happy, gentle Damon. She wakened early, to lie half dozing in bed, her dreams still vivid. Then, remembering Damon's early morning rides, she jumped out of bed and ran to the window, hoping to see him.

Cherry had just pulled back the drapery when she heard a harsh scream. For an instant she was startled; then, realizing the sound came from her right, she rushed across the chamber floor and pushed open the dressing room door. Another horrid sound seemed to echo and reecho in the small room. Quickly she opened the door to Damon's bedchamber.

In the dim light she could see him thrashing about in bed. Cherry sped across the floor to his side. Beads of sweat covered his forehead. His one hand was clenched tightly. His face showed a horrible grimace of pain.

What was happening to him? Why was he suffering so?

She wanted to hold him in her arms and comfort him, but fearing that such action on her part would waken him, she quickly knelt by the bed and put one hand on his head, the other on his arm. Then, leaning over, she brushed his lips with hers.

Instantly Damon quieted. His body lost its tenseness, his hand unclenching to lie relaxed on the sheet. His breathing, which had been ragged, became regular and even. His face smoothed out, becoming tranquil.

She remained until he was sleeping quietly, then, in a disturbed frame of mind, returned to her own chamber. Had Damon been having a nightmare? It must have been a horrible one, for a man like Damon to scream in pain. What could have caused such an ordeal?

Suddenly Cherry's knees gave way and she sank into a chair. Stupid! He had told her. Hadn't he likened his experience in Spain to being in hell? How he must have suffered . . . and must still be suffering if he was reliving that horrible experience.

Cherry felt as if a knife was twisting within her, as she realized how shallow and selfish she had been. She had no conception of the agony he had withstood. It had been much easier to blame him and hate him for his actions than to try to understand him. He had quieted at her touch. Had he needed Nicole for the same reason?

When Cherry came downstairs that morning, Damon was waiting again. Eagerly she glanced at him, seeking to discover whether his eyes still had that haunted look of yesterday. Their eyes met and it seemed as if their glance was a physical thing locking them together. For a long moment time seemed suspended . . . then her foot faltered on the stairway. Cherry had to grab the railing to keep from falling and the spell was broken.

As she joined him, he put his arm about her waist, propelling her forward. About to protest that her ankle had not been twisted on the steps, Cherry changed her mind. It was such a small deception and she didn't want him to remove his arm. She didn't want to meet their callers, either. She just wished this moment could continue on forever and ever.

Cherry was in a daze. She must have spoken, but she could not remember speaking. She only remembered Damon, greeting his guests, chatting to them, pouring wine. Her entire being seemed focused on him. She saw him smile and her spirits lifted, even though she knew the smile was for their guests, not for her.

That night before she drifted off to sleep she prayed to waken early. And her prayers were answered, for when she peeped into Damon's bedchamber the next morning, he was moving about in bed, but no screams came from his lips. She quickly ran over to the bed on soundless bare feet and touched his arm and cheek. Again he quieted at her touch and again she remained until he was sleeping peacefully before quitting his side.

Twenty-nine

Nicole opened her eyes drowsily and looked about her. The bedchamber was bright with sunlight—that was not unusual, for she never rose before eleven—but Marie was sleeping in a chair beside the bed. Why should her maid do that? And why did she feel so weak, as if drained of all energy?

She tried to sit up and a piercing pain brought her to full consciousness, a consciousness in which events tumbled about in disorder: a journey in Varian's coach; the humiliation of retching in the dining room; the highwaymen; Varian sitting on her bed; her jewel box; the shot; and then the agonizing pain that seared her soft body like a burning brand.

Gradually she sorted it out. She had been shot by highwaymen trying to steal her jewels and had been brought back to Varian Court where she was now. Where it was not safe for her to be!

Nicole had never before known fear. Always there had been males to succumb to her smiles and seductive glances. But this time her charms had not worked. She had met men willing to kill for a box of jewels, men willing to kill *her*. Her fear began to grow.

"Marie," she hissed. "Wake up. What day is this?"

The maid stirred, then sat up with a start, rubbing her eyes as if in disbelief. "*Je regrette que—*"

"Oh, do not apologize, Marie. I, too, have been sleeping. For how long?"

"*Pardonnez-moi,* madame." Marie spread her hands in a supplicating gesture, then asked eagerly, with a smile wreathing her face, "You are better, *n'est-ce pas?*"

"I am better, yes, but how long has it been? I am hungry and as weak as an infant."

"*Oui,* madame." Marie nodded. "The fever, it lasted three days, and then you slept for two more."

Nicole stared. "Five days?" It seemed unbelievable.

"*Oui.* You have been very ill. The wound itself, it is healing, but the fever, that was bad. We were up many nights, madame, the two housemaids and I, putting wet cloths on your head and body. But now that you are awake, you need food."

"Yes, yes, and to leave here."

"Leave? But, madame, you cannot. The physician, he said you must rest."

"Rest, yes. But not here. When his lordship comes I'll tell him so. He must take me to London."

Marie sat back in the chair, her lips tightening. Her silence was suspicious and Nicole's eyes narrowed. "What is it?"

The maid shrugged, spreading her hands helplessly. "It is just that milord has not been here."

"Not been here? He has not been to see me, not once?" This lord, who could not live without her but must needs

238

bring her along on his honeymoon, now when she is ill, does not come to see her! *Mon Dieu!*

"Bring me a mirror, hurry. Hold it here, where I can see . . . Ah!" Nicole shrieked. She did not recognize herself in the ravaged face that met her eyes. Her hair hung limp; the bones of her face stood out; her cheeks were hollowed; and lines showed around her eyes.

Nicole closed her eyes, her anger somewhat tempered by relief that Varian had not seen her looking like this, and waited for Marie to return the mirror to the dressing table. "And my jewels? Were they taken?"

"*Oui,* madame. All of them, except for the pearls."

"All my beautiful jewels gone, and my looks gone, too. Oh, Marie, what am I to do?"

"Eat, madame. You have been days without eating. You need rich food to repair the damage. With your looks recovered, the jewels will come."

Nicole smiled wryly. "I fear it will not be so simple, *ma femme.* But hurry, send for some food. I am starving."

"And milord?"

"I will send for him when I am stronger, Marie." It would be wiser to wait until her appearance had been improved, for it began to appear as if she would need all her beauty and feminine wiles to regain Damon. His acquiescence to her departure for London had not been mere caprice. His absence since the shooting proved that.

Two days later, propped up on pillows and with her hair covered by a fetching lace cap and her bandage hidden by her most opaque dressing gown, Nicole waited for Varian. She had sent Marie with a message, then dismissed her maid.

As the minutes passed and he did not come, her still smoldering anger increased. There was nothing here in this country house to rival her. She was his mistress, was

239

she not? He was responsible for her being here, was he not? Then why did he not come?

When he finally stood at her bedside, she exclaimed petulantly, "You might have come earlier, m'lord."

He bowed his head. "I deeply regret that you should have suffered this attack, Nicole."

"That's all very well, Damon," she said peevishly, "but it should not have happened."

His eyebrows rose. "I admit I was remiss in not providing outriders," he said stiffly.

"Outriders! What use would they have been?" she asked scornfully. "Would they have been of more use than your other servants? You should have been with me."

Even as she said these words, Nicole knew it was a mistake, for Varian's face became aloof and haughty. She should have known better. At best he was a touchy, arrogant aristocrat.

"May I remind you, Nicole, that it was your idea to return to London?"

She turned her head away. Varian had changed. He was not the same man she had known. Before he had been eager to do her bidding. Now he was cold. She sighed. Always this was the way with men. Their passions, so hot at the beginning, cooled, and she was left with nothing. And now, she had no beauty with which to win him back.

"And still my idea, Damon," she whispered.

"Don't be foolish, Nicole. You are not strong enough to leave."

"If I stay, I will die. Your servants first try to poison me and then they do not protect me from those *canailles.*"

"As I said once before, Nicole, my servants did not poison you." His tone was one of patient forbearance and it irked her.

"No? I lie here and eat. For the past two days I stuff

240

myself, trying to regain my lost figure, and I am not sick. And do you know why, my lord? Because I sent word to the kitchen that the maids, *your maids,* will taste of my food before I eat it."

"I refuse to accept your accusation, Nicole. If you are not increasing, then you had indigestion. There were no attempts made to poison you. And no harm would have befallen you if you'd handed over the jewels."

"Handed over? Handed over? Just like that!" She stared at him. "You expect me to calmly give my jewels to foot-pads? It is easy to see, my lord Varian, that you have never wanted for anything." Her voice was scornful.

"Are your jewels more important than your life, Nicole?" he asked dryly.

Her eyes were wide as she looked at this uncom-prehending peer. "They are my life, Damon," she whispered.

He merely nodded, as if her words had not been unex-pected. "Very well. As soon as Dr. Hughes says you may travel, I'll send you to London, with outriders this time." He turned away. At the door, he said formally, "I'll also direct Grimes to make over the deed to the house on Albemarle Street to you."

She stared at him. So it was over. Just like that. All the nights of passion they'd shared, forgotten as if they'd nev-er been. She was being cast off with no regrets. She wished she were an emotional woman, for she wanted to weep at the indignity of it all. A man sets up a woman as his mistress, at his convenience, at his urging, and then, when it suits him, he discards her. Indeed, the world was cruel, very cruel.

"I suppose I should be grateful, m'lord, but a house does not buy food. And how can I find another lover with this brand on me, eh?" She pulled apart her dressing gown and lifted the bandage to reveal a long red scar across her chest and shoulder.

His lips tightened. As he lifted his head to meet her accusing gaze, Nicole was shocked to see mirrored in his eyes a similar accusation.

"I doubt it will hinder you, Nicole. The scar will not be seen in the dark, but it will be a reminder to you of your own greed. However, I was remiss in not providing sufficient protection when I knew highwaymen were holding up coaches. Therefore, I will accept responsibility and make you a settlement. Will a draft on Drummond's be satisfactory?"

The door was closed quietly behind him and Nicole was left to her own disquieting thoughts.

Thirty

A dispirited Cherry climbed into the coach, shuddering as she looked about for bloodstains. Then she realized that the coach would have been cleaned before taking Nicole to London. Nicole! Gone, but for how long?

Nothing had really changed. Those harmonious days when she and Damon had dined together in peace and greeted their callers in amicable civility were all gone, as if they had never been. With Nicole's departure, Damon had become his old self again.

At dinner the evening before he had announced, "We leave for London tomorrow." When she'd protested, asking, "Why? We've just arrived," he had replied arrogantly, "Because I wish it."

He didn't have to give a reason. She knew he was going after Nicole. Why else would he follow her to London immediately after her departure? He couldn't bear to be separated from her!

Then Cherry smiled wryly to herself. She had said she wanted his happiness, hadn't she? Well, if a mistress was necessary for Damon, she would have to learn to accept it. But the thought of sharing him with another woman hurt. Other women, wives in name only, could be caught up in a marriage of convenience. She wanted none of it. Then she sighed. What she wanted, she could not have. Damon would never love her.

She glanced out of the corner of her eye at her husband. He was frowning, so she decided it would be wiser not to ask questions. She wanted to know whether Hetty and Hartley would be following in a second carriage with the luggage. Hetty had said nothing about packing her clothes. Indeed, she had been most reticent this morning as she helped Cherry dress. But if Cherry asked Damon, she might get a sarcastically raised eyebrow and harsh words.

She sat quietly, her hands folded in her lap, but inwardly she was grieving. She didn't want to go to London. It would be far worse than Lincolnshire, for there Damon would find too many entertainments to keep him away from her. And there would be nothing for her to do. She couldn't appear at any public parties, if there were any. In the summer most families left London for the country. She would either have to stay indoors, with nothing to occupy her time, or walk in the Park, and Cherry was becoming mightily bored with her own company.

Could she ask Damon for the use of a carriage? If she had any money, she could hire a hackney, but she had none. She didn't even know if she was to receive any pin money. It was customary, according to Mama, for the marriage contract to specify the details of the wife's allowance, but Uncle Geoffrey had failed to inform her of such practical matters, if he had remembered to include them in the contract at all. And she couldn't ask Damon. Granting that their newfound harmony had been damaged by

Nicole's remove to London, she didn't want to destroy it totally with awkward questions, as she had done before.

But she could ask her uncle! She was no longer Miss Hilliard, the poverty-stricken daughter of a younger son, but the Countess of Varian. Tomorrow she would send a footman with a note to ask her uncle and aunt to tea. They'd come—of that she was sure. And with her new rank to give her added prestige and confidence, she could question her uncle and expect answers.

Cherry gave a sigh of relief—that matter was settled—and sank back against the squabs. If only other problems could be settled as easily, she was thinking, when a sharp noise rang out and the coach was pulled up abruptly. She had to fight to keep from falling forward and became aware of a great deal of shouting outside. What had happened?

Just as Cherry turned to Varian to inquire about this strange occurrence, the door of the carriage was jerked open. The figure of a man appeared, pointing a pistol at her.

"Well, well, have I interrupted a love tryst?" a voice asked.

Cherry recoiled. It was the voice of Jack Keene. "He's the man," she whispered to Varian, but the highwayman interrupted her with a gesture of his pistol. "If you would please get down, my lord?" he asked with exaggerated courtesy.

Cherry's heart stopped. He had attacked her once before. What did he intend doing now?

Varian shrugged, stepped out of the coach, and helped her down. This time she was grateful for his hand on her arm, for her knees felt dreadfully weak. She glanced fearfully at the highwayman, whose face was covered by a kerchief.

"We meet again, my sweet," his voice purred. It sounded hateful, as did his words.

"Keene!" The name burst from Varian's lips. "So you're behind these holdups! Is the easy money attracting you again? There's no need for a mask, I recognize your voice."

"Do you know him, Damon?" Cherry asked. "He's the man who broke into my room at the inn."

The earl nodded. "He was a dragoon under my command before he turned traitor, selling information to the French."

An ugly laugh came from the highwayman. Then he reached up and pulled the kerchief from his face. "And it is to you, my lord, that I owe my discovery. Had you arrived ten minutes later, I would have been gone, five hundred pounds richer."

"Sorry, Keene. We had you under observation from the time you left camp."

The highwayman swore, then turned his gaze to Cherry, his eyes raking her, dwelling overlong on her body. She shivered and moved closer to Varian.

"And this delightful piece?" Keene asked.

"Is Lady Varian," the earl said stiffly.

"Your wife, my lord? How very fortunate." Keene rapidly reassessed the situation. The other woman in Varian's carriage must have been his doxy, sent off after the marriage. This was much better. He could profit financially as well as have his revenge. The widow Varian would pay handsomely to keep anyone from learning that *he* had been her lover. He smiled complacently.

"I had hoped my French friends had finished you off until I heard your voice the night I—ah—happened to—ah—visit this delectable article. You interrupted me, my lord," he snarled, his eyes narrowing, "just as you did in

Spain, both times before I could collect my prize. You bested me then, but now—now I can settle the score."

While Keene had been talking, his two companions began edging their mounts closer and closer, still keeping their pistols leveled at the coachman and groom on the box. "Why's Jack gabbin' so long wi' a gentry cove, Jas?" On receiving a shrug, Ben moved up to overhear the conversation, followed by his equally curious partner. Keene's identity as a former soldier did not surprise them. Many men were forced into crime because of circumstances beyond their control. However, his identity as a traitor was a shock. They may be footpads, but they were Englishmen. Equally disturbing were his next words. "I fear, my lord Varian, there will be an unavoidable accident." So Jack Keene was willing to kill to prevent disclosure of his dealings with the French? Yet he had rung a peal over Jasper for an accidental shooting. The eyes of the two highwaymen met in silent consultation.

"And as for you, Lady Varian, I'm sure his lordship has provided for you properly. He surely wouldn't want his widow to suffer from lack of his generosity. We can have a bit of fun, you and I, and if there's an *heir*"—he laughed suggestively—"you and I, my sweet, will be in clover."

Cherry wasn't sure she understood this man. He couldn't really mean what his words signified, that he would kill Damon and—and did he mean he would make love to her as Damon had done? Was *that* what he had wanted when he came to her bedchamber? Her mind reeled from the impact of her thoughts. This whole situation couldn't be happening. It was unreal, like a nightmare from which she'd waken soon. Then she saw Keene raise his pistol and point it at Varian. That was real, horrifingly real.

"No," she screamed and threw herself in front of Damon, clutching him around the waist. "You'll have to kill me first!"

"I just might do that," Keene snarled, furious that she was escaping him again, when his attention was caught by the sound of hooves drumming on the road. He lifted his head to listen and missed Jasper's words. "T'cove's got a snapper."

Varian gave Cherry an abrupt shove and she fell heavily to the ground. From there she saw him pull a pistol from his pocket.

Meanwhile, Dalton, who had been smarting from the reprimand from his lordship over his lack of courage during the earlier holdup, saw his opportunity when the highwaymen's attention was diverted. He drew his pistol and fired.

Jack Keene staggered and clutched his chest. Blood began to ooze from the wound onto his brown coat and his fingers. As Cherry watched, her senses reeling from a mixture of fear, relief, and horror, he collapsed, not three feet from her.

"Pike off," Jasper yelled to Ben and slapped his horse's flank with his pistol. The two highwaymen raced off, pursued by the oncoming group of horsemen, one of whom rode up to Varian. It was Sir Francis.

"Sorry we're late," he panted. "Held up—damn cattle in the road." He dismounted and quickly walked over to stand looking down at Keene's body. "You got one of 'em," he gloated. "We should have the others shortly. This plan of yours—" Then he stopped talking, as his lordship was obviously not attending to him.

Varian was bending over Cherry, who was still lying on the ground. He pocketed his unused pistol, then knelt down next to her and turned her over. Her eyes were closed and she seemed unconscious.

He thrust his right arm under her shoulders and lifted her to a half-sitting position, then cradled her in his arm, her head resting on his chest. "Cherry! Cherry! Good God, have I hurt you?"

She stirred, slowly opened her eyes, and stared blankly at him. Varian helped her to her feet, then guided her to the carriage. "Take care of it, Francis," he called, nodding toward the body.

In the carriage, Cherry sat stunned, her face white. Damon was going on to London as if nothing had happened, while her world had almost been shattered. If Damon had been killed—the horror of that thought overwhelmed her. Life without him was not worth living. With this realization came another. She was willing to accept Damon on any terms, just so long as he lived. She would have to learn to accept his mistresses, and his hatred of her. There was nothing else to do.

Cherry was so engrossed in her thoughts that she was unaware that the carriage was returning to the Court. When it stopped, Varian pulled her upright and led her down the steps. At his touch Cherry woke from her reverie, but, not wishing to do anything to spoil this thrilling moment, she allowed him to lead her into the house and up the stairs to her bedchamber.

She did not protest when he told Hetty, "Lady Varian has had a shock. Put her to bed." Although she wanted to run after him when he left, she suffered Hetty to undress her and put a bedgown on her. Still bemused by his consideration for her, his detested wife, she climbed into bed.

Hetty had just finished tidying up when Damon entered from the dressing room, decanter in hand. "Hold up that glass," he instructed, gesturing toward the glass on the table next to the bed.

Hetty did so and Varian poured brandy into it. Then he

sat down on the bed next to Cherry. "Put the glass on the table, then you may go," he directed Hetty.

Cherry was lifted against Varian's chest, and the glass held to her lips. She swallowed automatically, then sputtered at the remembered taste. She didn't like spirits and had no intention of drinking any more. She shook her head and pushed the glass away.

"I admit it tastes vile," he said in an amused voice, "but it seems to be the only way to get you to respond, Cherry."

She held her breath, her entire body motionless. He had called her by her name! It didn't make sense. Always before it had been "my lady."

Then she was laid back onto the pillow and Damon, his face anxious, said, "Don't withdraw from me, please, Cherry." He reached over and gently touched her cheek. "I know I've given you no reason to feel aught but hate for me, but please, speak to me. Don't withdraw from me."

Cherry sat up. "I wasn't withdrawing from you, Damon," she exclaimed indignantly. "I just didn't want you to stop being nice to me. I was so afraid you were going to London to find Nicole, or another mistress."

He shook his head. "The roads would not be safe until the highwaymen were caught. I decided to provide them with bait. Since I had no way of knowing who they were, or how much they knew of what was going on, and didn't want them to suspect a trap, I had to take you with me." His expression changed. "How could you believe that of me? Didn't you know I'd changed? Surely my actions—"

"I thought you still hated me," she whispered.

"Hate?" he asked, his lips twisting bitterly. "I wanted to. Oh, how I wanted to hate you, Cherry, but the truth is, I was falling in love with you and wouldn't admit it to myself. I had to keep reminding myself that I had reason to hate you and I had to keep hurting you to prove to myself that I didn't love you. I was afraid I would give in and admit my feelings for you. And then later I could not bring myself to admit I'd been wrong." He sighed. "A man's pride is a fearful thing, my dear. I did try to show you . . ."

Cherry stared at him, not at all comprehending. This couldn't be Damon speaking to her, telling her of his love. While her heart had yearned for him to love her, never in her wildest imaginings had she expected it to happen. Damon love her? "I . . . I th-thought you were t-trying to make a good impression on your neighbours," she stammered.

He laughed. "Cherry, must you constantly misinterpret everything I do?"

"How was I to know? You told me you would make me suffer."

"I know. Can you forgive me?"

"And I thought you loved Nicole," she protested.

"I thought so, too," he admitted wryly, "until I began to compare my feelings for her and my feelings for you. I discovered that passion is a poor substitute for love, my dear. Passions end, sometimes quickly, but love"—he picked up her hand and carried it to his lips—"grows."

Cherry still found it hard to believe Damon, though the expression in his eyes was tender and warm. "But how can you love me? My father hurt you."

"Did he? I'm afraid my hatred blinded me to the truth. Even if your father had died there at the ambush, my arm would still not have been saved. I cannot blame him for the loss of my arm, Cherry. And who knows, he may have regretted his impulsive action."

"He did die bravely, Damon. The letter Mama received

251

said he'd rescued two officers. Do you suppose he was trying to make up for leaving you?"

"I don't know, Cherry, but I'd gladly give my arm for two lives." He reached over and covered her hand. "What he did that day is no longer important, not to us, Cherry. What is important is what you are, and you, my sweet, besides being a beautiful woman, are no coward."

Cherry thrilled to hear Damon's words, but her innate honesty caused her to object. "But I run away, too, Damon."

"Do you?" he asked with a smile. "You have a strange way of running, then. I seem to remember this chin"—he reached out and touched it lightly—"lifted in defiance of me and these eyes glaring at me."

"I didn't glare," Cherry protested, "did I?"

"Indeed you did, most fearfully."

Cherry smiled in response, but her expression immediately changed to one of apprehension. "What about . . . when . . . I . . ." she faltered.

"When you withdrew into yourself?" Damon supplied the words.

She nodded. "Isn't that running away, Damon?"

"What were you thinking of, just now, in the carriage as we returned home?" he asked.

"That I could not live if you died," she whispered.

"And before?"

"I wanted to drown myself, because you preferred Nicole and hated me."

"Oh, my poor, poor darling. I was a fool, Cherry, an utter fool. I wanted to believe that Nicole wanted *me*. My pride would not allow me to admit that she preferred money to me." He took her hand and again lifted it to his lips. "There is one thing that puzzles me. If you thought

252

I hated you, my lady Varian, why, I repeat, why were you so ready to give your life for me?"

Cherry blushed and lowered her eyes. How could she admit to Damon what she felt for him?

"Well?" A finger lifted her chin.

Cherry raised her eyes. Damon was smiling so warmly at her, she no longer felt afraid. "Because I love you," she said simply.

"Somehow I suspected that," he teased. Then he leaned over and kissed her lightly on the lips. "Every morning for the past week you've been telling me so."

"Damon!" she exclaimed. "I thought you were sleeping."

"I always waken with human contact."

"Oh, Damon," she cried. "Do you always have such horrible nightmares?"

"I hope not. Perhaps now I will be free of them. Mayhap because I hated and would not forget, that incident preyed on my mind. I do not pretend to understand the dark recesses of my soul, Cherry. But if they do not cease, at least I will have you beside me."

She blushed, and then, because she did not want their newfound love disturbed by any lingering doubts on his part, she asked, "Are you sure, absolutely sure, that my withdrawing isn't running away?"

"Well, perhaps, just a little bit." Then, at the sight of her dismayed expression, he said firmly, "I believe that you are capable of concentrating so hard on your thoughts, Cherry, that you shut out all outside, extraneous distractions. I hope in the future you can share your problems with me, my sweet wife, and not withdraw into yourself by shutting me out. I want to be part of your life."

He was sitting so close to her, she reached up, smiling, and touched his face. "Don't be so humble, Damon. I was as much to blame as you. I resented you and hated you, too, for a while. You hadn't courted me."

He grinned then, mischievously. "Do you wish me to court you now, madam?"

She shook her head, then daringly lifted her hands to finger his cravat. Too shy to speak, for their new relationship had developed so suddenly, Cherry was still unsure of herself.

"You have the advantage of me," he said softly.

When she looked up questioningly, he said, "*You* are in your bedgown."

"Oh!" She blushed and looked apprehensively at her husband, but as he continued to smile at her, his eyes warm, Cherry gathered her courage and began to fumble with the knot of his cravat.

Love—the way you want it!

Candlelight Romances

Dell Bestsellers

- [ ] **RANDOM WINDS** by Belva Plain \$3.50 (17158-X)
- [ ] **MEN IN LOVE** by Nancy Friday \$3.50 (15404-9)
- [ ] **JAILBIRD** by Kurt Vonnegut \$3.25 (15447-2)
- [ ] **LOVE: Poems** by Danielle Steel \$2.50 (15377-8)
- [ ] **SHOGUN** by James Clavell \$3.50 (17800-2)
- [ ] **WILL** by G. Gordon Liddy \$3.50 (09666-9)
- [ ] **THE ESTABLISHMENT** by Howard Fast.......\$3.25 (12296-1)
- [ ] **LIGHT OF LOVE** by Barbara Cartland \$2.50 (15402-2)
- [ ] **SERPENTINE** by Thomas Thompson \$3.50 (17611-5)
- [ ] **MY MOTHER/MY SELF** by Nancy Friday \$3.25 (15663-7)
- [ ] **EVERGREEN** by Belva Plain \$3.50 (13278-9)
- [ ] **THE WINDSOR STORY**
  by J. Bryan III & Charles J.V. Murphy \$3.75 (19346-X)
- [ ] **THE PROUD HUNTER** by Marianne Harvey ..\$3.25 (17098-2)
- [ ] **HIT ME WITH A RAINBOW**
  by James Kirkwood \$3.25 (13622-9)
- [ ] **MIDNIGHT MOVIES** by David Kaufelt \$2.75 (15728-5)
- [ ] **THE DEBRIEFING** by Robert Litell \$2.75 (01873-5)
- [ ] **SHAMAN'S DAUGHTER** by Nan Salerno
  & Rosamond Vanderburgh \$3.25 (17863-0)
- [ ] **WOMAN OF TEXAS** by R.T. Stevens \$2.95 (19555-1)
- [ ] **DEVIL'S LOVE** by Lane Harris \$2.95 (11915-4)

At your local bookstore or use this handy coupon for ordering:

Dell **DELL BOOKS**
P.O. BOX 1000, PINEBROOK, N.J. 07058

Please send me the books I have checked above. I am enclosing \$ _____
(please add 75¢ per copy to cover postage and handling). Send check or money order—no cash or C.O.D.'s. Please allow up to 8 weeks for shipment.

Mr/Mrs/Miss _____

Address _____

City _____ State/Zip _____